End of a New Life

End of a New Life

Heroes of Grant's Crossing
Book 3

H.M.S. Brown

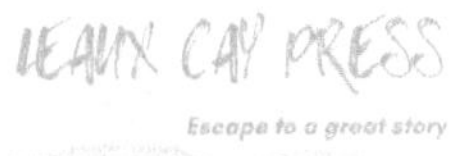

Also by H.M.S. Brown

Heroes of Grant's Crossing

(Can be read as standalones)

Wayward Guilt

MILITARY FICTION AT ITS BEST! - Amazon review

Safe Now

ANOTHER WINNER. - Goodreads review

End of a New Life

Grant's Crossing Romance (M/F)

Don't Call Me Sugar

☆ ☆ ☆ ☆ ☆

"... HANDS DOWN THE BEST ROMANCE NOVEL I HAVE READ IN A LONG TIME." - Goodreads review

Don't Call Me Ma'am - Coming Spring 2026

Leaux Cay Tavern Romance (M/M)

Leaux Cay Tavern - Coming 2027

Sandusky Psychedelics Cozy Mysteries

Face-off to Murder - Coming Autumn 2026

Foreword

It may have taken me a lot longer to get Derek's post-active-duty story out, but it finally happened, and I think it's worth it!

I'll start by asking for your forgiveness for a few author indulgences. The main facts of the story - those that truly matter, such as situations on paramedic calls and how someone copes with PTSD and alcoholism - are as based on fact and rooted in reality as much as I can possibly make them. Any mistakes are my own.

Previous books in my Heroes of Grant's Crossing have spanned over many years, even decades. End of a New Life, however, spans only a couple of years, and it all takes place after Derek is honorably discharged from the U.S. Army.

No one is immune to trauma and the immeasurable amount of stress that comes with it. It's how we handle it that gets us through. Some of us handle it well, and some of us don't, whether or not we have a good support system of friends and family.

Derek Mitchell is one such person with that support system, but damn if it doesn't take him a long while before he truly realizes it. I put him through the ringer, but his friends and family continue to have faith and don't give up on him.

Perhaps it's the friends and family who are the true heroes in this story.

   - Heather

Perhaps it's the friends and family who are the true heroes in this story.

   - Heather

Content Warning

Topics discussed in this book may be triggering to some readers, including alcoholism, grief, PTSD, brief reference to suicidal ideations, discussion of combat violence, and combat death.

If you suffer from PTSD and want help, please reach out to https://www.ptsd.va.gov.

In addition, the Veterans Crisis Line offers 24/7, confidential crisis support for Veterans and their loved ones. You don't have to be enrolled in VA benefits or health care to connect. You can dial 988, then press 1. Or you can text 838255. Texting charges may apply.

Online chatting is also available. For more information, visit
https://www.Veteranscrisisline.net

If you need help and are considering suicide, please talk to someone now via text at 988 or call 1-888-628-9454. https://988lifeline.org/

Reach out to family or friends. You are not alone.

To all those who made it home from battles waged

and

to all those who made it home, still waging battle

Crisis Line

Crisis Line: You've reached 988 Suicide & Crisis Lifeline, this is Skylar. How may I help you?

Caller: um... Help? I can't...

Crisis Line: Can't what?

Caller: Live with it.

Crisis Line: What did you do?

Caller: I killed him.

Crisis Line: Killed who?

Caller: (...)

Crisis Line: Are you still there?

Crisis Line: Hello?

Prologue

AFGHANISTAN - AUGUST 17, 2014

"JOEY!" Sergeant First Class Derek Mitchell's eyes focused on the blood seeping out of his best friend's shoulder. He tore open the shirt to inspect the wound. "Hey. You're okay. You're okay," he assured Joey as the weapons fire continued. "It's just your shoulder. Nothing vital."

Joey winced in pain. "Hurts like a son of a bitch."

"I bet," Derek looked at Joey's back to see where the bullet exited. "Looks like it went straight through. You're going to be fine."

"I can still fight," Joey grunted as Derek applied pressure to his shoulder.

"Roger that." Derek finished taping a bandage over his wound. "You're good."

Joey returned to his position and fired off a few shots when someone yelled, "RPG!"

With no time to dive away, the men in front were all forced back by the explosion, momentarily stunned by the blast. The Rangers in the wings closed in to make sure they were protected until they could rejoin the fight.

Derek heard shots ringing out in the distance, but the sounds were muffled, as if being projected through a thick pillow. He had the wind knocked out of him when he landed hard on his back. Gasping for breath, he struggled to suck air into his lungs. Looking straight up, he took in the bright light of the sun, trying to shine through clouds of orange and brown dust-filled smoke.

With a near-Herculean effort, he finally drew in enough air to catch his breath, but a searing pain demanded his attention. Still on his back, he turned to see something sticking out of his left arm. He slowly secured his weapon against his chest and reached over with his right hand to pull it out of his left bicep; blood, fortunately not too much, trickled down his arm.

"Shit." He coughed and examined the jagged piece of metal he'd just pulled out of his arm, and dropped it on the ground as the gunfire continued all around him.

Derek took a deep breath and flipped onto his stomach to regain his bearings and take in the situation. He flinched when he rolled over his injured arm, squeezing it again with his right hand but quickly determining he could go on. He left a streak of blood when he wiped the sweat off his brow.

Blinking a few times to focus, he turned his attention to the men to see who had been hit.

He crawled over to Jonesy, who was equally as stunned. "You okay, Jonesy?" Derek patted him on the chest and helped him up to a crouched position.

"Yeah, Doc." Jonesy coughed a few times as he steadied himself.

"Stevens?" Derek felt for a pulse on the lifeless lieutenant, who seemed to have taken the brunt of the blast. After a few seconds, he dropped his hand.

The man was dead.

"Doc!" Rass yelled. "It's Parker!"

Derek spun to see that Joey was on his back, his legs gone below the knees. Blood leaked out of multiple spots on his body, and Joey was gasping, desperately fighting for air. Derek fought back his initial panic of seeing his best friend so severely injured and turned to his training that had served him so reliably over the years.

"SHIT!" Derek rushed over and, without hesitation, tied tourniquets around Joey's legs to stop the filthy ground from turning even redder before methodically examining his other injuries.

"He pushed me out of the way. I would have been right there when it hit," Rass choked out in his Texas drawl. "What can I do?"

Derek set up an IV with medicine to curb the bleeding as the shooting died down. "Hold this up," he commanded Rass as he shoved the saline bag into his hands. There was a new shoulder wound, this time to the left shoulder. Derek packed it off, knowing some shrapnel was still inside.

"Hold on, Joey," he spoke softly as he worked.

"Logan." Joey coughed. Blood dripped from the corner of his mouth.

"You'll see Logan soon. Stay with us." Derek ripped Joey's uniform open to find wounds on his torso.

"D? You there, D?"

"I'm here." Derek grabbed Joey's shaking hand. "You're okay, Joey."

Joey gasped for air, "D? Help me."

"Look at me, Joey. I've got you."

"Help me."

He was still losing blood, but Derek couldn't find it. He rolled him onto his side and found yet another wound in his torso. The blood was quickly turning the ground a deep red.

Fuck. Fuck. Fuck.

Derek couldn't lose his best friend.

Training, Derek. Use your training. You know what to do.

He reached into his pack for another bandage to stop the bleeding, but it was too severe a wound to repair in the field.

"Tell Logan I love him, D."

Uncharacteristically, Derek's voice shook as he pressed

bandages to the gaping wound in Joey's chest. "You can tell him yourself when we get back."

If he could just stop the bleeding.

The shooting ceased, and the acrid smoke drifted away. The chirping of birds in the distance filled the sudden silence. Their captain called out orders as the enemy either fled or was dead.

"I wasn't there for him, D," Joey grunted, his pain obvious. "He tried … to kill himself because of me."

"You were there, Joey. It's not your fault. It was never because of you." Derek filled a syringe and injected pain meds into Joey's arm. He then returned to pack the shoulder wounds as best he could. There was too much blood loss already, but Derek would never give up trying.

His friend's eyes darted around as if he were looking for something or someone, not really seeing the men who were there with him. "Mom. Where are you, Mom?"

"Don't go there, Joey. Stay with us. You've got to get home to Logan, remember? I'm not supposed to tell you, so you have to act surprised, but he's going to propose. You're gonna get married." Derek's voice shook as he pressed harder on the wound on Joey's chest.

The other rangers gathered nearby to maintain a silent vigil for the fallen and injured soldiers.

"Mom. Mom."

Working like hell to pack his wounds, Derek put another bandage over his torso.

"Hold this down," he barked at Jonesy.

"Doc," Jonesy started to say.

"DO IT!" Derek ordered.

Jonesy released an exasperated sigh as he pressed down on the bandage covering Joey's chest.

"Mom," Joey called out again.

Derek grabbed Joey's hand. "No, no, no. Joey, don't do this. You stay with me. Look at me."

"D," Joey's voice sounded weaker as he called out. His voice slurred. His eyes flitted back and forth without ever landing on anything around him. "Mom ... Mom ..."

Derek's throat tightened. "Come on, Joey."

"Mmm ..." Joey's eyes glazed over.

Derek leaned down. There were no breath sounds. "FUCK!" Derek called out as he shoved Jonesy away and started chest compressions.

Joey wasn't moving.

"Don't leave me, Joey," Derek's voice cracked as he yelled, no, commanded his friend to stay alive. Desperation drove him.

Joey's lifeless eyes stared up at him, but Derek didn't stop. "Don't go, Joey," he begged. "Please," his last word came out as a raspy whisper.

"Doc." Jonesy reached out to stop him. "He's gone."

"No!" Derek shoved him backward and continued pressing on his chest to make his best friend's heart start beating again. "Come on, Joey," he pleaded. "Come back."

Chapter 1

Nightmare

Ten months after Joey Parker died

Grant's Crossing, Ohio - June 2015

"SERGEANT!" Juan "Tank" Palacios' voice was much closer as Derek shot up in his bunk, panting as if he'd just run a marathon, his gray T-shirt darkened with sweat.

Derek couldn't move. Nor could he catch his breath. His eyes welled with tears as he scanned the area in the hopes that he'd wake up somewhere else and discover this wasn't real.

It had been almost ten months since his best friend died on that filthy battleground in Afghanistan, and he still couldn't shake the guilt he felt at not saving him.

After all, that was his job: to save people. Bring his fellow Rangers back alive. Bring a man back to base with a heartbeat, and that man had a 92% chance of making it home.

The Taliban sure fought hard for that 8% that day because Derek lost two men in that sweltering heat before it was all said and done.

Derek blinked a few times, finally registering that someone had spoken to him. The red glow of the wall clock read 2:25 AM in the station bunk room, but Derek could only stare at his friend and fellow firefighter-paramedic, who held a vice-like grip on his shoulders.

"Doc. You with us?" Tank, the only one who called him Doc, his nickname from their Army days together, switched his expression from surprise to mission-ready to worried.

"Tank?"

Derek stared back like a deer in headlights. Confused by his surroundings, Derek's face contorted, fluctuating from shock to anger to fear, as if the battle being waged in his mind had just turned futile.

When Tank released his shoulders, Derek ran his fingers through his sweat-soaked hair, then stared at his hands, unable to comprehend how they were so damp. He still hadn't caught his breath when his head shot back up at Tank.

As his eyes scanned the room to regain his bearings, he could almost make out the outlines of his fellow firefighters he'd just awakened.

He had hoped the nightmares were gone, but deep down, he knew better. Even in the darkness of the Grant's Crossing Fire Station, Derek still couldn't stop his friend from dying.

Again.

Fucking nightmares. Would they never be gone?

Illuminated solely by the small light attached to the wall between their bunks, Kiro Marinov, the senior paramedic on B-shift, propped himself up on his own bunk, wearing a worried expression.

"You alright, Mitchell?" Emerson's sleep-laden voice called out from the darkness.

Disoriented, each man grunted as he sat up to find the source of the sound. It wasn't the first time this had happened. Not the first time they were awakened in the middle of the night by something other than a call dispatching them to a fire or other emergency.

Tank addressed his fellow firefighters while still seated on Derek's bunk. "Back to bed, men. Get some sleep."

Despite their concern, they settled back in their bunks.

In the far corner, Marine veteran Steve Cook stared up at the ceiling. He understood the nightmares. He knew what they could do to a man, how they could deprive him of sleep, of his sense of well-being.

Of his sanity.

Tank lowered his voice so only Derek could hear. "You were calling out for Joey again."

Derek dropped his chin. "Yeah."

"He's gone."

"I know."

"It's been a while since you've had a bad one, hasn't it?"

"Yeah," he lied.

It hadn't been a while. They came every night.

Derek slouched with his forearms resting on his knees. He inhaled deeply and scrubbed his face with his hands.

"Doc."

Still leaning up on his neighboring bunk, Kiro listened in silence.

Reaching out a hand, Tank grabbed Derek's shoulder again. "Doc!" Tank tilted his head to force his way into Derek's line of sight. "Remember all the men who are alive because of you." He looked straight into Derek's eyes and shook his head. "The Taliban killed Joey. Not you."

Derek's eyes shot up, and his forehead creased. "That's what Dad said." His words slipping out as a hoarse whisper.

"Your dad's a smart man."

Derek sat up a bit straighter, took a few seconds to focus on Tank, and just nodded.

"You with me?" Tank held up his hand.

Derek's thoughts took a few seconds to move from his nightmare, as if witnessing his friend's death for the first time, back to the present, when it hit him that someone had asked him a question. "Yeah." He barely spoke over a whisper as he met Tank's eyes. "I'm with you." He clasped Tank's hand.

"Alright. Good. And Doc?"

"Yeah?"

"I've got your back, okay?" Tank broke the handshake to give Derek a friendly slap on his cheek.

When the station alarm went off, calling them all to a factory fire. The men all groaned as they hurried out of the cold room.

Tank stood and reached out his hand to help Derek up. "Come on. We've got work to do."

Chapter 2

Breakfast at Baba's

AFTER A LONG NIGHT FIGHTING A FACTORY FIRE THAT KEPT them working beyond their usual 24-hour-long shift, Derek, Kiro, and Steve trudged their way into Baba's, the diner owned by the Marinov family. Since Derek reentered the civilian world the previous Christmas, it had become tradition to have breakfast together after every shift for a hearty meal before returning to their respective homes for a well-earned nap.

"Hi, Mrs. M," Derek said to Kiro's mom, Anna, greeting her with a hug and a kiss on the cheek.

Steve, the newest firefighter-paramedic at the station, returned her friendly greeting and, yawning, followed Derek to a corner booth.

"*Zdrasti, Maiko.*" *Hi, Mom.* Kiro Marinov spoke in his parents' native Bulgarian, dropping a kiss on his mom's cheek.

Anna tilted her head and gave them a motherly once-over as they each collapsed in a bright red, chrome-lined booth.

"You look tired, *Milo,*" Kiro's mom, Anna, stretched out the *MEAL-oh* in her endearment. She shook her head at them. "And hungry."

"I'll get coffee." Kiro started to rise when his mom held him in his seat.

"No. I'll get it. Sit."

With no argument, Kiro leaned back and closed his eyes as his mom fixed them coffee. She gave each man a warm smile after she dropped it off. "I'll get you boys something to eat."

"Thanks, *Maiko*," *Thanks, Mom,* Kiro said on an exhausted exhale.

Equally as spent, Derek and Steve muttered their thanks.

The door opened again, drawing their weary eyes to Abe Mitchell as he walked into the diner.

"Hi, Abe," Anna greeted Derek's father with a warm smile. "Don't usually see you here this time of day."

"I had some free time, so I thought I'd treat myself."

Abe made a beeline for his son, Derek. "It's after 11 AM. Are you just now getting off shift?"

The exhaustion in their faces, combined with their sagging shoulders, left no doubt as to the answer.

"Have a seat, Dad." Derek made room for him to sit down just as Anna set a cup of coffee in front of Abe and took his order.

Abe turned his attention back to the table. "Bad night, huh?"

"Yeah. Four-alarm industrial fire by Ostrander. We took one burn victim down to OSU Med." Derek said, referring to one of the three Level 1 trauma centers in Columbus, Ohio. He sipped his coffee. "Then, we spent the rest of the time shuttling firefighters back and forth to Grady with smoke inhalation."

"Any of yours?"

"Yes. All treated and released, though, so they'll be okay." Kiro added, receiving nods of confirmation from Derek and Steve. "Haven't heard about the guys from the other stations, but they didn't look too bad, all things considered."

"Fire laid waste to the factory," Steve said.

"Oh yeah?"

Derek shrugged. "Yeah. Not much was left by the time we left the scene."

Anna set their food down on the table. "Here you go, boys!"

Kiro pulled his plate closer and stabbed some eggs with his fork. "Thanks, Mom."

"Thanks, Mrs. M," Derek and Steve added as they dug into their meals, trying to get a few bites in before they collapsed from exhaustion right there at the table.

"What do you have going on today, Dad?" Derek asked.

Abe ate at a more leisurely pace, pausing for a sip of coffee before responding. "Heading over to the Mason Avenue site to check on a few things, then over to Brockmoor to close things up."

"Close things up? But you only just started." Since his carriage house apartment was part of the Brockmoor property, Derek perked up. Gutting and renovating the main house was Mitchell Contracting's biggest project. Their work in bringing Victorian homes back to life made them the most sought-after renovators in central Ohio.

"Carriage House is done, and permits are all ready to go." Abe took another sip of coffee. "But we received word that the owner isn't well, so everything is on hold until they figure out who can come out and oversee renovation."

"Wow." Derek shoved a piece of bacon into his mouth. "Still need me to take care of the lawn?"

"Yes. They said they'd probably call in a lawn care company for the landscaping when it came time to do the actual renovation, but didn't offer me a timeline." Abe leaned back in his seat. "The attorney who called told us they are working out the details, but it could take a while. Anyway, I have no idea when they'll get back out here, but if all goes well, they'll still want us to do the work."

"I'm sure they will, Dad. You're the best man for the job."

"Thanks, son," Abe smiled in appreciation. "Plenty of work to go around in the meantime. Won't be any trouble reassigning the crew to another job. Looks like you'll have some more time to settle into your new apartment without having us around to make noise."

Chapter 3

Independence Day

11 months after Joey Parker died

July 4, 2015

Derek pulled himself up off his couch and raked his fingers through his dark, wavy hair, not bothering to stifle the huge yawn that escaped his mouth. He originally had no desire to do anything more than head home for a much-needed nap after his shift ended, but plans changed when Tank invited him to the annual *Familia* Palacios cookout. Derek was pretty sure there was another fancy name for it in Spanish, but he couldn't repeat it without accidentally insulting someone, so he stuck to English.

They'd stopped work on Brockmoor, the large, Victorian home that sat abandoned, clinging to some vestige of grandeur outside his carriage house apartment. Ever since then, he'd been going out less and less with the guys outside of their shifts and spending more and more time at home inside his own head.

Apparently, Tank had noticed.

Tank's invitation aside, Derek still had his usual breakfast with Kiro and Steve at the diner. He didn't want to worry Kiro's mom, after all. But in reality, he just didn't want her to show up on his doorstep with a bag full of food, because she didn't think he was eating enough.

On the other hand, she was an excellent cook.

But then again, so was he.

In the six or so months since Derek started working at the Grant's Crossing Fire Department, he'd quickly established himself as the best cook on B-shift.

Last night, he served his famous jambalaya, a variation on the recipe his mom taught him as a teenager. He didn't make it very often—too much prep work. On shift, he couldn't count on having the time needed for all the chopping and such, much less for standing over a hot stove for it to properly simmer. In addition, the firefighters in the station were wimpy when it came to spices. Except for Tank, most of the guys at the station couldn't handle hot sauce from a Mexican fast-food restaurant, much less the real thing. But despite their lack of adventure when it came to spices, his Cajun and Creole cooking was always a hit.

The last couple of shifts had kept them busier than usual. Independence Day was this week, which meant there had been more injuries from people setting off their own fireworks without the necessary safety precautions—hell, without any safety precautions. It was amazing what sort of idiotic things people could do with a small incendiary device and a match.

Despite having exactly the kind of calls they'd all expected, he was dead tired. Going on a bender the night before the shift probably didn't help his cause. Nothing that some eye drops and a few ibuprofen couldn't take care of.

Waking from his post-shift nap, he sat up and slid his bare feet out from underneath the throw blanket to the carpeted floor below. He spent a few moments squishing the warm fibers with his toes. A quick glance at his watch revealed it had only been a few hours since getting off work, which explained the early afternoon sun coming in through the windows. Oh well. Some sleep was better than nothing, he supposed.

Growing up, he had always loved watching the colorful

fireworks with Joey and his family on the Fourth. But this year, things were different. He had no desire to celebrate with throngs of people who actually enjoyed the bright colors and loud booms.

Thirteen years in the Army gave him more than his fair share of loud bangs and explosions. Voluntarily subjecting himself to an evening of them was no longer Derek's idea of a good time.

He'd seen enough battles.

He'd heard enough explosions.

He didn't need a reminder of what they were like, not even under the guise of celebration. He knew what they could do, how much they could damage, and every last one of them reminded him of the RPG that took Joey's life last year.

Nobody in Grant's Crossing was there with him when Joey died on that battlefield in Afghanistan. They didn't see the aftermath of the ambush.

And except for a minuscule number of friends who had also served, yes–Tank included, nobody else remotely understood.

The cost of freedom was too damned high.

———

Derek hadn't wanted to be around people, but he enjoyed his afternoon and evening with the large and boisterous *Familia* Palacios, anyway. He always did whenever he was there. Tank had married his high school sweetheart, Araceli, and now had the large family they'd always wanted. Araceli was the happiest person Derek knew, and their children were adorable. Sweet kids, every last one of them. Rocio was the oldest at seven and a half, and Daniel was five. Diego was two, and Maria Elena was barely three months old. They were already calling him *Tío* Derek. Well, those who could talk already, but Maria Elena would learn.

Derek and Tank grew up in their idyllic small town in central Ohio. They enlisted and trained together to become Army Rangers.

While Tank had deployed to both Iraq and Afghanistan, Derek had only ever deployed to Afghanistan thanks to an extra year of combat medic training.

Since its founding a decade after the Civil War, Grant's Crossing had seen more than its fair share of men and women serving in the military, so instead of fireworks, a handful of combat veterans opted for peace and quiet indoors, usually at Jo's Bar & Grille downtown. At Tank's urging, Derek joined them this year.

While the rest of the family worked their way toward the festivities, the combat vets hung out and traded stories.

Derek took a seat next to Tank, who placed an order for nachos and opened the tab with Mike behind the counter. A decade or more older, Mike had served in the Army in Desert Storm. And like Tank, he, too, had spent time at Walter Reed.

They wouldn't drink much tonight - Tank never did - but they'd have one or two while the family was elsewhere. Most of the family, at least.

When Derek first arrived, the conversation concentrated on Tank's large family, which included little Maria Elena, who sat in her car seat on the corner of the bar. It was a small town, so Tank could get away with bringing in the baby. He was thrilled when she instantly became the center of attention. It wasn't just combat veterans who didn't care for the loud bangs of the fireworks.

While she slept, Tank covered her with a light blanket, more the size of a hand towel, since she was still so tiny. He spent the majority of the conversation with his hand on her leg to make sure she knew her *Papá* was always there. A short while in, he took her to the men's room for a quick diaper change, grateful Mike and Jo had added a changing table in the men's room as well. With four kids, he happily cared for his youngest while his wife, Araceli, took the other three children to the fireworks with their aunts, uncles, and cousins. Heck, if given the option, he'd stay at home with them full time, but between her nursing schedule and his firefighter schedule, it wasn't yet in the cards. Fortunately, they had two sets of doting grandparents nearby, so their children were always loved and cared for. Half the time he had extra nieces and nephews running around the house, and he loved it.

As for Derek, he was still adjusting to civilian life and had no plans to start a family anytime soon, if at all. He'd been home for just shy of seven months now, having been honorably discharged on Christmas Eve of last year. Still, he had yet to learn how to be a civilian as an adult.

Derek, Tank, and Joey were still teenagers when they enlisted after 9/11. Derek was the youngest of the three, turning twenty during boot camp. Now he was closing in on thirty-four but truly living on his own for the first time. It was definitely an adjustment from the barracks or shared apartments he'd lived in while on active duty. Though he didn't miss the extra snoring from some of his fellow Rangers, his apartment was almost too quiet for his liking.

He did appreciate its advantages. Anytime he wanted to take a date back to his place, he could.

Maybe not tonight.

The bar was so empty, there weren't any women inside to even think about picking up, except for Angela, who'd actually turned him down in the past. It was too bad, too. She had long blond hair, gray eyes, and the most gorgeous–.

A smack to his upper arm interrupted Derek's thoughts. "What?"

"Hey, Doc. Make room. Nachos are here."

Derek pulled his elbows off the bar and leaned back as Mike placed a heaping plate of nachos in front of them. "Yeah. Sorry." He smiled as his stomach reminded him it had been a while since he'd snarfed up empanadas and all the other delicious food they'd consumed at Tank's place. He grabbed a chip covered in cheese, salsa, shredded chicken, and extra jalapeños and smiled as he chewed the delicious treat. They weren't as good as Tank's nachos, of course, but they were pretty close.

Mike twisted off the caps and set cold bottles on the counter in front of them. Shaking his head, he lamented the food they ate, despite having been the one who created the bar's appetizer menu. "I have no idea how you both can stand all those jalapeños on there."

Derek and Tank exchanged a conspiratorial look as they both shoved hot pepper laden chips into their mouths.

Derek tilted his bottle and clinked it with Tank's. "Thanks."

"You bet."

Mike had treated himself to an order of cheese sticks with marinara sauce. He laughed as he chewed off a gooey bite of cheesy goodness.

For the next hour or so, Derek, Mike, and Tank talked about their various deployments. Mike and Tank occasionally offered some good advice on returning to the civilian world, for which Derek was grateful, but he didn't care to dwell on it for too long. His leg bounced on the footrest at the base of the bar while they spoke, the agitation in his gut growing as the evening progressed.

Their conversation continued a while longer when Angela stopped behind the register to ring up an order for a newly-arrived couple sitting in a booth by the far windows.

"Hey, Angela." Derek turned on a charming smile, drawing another eye roll from Tank, who continued talking with Mike and a couple of older guys sitting around the corner of the bar.

She returned his smile. "Hi, Derek." And just as quickly, she was gone, carrying a tray of whatever cocktails Mike mixed for her new customers.

Derek's face dropped the moment she turned away, as if being relieved of a mask he was forced to wear. He had so many of them, he almost didn't know how to function without one.

It was disappointing that she was involved with someone, but

Derek would be happy to swoop in and ask her out again if they ever broke up. From what he heard, she and her current boyfriend were on the outs anyway, so maybe it was only a matter of time. Plenty of other women to go around in the meantime.

Biding his time, Derek stayed until they knew the fireworks were well underway before deciding he'd spent sufficient time with his friends. Once he finished his beer, he said his goodbyes, gave a few smiles and tickles to little Maria Elena, and made a quick exit out the back door. Once outside, he sucked in a large gulp of fresh air and started walking. On the short walk home, he stepped up his pace upon hearing the last of the grand finale in the distance.

Chapter 4

Sarah

Safely inside his one-bedroom carriage house apartment, Derek closed his eyes and leaned back against the door with a prolonged exhale as if narrowly escaping danger. A few more deep breaths later, he took stock of his simple yet comfortable apartment. He unbuttoned his shirt on his way to the bedroom, then tossed it into the closet and replaced it with an old wrinkled Myrtle Beach tank top he picked out of the bottom drawer of his dresser.

Leaving the shirt untucked, he walked over to the fridge to grab the first of what was sure to be several more beers that night.

"Welcome to another Saturday night bender, Mitchell," he muttered as he popped the cap off and took a healthy swig of beer after dropping himself down on the couch. Grabbing the remote, he flipped through the channels to find some inane TV show he knew he wouldn't bother watching.

"Good." He dropped the remote next to his phone on the coffee table. "Ballgame's starting."

Downing another swallow, he leaned back and propped up his sock-covered feet on the coffee table.

While enjoying his second bottle at the bottom of the third

inning, his phone lit up with a call. Grabbing the phone off the coffee table, he answered. "Hey, Sarah"

"Hey, Derek. Didn't see you at the fireworks tonight. Thought I'd bring them to you."

"Yeah. Sure." He leaned forward on the couch. "Come on over."

"On my way."

He ended the call and tossed the phone back onto the coffee table.

Standing up and walking into the bedroom, he opened the drawer on his nightstand and grabbed the box of condoms. Giving it a shake before looking inside to see that plenty were left, he tossed it back in and shut the drawer. Finishing off his bottle, he returned to the kitchen to open another.

He was barely into his latest bottle when Sarah texted him.

Sarah: Downstairs

Beer still in hand, he walked downstairs to let in the attractive brunette. As soon as he opened the door, she jumped up and wrapped her legs around his waist, drawing him into a long, sloppy kiss before his hand let go of the doorknob.

Carrying her upstairs to his apartment, Derek neither paused their kiss nor dropped his beer before he tossed her on his bed,

Without taking his eyes off her, he took a healthy drink as she sat up and grabbed his waist. Unfastening his shorts, she offered up a mischievous grin as she reached in with her hand and leaned her head forward. With a sudden inhale, his right hand pulled her head against him as he closed his eyes. Letting his head fall back with a moan, he struggled to maintain his balance yet still managed to set his beer down on the nightstand without spilling.

Already panting, Derek pushed her down on the bed and pulled his shorts down enough to roll on a condom while she rushed to pull down her skirt and panties. As she backed up further onto the bed, he crawled on top of her, covering her mouth with his as he reached his arm underneath her. Bringing her closer, he pushed himself inside her, eliciting an annoyingly high-pitched, whiny squeal from her lips.

Sure. Her squealing annoyed him, but she delivered. She came to his place, so he couldn't argue. Inwardly, he rolled his eyes, but he was getting off, so he could put up with it for a while.

Thrusting in and out, he increased his speed until he gave a final push, collapsing with a loud exhale before rolling over on his back. She closed her eyes and smiled.

After a few minutes of nothing but the sound of their breathing, she rolled on her side to wrap her arms around him. He remained still and stared up at the ceiling, fighting against his urge to gag on the overpowering floral scent of her perfume.

Did she have to wear the whole bottle?

While pondering that question, he debated how long he wanted her to stick around.

Deciding it wasn't long, he turned away and sat up at the edge of the bed, taking a moment to tuck himself back into his boxers.

With a deep breath, he ran both hands through his hair before gulping down the rest of his beer.

"Still kind of cold," he muttered, studying the empty bottle.

Setting it back on the nightstand, he glanced behind him to see her give him a pouty look that quickly turned into a suggestive smile.

He grunted, then stood and pulled his shorts up enough to walk into the bathroom. He tossed the used condom in the trash and finally relieved himself of everything he'd drunk since returning home.

Back into the bedroom, Sarah had rolled over and rested her head on a pillow, her light sweater still on, and her panties stuck around her left ankle that dangled off the bed. Her steady breathing indicated she'd already fallen asleep.

"Shit," he said, annoyed again.

He zipped up his shorts but didn't bother buttoning them on his way to the kitchen. Collapsing back on the couch with another cold beer, he propped up his still-sock-covered feet to watch the rest of the game.

A few innings later, Sarah emerged from the bedroom. Standing behind him, she wrapped her arms around him as he took another drink. Slowly running her hands down through his chest hair toward his stomach, she leaned in to kiss him, but he shrugged her off, causing her to pull away.

Undeterred, she circled to the front of the couch, noticing how he tried to look around her to see the game.

She pulled the coffee table out just enough for his resting feet to land on the floor. That irked him, but he remained focused on the current batter. They had two runners in scoring position with only one out.

His focus changed when Sarah clumsily fell to her knees and pushed his legs apart. He made no move to stop her as she unzipped his fly and started stroking him, gently at first, then harder until his body reacted the way she wanted.

Bringing the bottle to his lips, his expression didn't change when she dropped her head, taking him in until he felt the back of her throat. Her lack of a gag reflex was her best quality. He took in a deep breath as she hollowed her cheeks, then slowly pulled back up, closing her lips and fingers tightly around him as she did. He closed his eyes and leaned his head back as her head bobbed up and down.

He reflexively brought his hand around to the back of her head, his hips matching her motion as she sped up. His breaths drew shorter until he jerked upward with a moan as his body finally let go.

She slowly pulled her lips off him with a pop, his hand already resting lazily at his side. He opened his eyes just in time to catch her swallowing. He closed his eyes again with a loud exhale, letting his head fall back against the couch.

A few deep breaths later, he leaned his head forward to take another drink and grabbed the remote off the coffee table. He turned up the volume.

"Thanks for stopping by, Sarah."

Her smile vanished, but she rose without a word to retrieve the rest of her clothes from the bedroom. Holding her purse over her shoulder, she walked straight out of the apartment. Moments later, the carriage house door slammed shut, and her car engine came to life.

Derek's attention shifted to the boarded-up Victorian home outside his window, temporarily aglow from her headlights as Sarah backed out of the driveway. Relief washed over him when she drove away, returning the abandoned home to its rightful place among the shadows.

He adjusted his shorts as he stood up, finishing his beer on the way to the kitchen, where he opened another bottle and took a long pull. On a shelf against the far wall, a framed picture caught his eye. He crossed the room and picked it up. Three young men in uniform stared back at him.

In the picture, he and his two best friends, Tank and Joey, stood outside their barracks in full combat gear, having just returned from one of countless missions they went on while stationed at Bagram Air Base in Afghanistan. They were helping people.

They were doing what they loved.

Not long after that picture was taken, Derek and Joey reenlisted, and Tank nearly died. It was a cold day in February when Tank was on the receiving end of a Taliban attack. Simply put, he was at the wrong place at the wrong time, the last of a group of men trying to jump clear of unexploded ordnance. He almost made it before it went off, sending shrapnel in all directions, and bringing down the wall they'd been using as cover.

Derek's skills as a combat medic got Tank to the medevac flight, which ultimately got him back to the base for the life-saving surgery he needed. Sure, he had an extended stay at Walter Reed, over six months, but he made it home to his wife and kids.

Joey, on the other hand, wasn't as lucky.

After their final mission eleven months earlier, Derek could only escort his best friend home in a flag-draped casket.

Knowing he would visit his friend at the cemetery the following day, Derek cast a quick glance at the green coffee mug filled with loose change and chose four coins: a quarter, a dime, a nickel, and a penny. Squeezing the coins in his palm, he carefully returned the picture to its designated place next to the triangular-shaped case holding a neatly folded flag, inscribed with his best friend's name:

Sergeant First Class Joseph Miles Parker
August 7, 1981-August 17, 2014

Derek stacked the coins on the small kitchen island next to the keys he'd tossed there earlier.

Collapsing back on the couch, he leaned back and closed his eyes, not moving again until the sun came up.

Chapter 5

Errands

Two years after Joey Parker died

AUGUST 2016

Derek was out running errands when his phone buzzed with a text alert. Parking his truck, he pulled out his phone to see that Kiro was finally sending him their dinner plans.

> Kiro: Dinner at Hamburger Inn at 7.

> Derek: Ok

> Kiro: Food first.

> Derek:

> Kiro: Food, D. Then girl.

> Derek: Fine.

> Kiro: 7 pm

> Derek: 7. Got it.

Derek had every intention of meeting his friends for burgers in the nearby city of Delaware, Ohio, but he needed to make a couple of stops first. His first was to a drive-thru liquor store for a case of his favorite beer. In other words, any beer that could get him drunk.

The worker placed the case in the bed of his truck and took his payment, making him all set for a quick visit to Joey's grave at the cemetery on the other side of the Scioto River.

Derek drove his truck past the square in town to the bridge that took him toward the old Storley industrial complex across the Scioto River. Once a major employer in the county, it shuttered its doors in the mid-1980s when the last bags of Storley feed came off the line. Derek was barely in pre-school when it happened, but he knew his dad had hired several former Storley workers when he started his contracting business.

Faded from years of neglect, the paint colors that gave each building its name could still be discerned. Blue Storley was the largest, home of the main production lines. Red and Green Storley were the next largest, followed by Yellow and Orange Storley. Smaller red brick outbuildings were generically labeled as they were mostly used for storage or maintenance offices back in the day.

Derek turned into an old parking lot filled with weeds growing up through the cracks in the pavement in front of Red Storley. The faded red building was in pretty decent condition, all things considered, with a fair number of intact plate-glass windows in front. He shut off the engine and stared in the direction of the river, thinking back to all the time he and Joey were drawn here for all the important conversations boys had while growing up, such as their many X-Men vs. the Justice League debates, how many lawns they needed to mow before they could afford the junkers they wanted to drive, how sick Derek's mom really was before she lost her battle with cancer.

Anything, really. It was their spot.

Derek took a deep breath and rounded his truck to open the tailgate. He opened the case, grabbed a handful of beers, and headed down to the river. The hot August sun soared high in the sky, offering no relief to the stretch of 90-degree-plus temperatures they'd had all month.

The trees had grown tall since he and Joey first found this place as kids. The path by the water was overgrown with brush, but he made his way to the large rock on the river's edge.

He set down the beer, then popped the top on the first can. He grabbed a rock off the ground and side-armed it toward the water. It skipped three times before plopping into the river. He chugged half a can before skipping another stone.

Water lapped at the shoreline at regular intervals, thanks to a warm, steady breeze. Derek always loved the sound of the water. It calmed him. He closed his eyes and listened. Listened to the water hitting the shore, the birds singing as they flew by, and the sound of the leaves rustling.

Just like when he was a kid, he sought out water wherever he could find it.

He smiled at the memories of his childhood, when he and Joey would sit by the river and throw stones into the water, but his smile quickly dimmed. Joey was gone, and Derek still hurt. What could he have done differently? What else could he have done for Joey during that ambush? What if he'd treated Joey's wounds in a different sequence? Would it have helped? He knew he always let his training guide him, and it had never steered him wrong, but why didn't it work that day? Why couldn't he save Joey like he did Tank?

The more Derek scrutinized his actions on the battlefield two years earlier, the angrier he grew.

Anger at the loss.

Anger at the Taliban.

Anger at not saving his best friend.

Anger.

It always came down to anger. The easiest of emotions, it always won out in the end, until the guilt took over. When the guilt reappeared, not that it ever really left, the need to escape overwhelmed him.

Leaning down, he grabbed a handful of rocks. And like he did after his mother's funeral, he threw them as hard as he could into the water and screamed at the top of his lungs.

When his lungs emptied, and his chest heaved, he threw more rocks, took a deep breath, and screamed again. And again.

And again.

Finally, he refilled his lungs without the scream, but his breaths were short as he fought to rein in lingering feelings of helplessness.

"Fuck!"

Derek turned to find the makeshift trash can he and Joey had made one summer out of some fencing and scrap wood. It still stood —kind of—behind the large rock they used to sit on while debating life and other things important to preteen and teenage boys.

He emptied the first can, threw it in the trash as hard as he could, and, unsatisfied, popped the top off the next. Balancing the beer on his knee, he started scrolling through his phone until he saw an ad he'd seen many times before: a suicide and crisis hotline. A few moments passed as he stared at the ad inviting him to call for help.

Should he?

Derek had previously debated whether or not to call, even going so far as to type out the three-digit number, 9-8-8, a few times, but ultimately opted against it since he didn't consider himself suicidal.

It wasn't for him, right?

He didn't think so.

In other words, he chickened out.

Sure, he occasionally drank beer to escape, but not to kill himself. As for women? Safe to say, there were plenty. After all, they offered a decent, albeit temporary, escape as well.

He huffed out a laugh at the thought. Then, he turned off his phone and grabbed another rock, which he promptly tossed into the water.

What could he say? He liked to get off, and women provided a curvier and much softer alternative to his own hand. Beyond that, relationships just weren't his thing. The Dear John letter he received from Kaitlyn Sutters during his early deployment at Bagram taught him that lesson. Sex? That was definitely his thing. But relationships? No way. That's why he didn't want women to stay the night. He never enjoyed the morning after. He'd have to cook them breakfast. They would read into it, and then they'd want more.

Not worth the effort.

Derek laughed again, but it didn't last long. His thoughts wandered to all the times he and Joey spent talking and sitting on this same rock. God, he missed his friend. He took a deep breath, held it for a few seconds, and released it slowly.

He finished the beer, crushed the can in his fist, and then tossed it into the leaning trash can. Standing up, he stared at the sky for a few moments before kicking at the dirt and returning to his truck.

He had one more stop to make.

Chapter 6

Help Me

D EREK LEFT THE RIVER BEHIND AND DROVE TO THE CEMETERY, just a few miles away from the abandoned factory. Joey's grave was right next to his mom's, just beyond a curve by a huge oak tree. A good forty to fifty feet high, it towered over the northwest corner of the cemetery, offering shade to the nearby gravesites.

He pulled up beside the tree, which was barely outside the narrow lane winding through that corner of the cemetery, and hit the brakes. One of the unopened cans rolled onto the floor of the passenger seat.

"Shit," Derek said as he leaned down to retrieve it, but the truck bucked and shot forward into the tree trunk. He shot straight up and looked forward to see what hit him. "Shit!"

His foot had slipped off the brake before he put his truck in gear. Fortunately, he was only a foot or two away when his truck lurched forward. Frustrated, he quickly shifted it into Park with a few choice curse words and retrieved the can that was still on the floor along with several others that had just joined it. He shoved it back in the case and grabbed another one, which he opened and started to drink.

A few sips later, he opened his door and stepped out, case of beer in hand. Before walking too far, he stopped and made an about-face, reaching inside the truck to grab the coins resting on the console. The movement disturbed a pair of cardinals flitting about, catching his attention until they disappeared through some trees across the cemetery. Joey's grave wasn't too far away, just on the other side of the enormous oak tree now blocking his truck.

He leaned over and set the case of beer down next to Joey's grave, which still looked shiny and new. Derek reached down and pulled a weed, which he tossed away from the graves in the row. He knelt down and traced Joey's first name on the stone.

JOSEPH MILES PARKER
SERGEANT FIRST CLASS
U.S. ARMY
AUGUST 7, 1981 - AUGUST 17, 2014
LOVING SON • BROTHER • FRIEND

Standing, Derek opened his hand to reveal the loose change. He bounced the four coins a few times before stilling them in his palm. With a heavy heart, he first pinched the penny between two fingers and then placed it atop Joey's gravestone.

One penny for visiting his grave.

One nickel for going through bootcamp together.

One dime came after, for having served together.

Derek took a deep breath and stared at the quarter that remained in his palm. Hesitating, he finally placed it next to the others.

One quarter for being with Joey when he died.

As if he'd ever forget that. If nothing else, Derek was going to show his respect for his best friend, even if the whole world knew he was the only one in town who was with him when he died on that battlefield.

With his fingers still touching the gravestone, he closed his eyes. "What am I doing, Joey?" he asked out loud, knowing he wouldn't get an answer. He drank the remains of his can and shifted to sit cross-legged in the grass that had grown over the top of Joey's final resting place. "I don't want to get used to you not being here."

Derek sniffed and wiped his nose with the back of his hand. "Damn, I miss you. And, uh, I don't think I'm doing very well. I'm not sleeping. And maybe the guys were right because I'm fucking every woman I can, just to forget, but it doesn't work." He chugged another gulp of beer. "Nothing works, and I don't know how long I can keep this up, you know?"

He blinked back tears and stared up at the sky that dimmed when clouds passed in front of the sun.

"I'm so sorry, Joey. I'm so sorry I didn't do better."

Movement drew his gaze, and he shifted. Wincing, he pulled his phone out of his pocket while a few birds flew by and landed on Joey's gravestone. Two yellow finches. Derek smiled, though it didn't reach his eyes. "Message?"

He turned his phone back on and stared at the texting app. Maybe he'd try calling this time rather than texting. No. Who was he kidding? He wouldn't call. He'd tapped those three numbers so many times before, but he'd never actually hit send.

Until now.

Crisis Line: You've reached 988 Suicide & Crisis Lifeline. This is Skylar. How may I help you?

Derek: Um … Help? I can't

Crisis Line: Can't what?

Derek: Live with what I did.

Crisis Line: What did you do?

> Derek: Killed him.

> Crisis Line: Killed who?

Derek's heart raced, and he paused to consider whether or not he should finish his confession. He held his phone out and stared at it.

> Crisis Line: Are you still there?

"No." He quickly closed and stuck his phone in his pocket. He knew he needed something, someone, but wasn't ready. Not yet. Someday, maybe. Someday, he'd talk to someone, but not yet. Not today. "I'm sorry, Joey."

Derek wanted his best friend back. He pulled his phone back out of his pocket, stared at it for a few moments, then shoved it back into his pocket again, this time opting to leave it there. He finished the most recent can of beer, crushing it in his hand before dropping it to the ground next to his half-empty case. He checked his watch. 18:25. Six-twenty-five PM.

"I have time for another one before dinner." He popped open two more cans. "No need to rush." He took one and turned it upside down, pouring it out over Joey's grave. He held up the other as if to toast. "Here's to you, Joey."

Chapter 7

Graveside

"Have you heard from him?"

"No. Can't get him to respond." Kiro plugged in the code and opened the door so he and Tank could enter the carriage house, a long, rectangular building with two apartments on the second floor above a large garage area. "I was worried when he didn't show for dinner."

Tank jogged up the stairs and pounded on the door to Derek's one-bedroom apartment. "Hey, Doc. You there?" He turned to Kiro. "Do you have a key?"

"Yep. Abe gave it to me a while back, just in case." Kiro unlocked the door.

Flipping on a light, they both walked into the tidy apartment, noticing only the empty beer bottles out of place on the counter and coffee table.

"Found his backpack." Kiro picked it up off the chair and held it up for Tank to see.

"Shit." Tank rushed into the bedroom, checking both the bathroom and the walk-in closet. "He's not here." One look through the window revealed a conspicuously missing truck. "Tell me he didn't drink and drive."

"He might have," Kiro said, sounding defeated. "I just hope I'm wrong." He darted downstairs with Tank on his heels. "Come on. I'll drive."

"What are you thinking?" Tank asked as Kiro pulled out of the oversized driveway.

"It's just a hunch, but," Kiro shook his head and turned toward the edge of town. "How long has it been since ..."

Tank looked upwards long enough to confirm the math. "Yesterday would have been two years to the day."

"Right, but we were all on shift yesterday. He couldn't think about Joey while we were working." Kiro turned into the main entrance of Grant's Crossing Cemetery. The gravel crunched underneath his tires as he navigated the narrow lanes to the newer section. "There it is."

The last remnants of the late-setting sun shone down through the leaves, allowing them to make out the silhouette of a large, blue pickup truck.

Tank looked up to see Derek's blue Silverado parked diagonally across the lane, blocking passage for anyone who might try to get through. Seemingly undamaged, the grill rested solidly against the trunk of a large oak tree. The driver's side door hung wide open. Empty beer cans were strewn about on the ground below.

Before Kiro even stopped his SUV, Tank jumped out and sprinted to the other side of the tree to Joey Parker's gravesite. "No. No. No. No. No. Shit. KIRO!" Tank called out from the far side of the wide tree trunk. "OVER HERE!"

Kiro ran around in time to see Tank drop to the ground, where Derek was sprawled across his best friend's grave, face resting on the grass. More beer cans were tossed on the ground.

They were all empty.

Tank's quick glance revealed forty-one cents on top of Joey's headstone.

Kiro wiped his brow and joined them just as Tank rolled Derek over on his back, earning a faint groan out of Derek. Reaching down to feel his pulse, he haphazardly wiped some of the dirt off Derek's face. "He's breathing, but his pulse is weak. Let's get him out of here."

Derek stirred and turned to Kiro and Tank. "I think I'm gonna be late for dinner, K. Oh, hey, Tank," he said with a drunken smile before passing out.

"Let's get him up," Tank instructed as he ducked his head under Derek's arm.

Kiro helped lift Derek enough so Tank could carry him over his shoulders. A shorter man than Derek, Tank grunted as he stood. Derek's limp body draped down Tank's back as he took him to Kiro's SUV. Kiro ran ahead to open the cargo door and fold down the seats. Another moan escaped Derek's mouth as Tank carefully placed him in the back and climbed inside.

"Keep him on his side." Kiro shut the door and jumped in the driver's seat.

"Yeah. Yeah. I've got it." Tank snapped, trying to rouse Derek from his worse-than-usual drunken stupor.

"Hey, Tank. I'm gonna barf." Derek said just before dropping his head and puking his guts out in the back of Kiro's SUV.

"Ah, shit," Tank exclaimed. "He just puked back here!"

In response, Kiro muttered some choice swear words in Bulgarian.

"You're lucky you're facing away from me," Tank said, wincing at the putrid smell inside the vehicle. "Otherwise, I might be pissed."

On the drive back to Derek's apartment, Kiro broke all sorts of speed limits, grateful they didn't encounter any police along the way.

Despite his Ranger and firefighter training, Tank still struggled to carry Derek up the stairs to his apartment. He eased Derek onto the bed, got his shirt off, and turned him on his side to keep his airway open. "Pretty sure you weighed less when we were in Basic, Doc."

Kiro kneeled beside the bed and opened the med bag he always kept in his SUV. Taking his friend's vitals, he felt better when another groan escaped Derek's lips, though his breath made Kiro want to pass out from the stench. "Tank. Grab the trash can out of the bathroom. Whatever he drank will probably come back to haunt him again after a while."

Tank retrieved the trash can and set it on the floor by the bed. Then he took off Derek's shoes. "Well?"

"Well, what? " Kiro snapped. "He's weak. He's dehydrated. He's fucking drunk off his ass."

"Guess we just wait now, huh?"

"Yep. Let him sleep it off." Kiro responded without enthusiasm. "Not much else we can do except make sure he keeps breathing and doesn't choke when he gets sick."

"Jesus, Doc." Tank gently rested his hand on Derek's shoulder. "Why are you doing this?"

"He's gonna need fluids and nutrients. I'll stay and watch over him."

"Got a banana bag?"

"Yeah." Kiro nodded toward a small refrigerator in the corner of Derek's bedroom. "Already checked. He's got a couple in there."

"Okay. I'll head back to the cemetery to clean up Joey's gravesite and figure out how to bring Derek's truck back. I shouldn't be too long."

"No need to come back. I'll watch him tonight." Kiro offered, his expression as grim as Tank's. "Get back to your family. We can get his truck in the morning."

Tank's shoulders sagged as he dropped a hand to Kiro's shoulder. "Thanks, man."

"Yep." Kiro settled on the floor against the wall and scrubbed his face with his hands. A book on the nightstand caught his eye. "You and your spy novels, D."

Keeping Derek's bookmark in place, he opened the book to the first chapter and started reading.

Chapter 8

Bring You Back

Derek sprinted into the fire station with his backpack over his shoulder just as the A-shift firefighters were leaving.

"Hurry up, Mitchell," one of them encouraged him with a laugh.

He gave a halfhearted wave and zipped through the lounge as they laughed, making a beeline for the locker room. He'd almost finished changing into his uniform when Tank appeared.

"Glad you decided to join us today, Doc."

Fully dressed, Derek shot his friend a glare before reaching his hand into the top shelf of his locker and pulling out some eye drops. "I'm not late." He quickly dropped some of the refreshing liquid into each eye, blinking a few times as he stared up at the ceiling. Dabbing the excess under each eye with a finger, he screwed the lid back on and placed it back on the shelf.

"What do you want, Tank?"

Tank pointed toward Derek's locker shelf. "You really think that's going to prevent anyone from seeing you're hungover?"

"I'm fine." Derek grabbed a bottle of acetaminophen and popped a few in his mouth before shoving the bottle back inside. He slammed the locker shut and tried to slip past, but Tank grabbed his arm.

Derek snapped. "What?"

"You've gotta get some help, man."

"I said, I'm fine."

"You weren't fine when Kiro and I dragged you off Joey's grave, surrounded by empty beer cans."

"That was an exception. You know what day it was."

"I do." Tank paused. "Look. I know the VA isn't always the best, but you'll never get in to see a doctor if you never make the call to begin with."

"Tank ... " Derek shook his head. "You need to let it go. I've got it under control."

Tank scoffed. "I've seen your idea of control. Go see someone. There are people who can help you."

"Can they change what happened?" Derek shrugged his arm loose as Kiro appeared in the doorway.

"Doc." Tank took a step back.

Derek remained silent, so Tank continued. "He's gone, Doc. You know they can't. But you need to be able to deal with that."

Derek's heart started racing. "You mean I need to deal with having killed him?"

Tank rattled off a litany of curses in Spanish. "No. What you need is to get your head out of your ass and get help."

Derek glowered at Tank. His voice deepened while attempting to control his anger. "Drop it."

"No. I will *not* drop it." Tank got in Derek's face. "You have not yet messed up on the job, but at the rate you're going, it's inevitable. People's lives are at stake ... including Kiro's."

"I've never messed up."

Tank poked him in the chest. "And you also can't drive the ambulance if you get a DUI, either. You're lucky it was just a tree this time. You're gonna lose your job, man. Then what will you do?"

Movement caught Derek's eye. Tank followed his gaze to find Kiro standing in the doorway to the locker room.

"What's up, K?"

Sensing the tension in the room, Kiro's eyes darted back and forth between Derek and Tank.

"Chief wants to see you."

Derek's glare turned fierce. He shook his head at Tank. "Tell me you didn't–"

"Talk to him, Doc."

"Fuck!" Derek slammed his hand against the locker and stormed out of the room.

Tank met Kiro's gaze. "Did you talk to the chief?"

"Nope."

"Me, neither."

Derek knocked on the door frame. "You wanna see me, Chief?"

"Yeah." Chief Travis waved him in from behind his desk. "Come on in, Mitchell. Close the door."

Derek exhaled but turned to close the door behind him.

Chief Travis motioned toward the chairs in front of his desk. "Have a seat."

Derek sat down while the chief flipped through some papers on his desk, occasionally writing notes.

"How are things going with you?" he asked nonchalantly.

"Fine." Derek's response was curt.

"Everything at home okay?"

"Yeah," Derek assured him. "It's fine."

"Sleeping okay?"

"Like a log."

"Mmhmm," the chief grunted, not looking up from his papers.

"Seeing anyone?"

A crease formed on Derek's brow. "Not seriously, no."

"Hmm." Chief Travis gathered the papers together and tapped them against the table to arrange them in a neat pile. He set them down on his desk, folded his hands together, and finally met Derek's gaze.

"Are you talking to anybody?"

"What do you mean?"

"I know it's been tough since you came back."

Derek shook his head with a pronounced eye roll. "I don't know what you've heard, Chief, but I've been back for a while–"

Chief Travis held up his hand to cut Derek off. He reached into a drawer and pulled out a card, which he offered to Derek. "I know the VA is an option for you, but I also know that takes time. Here's someone who can help right away."

"I'm fine," Derek insisted.

"I'm sure you are."

"Chief, I'm fine."

"I saw your truck yesterday."

"What?"

"At the cemetery."

Derek froze in place as his stomach clenched.

"I was there putting fresh flowers on my mother's grave yesterday morning when I saw Tank in the distance. He was cleaning up a gravesite."

"Shit."

"And then I saw him drive away." Chief Travis took a breath. He continued in his usual calm voice. "Only, I saw him drive away in your truck, which made me wonder. Why would he do that?"

"It's been two years–"

"Two years since you lost your best friend," Chief Travis finished his sentence. "Have you ever talked to anyone about it?"

"I'm fine," Derek's voice carried much less strength than when he walked in.

"You're fine. Of course." He extended the card to Derek again. "Take the damned card, Mitchell. He's helped out a lot of first responders. Myself included. He's also a veteran, so he'll relate more than you think."

Reluctantly, Derek accepted the proffered card.

"He's expecting your call."

Derek stood up.

"But talk to him soon."

"Chief ... "

"Today, if you can. Or you'll be on full-time desk duty and inspections."

Derek winced at the thought. "Yes, Chief."

Chief Travis stood up as well. "I can only imagine what happened that would give Tank cause to clean up your best friend's gravesite and drive *your* truck home, but you don't need to risk your job or your life simply because you're too damned stubborn. There's no shame in asking for help, Derek."

Derek glared at the chief. "Will it help bring my best friend back?"

"No," Chief Travis answered solemnly. "But it'll help bring *you* back."

THERAPY 1

A New Doc

A MAN WITH SHORT, SALT-AND-PEPPER HAIR STOOD UP FROM behind the desk and approached Derek with a smile. He extended his hand in greeting. "You must be Derek Mitchell."

"Yes."

"I'm Dr. Zachary Majors." He welcomed Derek inside his office. "Come on in. Have a seat wherever you'd like and make yourself comfortable." He shut the door, walked back inside, and leaned against the front of his dark wooden desk.

While the doctor introduced himself and advised Derek to call him whatever he wanted, Dr. Majors, Zach, Doc, Doc Majors, etc., Derek found a spot on the side of the couch closest to the corner of the room. He leaned forward, resting his forearms on his knees while he scanned and took inventory of the room, like he always did when clearing houses in Afghanistan during a search for Taliban insurgents.

There were two doors, one he came through from the waiting room and another in the far corner that presumably led to a bathroom or the rest of the office. Three large windows let light in from one side of his desk until it almost met the couch. Each one could be opened and led out to a fire escape on the west side of the building, facing both the alley behind Lincoln Ave as well as a handful of houses leading out toward the Scioto River. The patient could sit behind the wall for cover, but the doctor was exposed. The small, half-sized refrigerator tucked between bookshelves covered with more books would have offered no protection.

"Your chief said you'd be stopping by. Said you needed to talk some things through."

"More like made me come, or he'd bench me."

The doctor smiled. "Something like that, yes."

Derek didn't respond.

"Before we get started, do you have any questions?"

"How long will this last?"

"Today?" He curved his lips into a thoughtful frown. "Maybe an hour or so."

Derek rolled his eyes. "So after today, that's it? You'll sign off and let the chief know I'm good?"

Smiling, the doctor rested his palms on the edge of the desk and crossed his legs at the ankles. "Probably not."

"I don't have time for this." Derek stood up.

"You'll want to make time," Doc Majors said with an air of nonchalance.

"I don't want to be here." Derek shook his head and started to walk out. "I don't need this."

"No one ever does, so I won't take that personally, but if you walk out of here without talking to me, you'll be taken off active duty before you make it out of the building."

That stopped Derek in his tracks.

"So you may want to sit back down and make yourself comfortable."

Derek's hand went up and scrubbed his face. After a few long moments, he turned around and returned to where he was sitting on the couch. "Fine."

"Your chief told me you don't always sleep well at the station."

"I sleep fine," Derek lied.

"Mmhmm." The doctor reached back on his desk for a narrow blue file and pulled out a few pages. "Said you'd been serving as a paramedic for about a year and a half now, is that right?"

"Sounds about right."

"And before that, you spent nearly thirteen years in the Army?"

"Just over thirteen years." Derek glanced over at the unopened mystery door.

Someone could come through the door at any minute.

"Right." The doctor's gaze followed Derek's interest in the corner door. He set the papers back down atop the folder. "And your DD-214 in your Army file says the same thing as your service record at Grant's Crossing Fire Department, nothing but exemplary service as a combat medic with the Army Rangers from basic training through an honorable discharge, December 24, 2014."

"Right."

"How many deployments to Iraq and Afghanistan did you have?"

"Too many to count."

"Too many to count?"

"We supported special forces. Where they went, we went. Our deployments weren't always as long as regular infantry, but we deployed more often."

"Mmhmm." The doctor paused to review the papers in his hand. "So, nearly two years of medic training, then you deployed overseas on multiple occasions from 2003-2014."

Derek released an annoyed sigh. "Right."

"Maybe even a commendation or two in there."

Joey earned the Silver Star, but it had to be awarded posthumously. It took up a permanent spot next to the triangular frame displaying the flag that covered his coffin. Both the flag and Joey's medal sat atop Derek's bookshelf.

"Two Bronze Stars. And a Purple Heart? Yes?"

"Yeah."

"If you don't like the couch, you're welcome to sit in one of the chairs."

Derek glanced over at one of the two tan-colored cushioned chairs but made no move to relocate.

The doctor's eyes followed Derek's gaze, but returned to his paperwork. "But you're fine, right?"

"Yeah."

"What's your favorite beer?"

"Huh?"

"Why are you here?"

Derek scoffed but answered with another glance at the unopened door. "You said it yourself. I come here, or I get benched."

"But you don't have a favorite?"

"What?"

"A favorite beer."

"No."

"Ahh." The doctor strode over to the unopened door.

Derek started bouncing his knee up and down. He glanced back and forth between the windows and the door to the small waiting area just beyond. There were windows in the waiting room, too.

If someone came in, the fire escape wouldn't protect him.

"Why are you here?"

"I told you already." Derek shifted uncomfortably in his seat. His heart raced.

Did the doc have any beer in the fridge?

"Chief said I needed to come here, or like you said, I'll be taken off active duty."

"Why hasn't he done that already?"

Derek's head snapped up. "What?"

"Why hasn't the chief taken you off active duty already?"

The doctor's overly calm voice was getting on Derek's last nerve.

His heart rate quickened, and he rubbed his hands on his thighs. "Because I'm fucking good at my job, that's why." He glared at the doctor but swallowed, still trying to catch his breath.

"Okay," the doctor acknowledged with an annoyingly indifferent tone. He paused a few moments while Derek shifted uncomfortably on the couch. "Anything else I should know?"

Derek's forehead creased, but he gave a subtle headshake. "No."

"Hmm."

Dr. Majors straightened a book on the shelf behind him but maintained a watchful eye on Derek, who glanced at the far door no fewer than three more times.

Finally, the doctor stepped over to the door and opened it wide, offering a full view of what lay beyond. "It's a twelve-foot-long hallway."

"What?"

"The first door on the left is a six-by-eight-foot bathroom."

Derek sucked in his first real gulp of air since entering the room while the doctor described what was beyond the door.

"Just after the bathroom is a small broom closet about four feet wide. And beyond that is another small lounge area about twelve feet by ten feet with a couch and two chairs and a window facing south, leading out to another fire escape."

The doctor continued adding details for Derek. "Turn north at the end of the hallway, past the small coffee station inside the room, and you'll be able to take the stairs. You'll come out on Grant Street."

Derek breathed in and out in an attempt to slow his heart rate, but it took effort. More effort than he thought it should. He wiped his hands on his jeans again, rubbing them up and down his thighs to his knees. After a few minutes, he finally started calming down. His heart rate finally slowed, and he could draw in enough air to relax enough to not want to jump out of his own skin.

Merely possessing the knowledge of what lay beyond that door was enough to bring himself the slightest semblance of calm.

He dropped his head in his hands. "Fuck."

Doc Majors returned the papers to the file folder and sat down in a chair next to the couch.

He leaned forward and spoke softly. "Why are you here, Derek?"

Derek lost all sense of control over his features and shot a pleading look to the doctor. He swallowed and cleared his throat, but could only speak in a whisper. "I ... I don't know, Doc." He swallowed again. "I don't know."

The doctor nodded in response. "Okay." He stood up and returned to his desk. "I'll see you again after your next shift, alright?"

"Yeah." Derek stood and took a few steps before making eye contact with the doctor. He opened his mouth to say something, but didn't have it in him to speak, so he nodded instead, exiting the room through the open, no-longer mystery door.

Chapter 9

Overdose

Two years and one month after Joey Parker died

September 2016

"Hey. Did you know that a deer can jump higher than a house?" Kiro asked while wheeling the gurney out of the hospital emergency department. There was never a doubt about how seriously he took his job, but he could never resist messing with his best friend and partner.

Derek gave him a weary glance. "Uh, no. Didn't know that."

"Not sure why you don't. Houses can't jump." Kiro said as he shut the doors and walked to the front. He was still smiling as he sat down on the passenger side of the ambulance.

"Shit, K." Derek's head dropped as he stood for a minute before heading to the front of the ambulance. "You need to stop."

Though rarely able to avoid Kiro's bad jokes, he endured them nonetheless as he sat down behind the wheel and fastened his seatbelt.

"You're going to be the next fire chief when Chief Travis retires, aren't you?" He put the ambulance in gear for the short drive back to the fire station. "We'll never be able to escape bad jokes. I mean, seriously. He's at least a dad. You? You have no excuse."

Kiro's laughter said it all, so Derek attempted a change of

subject while waiting for the light to change. "You know, it looks like I may have to move out of the carriage house."

"Oh yeah?" Kiro asked.

"Yeah. Not sure when, but pizza and beer for anyone who lends a hand. Pretty sure that's the going rate for helping friends move."

"Count me in. But, why so soon?"

"You know how the owner who had started fixing the place was really sick? Well, I guess they're finally sending someone out this week." Derek explained as an alert came across their radios.

"Dispatch to GC Medic."

Kiro placed his hand over the black radio hanging across his uniform and pressed the button. "GC Medic. Go ahead, Dispatch."

"Unconscious man in vehicle at the Blue entrance, Storley Industrial Complex. Possible overdose."

"Copy that. Medic en route."

Derek flipped on the sirens and lights and turned to cross to the other side of the Scioto River, hoping the rain would hold off until after the call.

"This week, huh?"

"Yeah. I just found out on Friday. Maybe they'll still rent it out and I can stay. At least dad has some space for me for the time being if I have to find a new place." Derek gave a short laugh. "Moving back home in my thirties wasn't exactly the plan, though I suppose it wouldn't be the first time."

"Pretty sure reentering civilian life doesn't count, D."

Derek nodded. "True that."

"Still." Kiro started laughing. "It would put a cramp in your social life."

"Speaking of which," Derek grinned. "I have a date with Angela tomorrow night."

Kiro shook his head and laughed. "She finally caved, huh?"

"You know women can't resist me."

Kiro rolled his eyes.

"But she finally broke up last month with her now-ex boyfriend."

"Seriously, man. Is there a woman in town you haven't slept with yet?"

"Yeah." Derek smirked. "Celeste."

Kiro shot him a dirty look. "Lucky for me, she has better taste," he said of his girlfriend.

"Her loss."

"Yeah, no. I don't think so."

Derek laughed. "When are you guys gonna get hitched, anyway? I mean, as long as she's technically single–"

Kiro added a warning, his face expressionless. "Never forget I have the ability to cut your balls off–with or without sedation."

Derek chuckled as he raised his fingers off the steering wheel in surrender. "Would never do that to you, K."

"See to it that you don't," Kiro said with a friendly glare that morphed into a laugh.

Passing by the last of the cornfields while heading toward the abandoned industrial complex, Derek started to speak, but Kiro cut him short, pointing to their left. "There's the car."

Derek killed the sirens as they eased into the narrow lane between a large, blue, U-shaped, abandoned industrial building. Lights still flashing, they stopped the ambulance near a parked blue sedan with two wide-open front doors.

They rushed out with their go bags to find a teenage boy hanging out of the driver's seat, occasionally gasping for air. Having just emptied the contents of his stomach, his face was still hanging above the ground.

"He's just a kid." Kiro reached down to feel his neck for a pulse. "Pulse is weak and thready. Hey buddy. Wake up! You with us?" He shined a light into the boy's eyes and mouth. "Pupils are constricted and non-reactive. Throat looks clear."

He gently fastened a collar around what appeared to be a young teenager, at best, barely old enough to drive, careful not to let his head move side to side. A quick glance to the passenger seat revealed a cell phone with the live 911 call next to an empty pill bottle.

Kiro rotated the bottle to read the label: *OxyContin® - extended-release tablets*

"Shit! He chewed Oxy. Help me get him out."

A faint moan escaped the boy's lips before his groggy eyes rolled up into the back of his head, and his body went limp. Kiro patted his face and, with a gloved hand, forced his jaw open to discover a hint of a white gritty substance. "Hey, kid. Stay with me."

Derek set the backboard he carried onto the ground and together, they carefully removed the boy from the car and placed him on the backboard so he was lying on his back. "He stopped breathing."

Kiro wasted no time reaching into his bag for the naloxone spray while Derek grabbed the oxygen mask to help the boy breathe.

"Yep." Kiro nodded simultaneously. "Pushing *Narcan*."

Derek lifted the mask long enough for Kiro to push the spray into the boy's nose before starting the oxygen back up.

"Come on. Come on."

The boy's eyes opened, and he took a weak breath.

"Welcome back, kid." Kiro leaned into the car and hit the speaker button on the phone. "Dispatch, this is GC Medic. We're on-site assisting the patient."

"Copy that, Medic. Disengaging call." Kiro set the phone on the gurney with the patient. "Alright. Let's get him up. We may have to hit him again on our way to Children's." Kiro grabbed his side of the backboard to lift him onto the gurney. Once raised, Derek continued with the oxygen as they wheeled him to the ambulance.

Kiro took care of their patient while Derek took the wheel to make the trip to Children's Hospital in Columbus.

In the back, Kiro hooked him up to the heart monitors and an IV in case he needed to administer naloxone again on the way to the hospital.

"GC Medic to Dispatch. Victim's a minor. En route to Children's." Derek relayed, sirens blaring.

"Copy that, Medic. GC Police are heading to the scene and will check in upon your return to quarters."

"Copy that."

Chapter 10

Breakfast

SUNRISE OVER GRANT'S CROSSING PROMISED TO TURN THE first sunny day in over a week into a beautiful autumn day. Sidewalks were finally drying out after a week of intermittent rainfall, the worst of which hit during Friday night's football game at Grant's Crossing High School. Drenched though they were, the Fighting Cannons came out on top thanks to some great passing by the star quarterback.

Downtown, across from the tree-lined square, friends and neighbors gathered at Baba's Diner for breakfast and to get caught up on the latest goings-on in town.

"Another coffee, Russ?" Anna asked in her mild, eastern European accent, carafe in hand.

A man with a gray buzz cut responded. "Yeah. Top it off if you would, please, Anna. While you're at it, can I have some more of your *mekitsis?*"

"*Razbira se,*" *Of course,* she rolled her Rs, responding in her native Bulgarian. "With raspberries?"

"Yes, please!"

"Coming right up," she said with a smile. "Alex!" she called back to her husband. "*Mekitsi, molya!*"

"*Dobre*," Alex confirmed in response.

"Good morning, Russ." A tall, black man with a deep, baritone voice extended his hand in greeting and took a seat at the counter.

"Hi, Nate!" Russ shook his hand. "Have a nice weekend?"

"Not so bad. Sure glad it stopped raining."

"No kidding!" Russ agreed. "Great game on Friday, huh?"

"Yes, it was," he agreed.

Anna placed a cup in front of him and filled it with coffee. "The usual, Nate?"

"Yes, please. Thank you!"

Anna turned around to put the order in.

"That precision pass in the fourth quarter was a thing of beauty." He leaned forward and held up his coffee mug, "I tell you, it was the final straw that broke the back of their defense. That Hunter kid sure has a bright future ahead of him."

"Yeah, he does," Russ agreed, taking a sip of his coffee.

"So, Russ. Did you hear that Brockmoor has a new owner?"

"You don't say. Who?"

"I dunno. Another person from out east, I hear." Nate shrugged. "Jackie was talking to my wife at church yesterday and mentioned that someone was coming in this week to pick up the keys."

"Hmm," grunted Russ. "I wonder what'll happen to it. It used to be pretty grand in its day, I hear."

"Yeah. It'll be nice to see another historic home in town brought back to life. With any luck, it'll be something other than offices or apartments."

"Or torn down," Russ added while Nate nodded in agreement.

The shop bell rang as Anna set the plates in front of Russ and Nate. She glanced up to see Kiro and Derek dragging themselves through the door.

Kiro's dad waved from the back as Kiro greeted his mom with a kiss on the cheek. "Hi, Mom," Kiro said, waving through the pass-through to the kitchen, "Hi, Dad!"

"Hi, Mrs. M." Derek leaned in and kissed her on the cheek as well. He nodded to Nate and Russ before collapsing in a booth by the front window.

Looking at the counter, Kiro offered a nod, "Morning, Nate. Morning, Russ."

"Good morning, boys," they responded in tandem.

"Tough night?" Anna asked her son as Derek dropped his backpack on the seat next to him.

"No more than usual," he gave an exhausted smile.

"Hungry, Derek?"

"Yes, ma'am!" he perked up with a tired grin.

"Where's Steve?"

"Had something going on with Tara before she opened her shop or something," Kiro said while Derek snickered, knowing exactly what Steve and Tara were up to. "We're meeting up with him later, though."

"Mmhmm. Help yourselves to some coffee, boys, while I get you both something to eat." Anna went behind the counter while Kiro filled two cups, giving one to Derek before taking a huge gulp from his own.

"Ahh," he exhaled. "I needed this."

"No kidding."

"What a night. I could fall asleep right here and now."

"Heh. Me, too. Think your mom would mind?"

"Probably."

Kiro was still chuckling as his mom set down two plates of food and glasses of orange juice. "Enjoy!"

"Thanks, Mom."

"Thanks, Mrs. M," echoed Derek.

Both men dug into their breakfasts like they hadn't eaten in days. Halfway through emptying his plate, Derek spoke first with his mouth full of food. "I wonder what's going to happen to that kid we took down to Children's. What's his name again? Caden?" He washed a bite down with some OJ.

"I think so. Yeah," Kiro replied, still chewing. "They'll probably keep him for a psych eval."

"I sure hope he's okay. Too much of that going around these days."

"More coffee, boys?"

"No thanks, Mrs. M," Derek answered as he smiled up at her. "I'm stuffed."

She patted him on the shoulder before moving on to the next table.

Stifling a yarn, Derek stood up and stretched. Before grabbing his pack, he tucked a few bills underneath the plate, knowing that Kiro's mom would never accept them if he handed them to her directly.

Kiro stood and ran his hands through his hair. He grabbed his pack. "I'm beat. I think I'll head upstairs to crash for a couple hours. I'll be over later for the game."

"Sounds good." Derek shook his friend's hand. "See you later."

Kiro turned and headed to the back of the dining area, disappearing behind an employees-only door to get to his apartment above the diner.

Derek shifted his pack over one shoulder and started toward the front door just as a beautiful woman in form-fitting blue jeans, a red cotton top, and a well-worn messenger bag walked in.

After nearly bumping into each other a few times, each going the same direction back and forth, trying to get past the other, she stopped moving and peered up at him.

Making eye contact, Derek took in her golden-brown eyes as his lips curled into a smile. He noticed a small scar over one eye, but didn't get out of her way until she raised an eyebrow and released an audible exhale.

Confident he'd have another opportunity, he stepped aside so she could pass.

"After you, ma'am," he said with a big grin, extending his arm in a formal bowing motion to welcome her inside, his eyes following her as she walked by. After he took a moment to look her up and down, he headed out the door.

Chapter 11

New Owner in Town

Derek buzzed Kiro into his carriage house apartment. Once inside, Kiro shoved a bag at him. "These are from Mom."

Derek opened the container inside to reveal some of Anna Marinova's famous baklava. He grabbed a piece and moaned as he took a bite. "I love your mom."

"Yep. She's the best." Kiro plopped himself down on the couch and grabbed the remote. "What station is the game on?"

"Six, I think."

Kiro scrolled through the channels until finding the commentators making their usual pre-game predictions. Tossing the remote on the coffee table, he picked up a book and read the back cover. "American Assassin. Is this the Mitch Rapp prequel?" he asked, referring to the series by author Vince Flynn.

"One of 'em, yeah."

"How is it? I haven't read this one yet."

"It's good. I just finished it. You can take it if you want."

"Thanks!" Kiro started flipping through the pages as if he were going to start reading it on the spot. Kiro turned and rested his elbow on the back of Derek's couch. "How'd it go today? Did you see the guy–"

"Yeah," Derek cut him off. "It was fine."

"Good," Kiro said. "So, I threw out this idea to Celeste the other day."

"Oh?"

"You know she's always rotating coffee flavors at the shop, right?"

"Yeah?"

"Well, she has her regulars, sure, but sometimes, she discontinues them in favor of totally new flavors. And well, that's great and all, but ... " Kiro couldn't hide his excitement. "I think she should occasionally bring some of the discontinued flavors back."

"Not a bad idea."

"So now she's thinking about it."

"Cool." Derek opened his refrigerator. "Want a pop?"

"Yeah. Thanks." Without looking, Kiro held his hand out behind him as Derek dropped a cold Coke on his palm.

Kiro popped the top and took a drink while starting the first chapter. "Anyway, I told her I think she should call them Has Beans."

Derek pressed his fingers to the bridge of his nose and groaned.

Proud of himself, Kiro chuckled and read the first page.

The buzz of the carriage house door pulled Derek out of his Kiro-joke-telling misery.

Steve arrived and made the same moaning sound with his first taste of the baklava. "I love your mom," he said to Kiro.

"For some reason, she thinks you both need more food."

Movement through the window drew Derek's gaze. Stepping out of the confines of the tree-lined street, a woman crossed the street and walked a few steps on the driveway and into the yard toward the front porch.

Derek crossed the room to his large bay window overlooking the wide drive and the main house on the property. "What the hell?"

Steve and Kiro's heads turned to follow his gaze.

"What's wrong?" Steve asked.

"Why do people just wander onto the property as if the no trespassing sign doesn't even exist?"

"To be fair, it's probably covered by all the vines," Kiro said, now just as interested to see what was going on. "You can barely see there's a fence there."

Derek's eyes glanced back toward the tall, black fence that lined the perimeter of the estate, and he shrugged. Kiro wasn't wrong. The fence was barely visible behind overgrown shrubbery, vines, and weeds on both sides, though the sidewalk side was far less unkempt. "True that, but there's a sign on the front door, too."

When his gaze returned to the house, the woman was gone. "Shit. Where'd she go?" A crease formed in the middle of his brow as his eyes darted back and forth to find her. "I'm going out."

Kiro smacked Steve's arm to follow Derek outside, too.

The three men rounded the back side of the main house to find a woman trying to pull off a loose piece of plywood to peek inside the house itself.

Knowing how unsafe the wraparound porch was in its current state of neglect, Derek called out to her. "Watch out for that–"

Startled, she turned around, stepped on a weak board that gave way, and unceremoniously landed on her backside. "Shit." Upon seeing the three men, she scrambled backwards and grabbed onto the splintered wooden railing as if she were about to fall through the tall front porch.

"Stay back," the determined woman warned. She tried to stand up, her feet struggling for purchase on the broken floorboards. The cracking sound of wood threatening to give way froze her in place.

A flicker of recognition crossed over Derek's face.

The woman from the diner.

He extended his hands in an effort to prevent her from moving. "Let me help you, ma'am. Don't move." Derek stepped up to the two or three rows of boards he knew were still sturdy enough to carry the weight of a full-grown adult. How he wished his dad didn't have to halt renovation efforts before replacing the front porch.

"Ma'am," she scoffed. "Did you just call me ma'am?"

Amused, Kiro and Steve stood back and observed from the other side, where she'd originally climbed the handful of precariously perched stairs to the porch. Her eyes widened at two more men flanking her. Nearly slipping, she popped one arm up and behind her head, grabbing at anything she could. She visibly grimaced in pain. "Ow! Son of a *bitch*!"

Derek's brows propelled straight up to his hairline, though he knew her expression was as much from pain as from a fear of being surprised by three men.

Taking note of her quickened breathing, Derek reached out his hands. "K? Steve? Stay back. It won't support all of us."

Kiro and Steve took a few steps back until they were off the porch. Kiro noticed blood dripping down her arm, probably from one of the nails sticking through the wood. "D, she's bleeding."

"I'm right here, you know," she called out while struggling to stay upright. "Shit!"

Derek tossed his keys to Kiro. "Can you get my kit out of the truck? I can take care of it when she's off the porch."

Chapter 12

Got Away

WHILE THEY RETREATED, DEREK EDGED CLOSER TO THE woman nearly frozen in fear. Whether it was from being surprised by three men or nearly slipping into the dark underbelly of a high front porch, he didn't know, but the boards weren't going to hold for long.

"Hi," he said to her frightened eyes, not nearly as confident as they seemed when they first encountered each other at the diner. "I'm Derek. I'm going to help you down, alright?"

"Just don't call me ma'am, okay?"

"I promise." He passed on laughing since he knew the boards were about to give in. She let out another small welp when another board cracked beneath her. Her white knuckles gripped the wooden railing behind her as if her life depended on it.

"Don't move," Derek was close enough to touch her. "I've got you."

"Tell that to the creatures underneath the floorboards."

Derek glanced down to see a few mice scurrying along the foundation below the porch.

A car backfired in the distance, making her welp again. She flinched when Derek's hand appeared in front of her. Holding on to one of the support columns, he held out his hand. "Come on. Take my hand."

She stared at his outstretched hand as if to study it, then, reluctantly extended her own just as a loud crack precipitated the collapse of the flooring below her. Derek's lightning fast reflexes caught her and pulled her against his chest. Over her shoulder, he glared at Kiro and Steve who stifled their laughter at the fact that he ended up with his arms around yet another woman.

Once he eased her off the stairs and onto the lawn, she shrugged herself loose and took a few steps to create space between them. "Let me go. Please."

Derek held up his hands and backed up a few steps as she haphazardly brushed the dust and wood pieces off her jeans, apparently not yet realizing how badly she'd cut her hand. "Oh my god," she said, holding her left hand out in disbelief. A nasty cut around her thumb was now dripping blood at a steady rate. As her breath quickened, her legs buckled while still trying to maintain her balance.

"It's okay. I've got you." Derek stepped in and caught her by the shoulders to prevent her from falling. "Don't like blood, huh?"

"It's better," she struggled to catch her breath, "when it's not mine."

She turned back at the new hole in the porch and started hyperventilating in earnest. "I could have fallen in there. Rats."

"Quite the change in cuss words–"

"No. There could have been rats." She eyed the porch in fear, still trying to step away.

"Mice? Yes. But rats?" Derek said nonchalantly, "Not that I've ever seen."

To prove him right, another mouse scurried along the wall where they'd been standing, causing her to startle.

He changed the tone when her breathing sped up again. "Hey. It's okay. You're okay," he repeated softly as he steadied her, recognizing the signs of an actual panic attack. "Here. Let the house support you until you catch your breath. Lean your head forward and put your hands on your knees."

He went down on one knee, supporting her with his hand on her shoulder while still holding her injured hand, palm up. "Easy now." His deep voice had a calming effect as he looked her in the eye. "Just put your head down and concentrate on your breathing. I won't let you fall."

She folded herself over, with her head down and one hand on her bent knees, easing down to a short stack of bricks. Derek held a steady grip on her shoulder, which was the only thing keeping her from falling flat on her face. He also held her left wrist up and away from her knee. Blood still dripped down her fingers onto the weeds below.

Jogging back, Kiro set the kit on the ground and opened it, grabbing a glove and a small bandage. "Here." He held a glove open so Derek could slip one hand inside. Then, he opened a packet, freeing a bandage that Derek used to start applying pressure to her hand to stop the bleeding from a cut down the side of the thumb and into her palm.

The woman winced but said nothing as she worked to get her breathing under control, eyes darting around as if unsure of where she was or where these men came from.

"Need anything else?"

"Nah, K," he shook his head as he worked. "I'm good, thanks."

Still applying pressure with a strong yet gentle hand while Kiro walked toward the carriage house with Steve, Derek checked to see if the bleeding had stopped. It hadn't. "How are you doing? Any better?"

She could only nod, her breathing only now beginning to slow down.

"You would've landed on your feet, you know. It's not that far down."

Her mouth formed a round O.

He used his teeth to tear open another packet. He pulled out a second bandage, which he used to replace the first, making a mental note of her conspicuously empty ring finger.

"Keep breathing. Try to take longer breaths as you're able," he instructed, a look of concern on his face. "I'm going to keep pressure on this for a minute."

She nodded again, still trying to catch her breath.

Derek's green eyes peered out from behind his wavy brown locks. "Didn't mean to scare you. Folks aren't usually as determined to see inside."

"I wanted to see what it looked like," her soft voice whispered.

He laughed. "If you wanted a tour, you could have asked. Not much to see otherwise. It's filled with junk and has been boarded up for a while now."

"Why were you here?"

"I saw you walk up."

"Saw me?"

"That so hard to believe?"

"Wait." She huffed out an exhale. "That was you in the diner earlier, wasn't it?"

Glancing up to meet her eyes, which still showed a tinge of fear mixed with a bit of defiance, he nodded. "Yeah." His lips curled up into a cocky grin. "That was me."

"Well, I'm moving in."

"To Grant's Crossing?"

"No, here. I mean, yes, Grant's Crossing, but also yes, here. Kind of. Ugh."

This time, his laughter was genuine. "Nobody's moving in here anytime soon. The place needs work."

"Don't believe me?"

Still laughing, he shook his head. "Nope."

"Why not? Aside from the porch, how hard can moving in be?"

She watched him as he continued to apply pressure to her still-bleeding hand. "Just need to pull down the vines, give it a paint job, and it'll be good, don't you think?"

"At least you're optimistic." He checked under the bandage. "Looks like the bleeding has stopped."

Derek opened another packet from his well-stocked first aid kit. "This is going to sting a bit, but I've got to clean it out."

"Ow!" she winced as he cleaned her hand off.

"Sorry." It took him a few moments to break her gaze before grabbing another to repeat the process. "You may want to hit up an Urgent Care if you haven't had a tetanus shot in a while. There's one across from Taft Park."

"Taft Park? You sure like your presidents here."

"That we do." His eyes met hers as she stared at him intently. "Your breathing is starting to sound better."

"Thank you ... for your help." Her eyes darted across the yard as if planning her escape route.

"You're welcome," he said, adding another bandage and taping it in place. Then he cleaned the rest of her hand and wrist.

After cleaning off his own hand, he picked up all the packaging and used bandages, collecting all the trash inside the wrong-side-out glove. He handed her another bandage and a small packet of tape.

"You'll want to hit up a drug store for more, but this will give you something after you give it a proper cleaning. Keep it bandaged for a couple of days at least. Doesn't look like you'll need stitches."

"Uh, thanks."

"Are you doing okay?" He took her hands and helped her stand up. "You look better."

"I think so." She lost her footing on the uneven ground and stumbled, catching herself against his chest. His hand quickly reached around her back to support her.

Her mouth opened, but she didn't let out a sound as he stared down at her brown eyes that sent a rush of heat between his legs.

He swallowed hard. "You sure about that?"

"Yes."

As if his chest were a hot stove, she jerked her hand back and stumbled backward.

He reflexively extended a hand to catch her when the stack of bricks in front of the siding caught her fall. Regaining her footing, she scrambled away. "I've got to go." Holding up her bandaged hand, she gave a half smile, "Thanks for your help."

"You're wel–"

"Bye!" She cut him off with a wave and hurried away, rushing down the street.

Stunned, he stood there and watched her disappear. "You're welcome."

Kiro slowly walked up behind him with a long whistle. "Not like you to let one get away like that, D," he said, earning a quick glare from Derek. "Where'd she come from?"

"No idea." Derek couldn't pull his eyes from the woman rushing down the sidewalk. "Probably wasn't planning to fall through the porch like that, though."

"Probably not." Kiro stared at the bloodstain on Derek's shirt sleeve. "You've got blood on your shirt."

"Shit." Knowing he'd had a nosebleed earlier in the day, Derek's hand flew to his nose. Derek glanced down and pulled a face when he found it clean.

He glanced up and focused on the boarded-up large Victorian. Paint chips fell from the siding. A handful of fallen shutters lay heaped in a pile next to the pile of bricks the woman had used to steady herself. The inside was worse, abandoned with the previous owner's belongings still inside like a musty time capsule from right before the economy tanked in 2008.

Still, he could relate to the abandoned home that sat a mere handful of yards outside his apartment. Brockmoor, as it was named, was a home with boarded up windows, a barely-kempt yard, and stacks of discarded construction materials around the exterior that reminded him too much of what he left behind after his and Joey's final mission. As if looking in a mirror, he saw too much of himself in the neglected structure, often wondering if it would be better to tear it all down and rebuild from scratch, rather than fix something so broken. He didn't like what he saw in himself, since returning from Afghanistan.

But this was his new life. And it was nothing like he'd imagined.

He cast another glance at the dilapidated home. At least the house could be fixed, but himself? That's another question altogether.

A crease formed in Kiro's forehead.

Derek blinked. "What?"

"The blood." Kiro motioned toward Derek's shirt. "It's probably hers." Derek reached down to grab his med kit, pausing long enough to gaze down the block to discover she'd already disappeared.

On the way back to the carriage house, it struck him that he didn't even get her name.

Chapter 13

Unexpected Meeting

Derek made himself scarce while his dad was showing the new owner, or the surrogate for the new owner, the inside of the house. He was doing his best to avoid meeting the person who was probably going to force him to need a new place to live, but he needed his wallet out of his truck, so he risked a trip down the stairs. He stuck his wallet in his back pocket just as one of his dad's foremen pulled into the drive.

"Hey, Joe," Derek greeted the forty-something man as he stepped out of his truck with a cylindrical case, presumably holding the blueprints to the big house.

"Oh hey, Derek. Your dad asked me to drop these off. I need to head out to my daughter's recital. Mind giving these to him?"

He shoved the tube into Derek's hands and jumped back into his truck without giving Derek a chance to say no. "Thanks!"

So much for avoiding the new owner.

Derek stepped into the house, sidestepping the abandoned furniture, boxes, and trash. He narrowly avoided stepping on a mouse as he hopped over an open drawer on an old toy chest of drawers against the wall. Wincing at the putrid odor that filled the house, he paused long enough to hear his dad's voice.

Abe and the owner descended the old servants' staircase from the attic to the second floor.

"I still can't believe there are six bedrooms but only one bathroom," a woman's voice said.

"Remember what I said about imagination?" Abe asked.

"Yeah?"

"This is where you need it. If we're gutting the place, adding bathrooms will be easy."

"Dad?" Derek called out from the stairs. "Where are you? Joe dropped off your … "

Derek reached the landing at the top of the stairs, stopping mid-sentence just as a familiar-looking woman and Abe turned around to see him jogging up, carrying the large tube in one hand.

The light was a little dim since some of the windows were still boarded up, preventing the sunshine from penetrating the hallway, but it was the woman who fell through the porch.

The woman from the diner.

Those brown eyes knocked the breath out of him.

"Hi," Derek said to her, taking a couple of steps forward to meet them.

She froze as well, as if surprised at seeing him again. She schooled her features. "Hi."

Not breaking eye contact with her, Derek spoke. "Dad, Joe dropped off the blueprints you wanted."

Abe creased his brow and pointed his index finger back and forth between them. "Have you two met?"

Derek said yes, and she answered no.

"Well, no. Not really." Derek conceded in tandem with her "Not exactly."

"Right." Unconvinced by their answers, Abe started the

introductions. "Callie, this is my son, Derek Mitchell. Derek, this is Callie Thomas. She's the new owner of Brockmoor."

"Oh." Derek extended a hand in greeting and smiled. "Nice to meet you, Callie."

Callie took his hand, managing a smile in return. "Nice to meet you, too, Derek."

"New owner, huh?"

"Yes." Her eyes dropped to their continued handshake and then back up at Derek with a half-smile and a cocked brow.

Derek let go. "Uh, how's your hand?" Derek half motioned toward her bandaged hand.

"Better." She waved it for him to see. "Thanks."

"Good."

Abe pressed his lips together to keep a straight face. "Derek has been living in one of the carriage house apartments. He's been helping me keep an eye on things here."

"Oh. Thank you."

"You're welcome." Derek still didn't break eye contact.

"Son, the blueprints?" Abe prompted.

"Oh, right." Derek handed them over with a quick glance, not otherwise moving.

"Thank you."

"Sure." Derek looked back at Callie, swinging his arms and bringing his hands together. "Uh. Guess I'll go now." He took a step backward.

"Careful!" Abe cautioned him before he reached the stairs

"Huh? Oh. Yeah. Bye." He glanced back with a wave before jogging back down the stairs.

Callie was still looking down the stairs when Abe spoke, "Care to head out to the carriage house?"

"Hmm?" She turned back in surprise. "What? Oh. Yeah." She furrowed her brow. "Right."

Abe motioned for her to descend the stairs, shaking his head in amusement.

Derek trotted down the stairs and navigated his way through the junk and out the front before looking back up to the second floor. He ran his fingers through his hair and winced. "Idiot," he berated himself.

Heading out to meet his friends, Derek stopped at the workshop entrance, across the long room from where Callie and his dad were speaking to the inspector at the far end.

"Long story short: nothing is up to code," the inspector announced.

Leaving a copy of the report, the inspector shook their hands and left.

Abe looked at Callie and smiled, "Well, on the bright side, we're going to be adding a lot of wiring and plumbing with all your new bathrooms anyway, so it might as well all be new."

Derek stood in the far corner, checking his phone while surreptitiously eavesdropping on their conversation.

"So, Callie," Abe asked. "What do you think?"

Callie took a deep breath and let out a nervous laugh.

Derek recognized the optimistic expression on his dad's face the moment he set down his clipboard and clasped his hands together. He knew his dad always loved for people to live in the houses he fixed up, but he especially loved an opportunity to bring them back to life.

"Look. I have no idea what you ultimately want to do: fix it and sell it or fix it and move in. Doesn't matter." Abe waved his hands back and forth. "I can help you with either option. But one thing you should know is that this is an amazing house."

Abe's face lit up with excitement, from the twinkle in his eyes to the broad smile he carried. "I mean, she's been neglected, don't get me wrong, but she's got a lot of potential. I'd love the opportunity to continue fixing her up so we can restore her to her former beauty. Or," he shrugged, "at least our interpretation of her former beauty. With some work, this place will be absolutely spectacular."

Callie puffed out a breath but nodded in agreement. "My grandfather wants to start by making it livable."

"Okay." Abe nodded in agreement. "Which starts with more bathrooms."

Callie put her hands on her hips and looked up at him with a straight face. "I'm not going to live that down, am I?"

"Nope."

Their laughter drew a smile to Derek's lips. Leaving them to discuss specifics, he snuck out and headed out to meet his friends.

"Wow. That's a lot to take in." Callie exhaled.

"Yeah, but you're going to have fun with this," Abe promised.

Callie rolled her eyes. "I'll have to take your word for that, so let me get past the overwhelming stage first, okay?"

He held up his hands. "Fair enough."

"I'm starved." Callie's hand went to her stomach when she heard it growl. "Where's a good place to grab a bite to eat?"

"I know just the place."

THERAPY 2

A Sense of Calm

"I feel crowded," Derek admitted, resting his right ankle over his left knee in his usual seat on the couch near the corner of the room. He liked this spot, or at least disliked it the least of all the options in the doctor's office. It offered a full view of the room, leaving all possible exits within his line of sight.

"How so?" Doc Majors asked while sitting comfortably in a cushioned chair across from the couch. A notebook rested on his leg, his pen poised for notes.

"For the last year, I've had my own place," Derek scratched his nose with his knuckles. "It's not big or anything, but it's mine. And it's quiet."

Doc Majors didn't interrupt when Derek spoke, allowing Derek to share his thoughts at his own pace.

"Nobody else is around because it's, uh, kind of secluded."

"Secluded?"

"Yeah. Quiet. Set back behind a large, abandoned house, away from the street. Away from people." Derek waved him off. "It's nothing fancy."

"Do you want fancy?"

"I want to be left alone."

"And you get that where you live?"

"I did."

"Hmm." When Derek didn't start talking, Doc Majors did. "What changed?"

"The owner," Derek took another drink from the water bottle. "The owner, somebody from out east, sent somebody out to fix up the main house."

"And that's not a good thing?"

"No. I mean, yes. It's a good thing, yes, but does she have to be *here*?"

"She?"

"Hmm. Supposedly, she's related to the actual owner or something."

"Why does that worry you?"

"I'm not worried."

"Okay. Why does it concern you?"

"I'm fine the way I am."

"Mmhmm."

Derek opened his mouth but decided against speaking.

"Tell me about where you live."

"What do you mean?" Derek gestured around the room with his hand. "You live here, too. Grant's Crossing. Small town. Everybody knows everything about everyone else."

"Your apartment. Where you live. Tell me about it."

Derek's leg started bouncing. With a deep breath, he started describing his home. "It's uh, it's a one-bedroom apartment in this big carriage house behind one of the old Victorians on Adams Street. The carriage house is just a big, red brick, rectangular-shaped building. Garage below, apartments above." A hint of a smile formed on his lips. "It's on an acre of land surrounded by trees and a black, wrought-iron fence. Kids used to sneak in around Halloween to see how long they could stay in the house." He released a humorless laugh. "It's kind of like something out of a horror story." Derek stopped talking and stared out the window.

"Do you like horror stories?"

Derek blinked and slowly returned his attention to the doctor. "What?"

"Do you like horror stories? Horror movies?"

Derek waved him off. "Oh no. Can't stand them."

Doc Majors smiled. "You say there's a house there?"

"Yes. It's a huge Queen Anne Victorian with a wraparound front porch with balusters, well, not so many anymore. Most are damaged by the elements or by termites. The roof is asymmetrical."

As if reminiscing, Derek described the empty home, smiling as he spoke. "There's a huge turret and a large dormer upstairs in the third-level attic. Nobody's lived in it for years. Nobody's cared." His smile dropped. "Windows are broken, shutters have fallen, it's overrun with mice." He furrowed his brow. "She doesn't like rats."

He cleared his throat and continued. "Outside, the paint is peeling, and inside, half the plaster is in pieces on the floors, exposing the wooden laths in the walls. It has water damage. It's filled with all sorts of old furniture and shit people have just left behind. Literal shit thanks to the mice and other animals that have worked their way in over the years. Not that it matters because you can't see it. You can smell it, but you can't see it. Hell. You can't even see the house or the fence. Everything's overgrown. The house itself is a dump. Should probably be torn down, but ... "

Derek didn't finish his thought for a few moments.

"But?" the doc prompted him.

"But it has character, I sup–" A pair of house finches landing on the fire escape outside the window captured Derek's attention.

"D? Help me."

He froze, but his heart started pounding inside his chest. His breaths shortened. A third finch landed, and his thoughts flew back to his final mission in Afghanistan.

Derek gripped the front handles of the stretcher carrying Joey Parker. Weary from the losses they couldn't prevent, the men not carrying the two fallen men or their gear held their weapons at the ready, remaining somber yet vigilant. One ambush was more than they'd bargained for that morning, and it was time to move before Taliban reinforcements came back for another.

Derek risked a final glance back to where he'd last seen his best friend alive. His gaze followed a trio of snow finches fluttering up from the blood-soaked ground toward the light of the rising sun.

"Joey," he whispered more to himself than to the doctor.

Doc Majors followed Derek's gaze to the window in time to see the birds flying away. "Derek?"

When Derek, still staring through the glass, didn't respond, he asked again. "Derek? Who's Joey?"

Derek gave his head a quick shake, then returned to his description of the house. "Um, the owner lives out east somewhere." Derek motioned toward the east, then took a drink out of a water bottle.

"Yes. So you said."

"The carriage house is fixed up, but he's never even come out to look at it. If he'd cared, he would have come out here. He'd still be here."

"Still? Or?"

"The owner."

"Okay. And you did the work on it? Did you work on the carriage house?"

Derek shrugged. "Yeah. Well, my dad and his company did, but I helped out from time to time on my days off."

"You worked for your dad?"

"Yeah. Once we turned eighteen." Derek paused to smile. "We started working for him. Until we enlisted, anyway."

"You both did? Or were there more of you?"

"What?" Derek paused. "No. Just me."

"You said 'we' a moment ago."

"No. It was just me."

Doc Majors wrote in the notebook resting on his lap as he spoke. "Do you still want to work for your dad?"

"Yeah. I do, I guess. I mean, I like working on old houses. I grew up learning how to fix things around old houses. It makes sense."

"So you're pretty handy to have around?"

"I guess so."

"So you want to work for your dad, but instead, you work for the city."

"I like to help people."

"Why?"

"I just do. I can." Derek took another quick swig from his bottle of water. "In my job, I see people at their worst." He leaned back against the couch. "I see people when their houses are burning down and they're losing everything. I see people when they're so sick they can't take themselves to the hospital. I see people when they hurt themselves doing stupid shit. I save them. People buy me drinks. Women want to go out with me," He breathed out another humorless laugh, but extended his arms. "Come on. You know what I do, Doc. I see people when they're having heart attacks. I see people who are shot. I see people whose legs are blown ... " Derek stopped mid-sentence as if the wind had been knocked right out of him. He sat frozen as if forced back in time while gasping for breath. "I see ... I see ...."

"You see?"

Derek inhaled deeply. "Nothing." He waved the doctor off. "I see nothing."

They sat in silence for a minute or so.

"And what do you want now, Derek?"

Derek shook his head without making eye contact. "Calm. I want calm."

Chapter 14

Dinner at Jo's

Jo's Bar & Grille was located on the corner of Adams and Grant Streets. Despite the popularity of Baba's breakfast and lunch crowds, Jo's was the hangout place in town once the workday ended.

Walking past the patio area, Callie Thomas approached the main door which was off the corner, inset diagonally. The outside tables were already filling up with families, which seemed surprising for a week night, but perhaps that was the norm here in Grant's Crossing.

Callie thanked the young boy who held the door open for her after his family exited. Having walked in from the bright September day, she had to give her eyes a minute to take in the space before heading toward some open seats near the end of the large bar.

"Hey Jo, any games on?" A man yelled out from a booth against the wall. Glancing over, Callie saw a booth full of potbellied, beer-toting older men all peering in her direction. Without changing expression, she met their gaze for a few steps before continuing on, eventually taking a seat toward the end of the bar.

"Welcome to Jo's!" A bartender greeted Callie. "Get you something to drink?"

"Diet Coke, please," Callie answered.

"Sure thing. Need a menu?" The lady asked.

"Yes, please," she answered as the bartender placed a laminated menu in front of her and poured her drink.

Coming back right away, she set the drink down on the bar in front of Callie. "Know what you want?"

"Not sure," Callie admitted. "You don't have any crab cakes by chance, do you?"

"No. Not many crabs in the Scioto River, but if you ever interrupt Russ and Nate while they're fishing the river, they might get crabby," she said with a smile. "Not the same, I imagine."

"No. Not so much." Callie laughed. "This is my first time here. Any recommendations?"

"Great! Welcome. My favorite is the grilled Turkey and Swiss, but this is a sports bar, so we have excellent burgers and wings! My husband and I both love the Bacon Cheddar Burger."

"Oh. That sounds good." Callie's mouth watered at the thought. "Bacon Cheddar burger it is, then," she ordered with an excited look.

"We cook it medium unless you want it more well done," the bartender said. "And it comes with fries and a pickle."

"Sounds perfect, thanks."

"I'll get that right out. In the meantime, my name's Jo, so yell if you need anything."

While sipping her Diet Coke, Callie took an opportunity to take in the deceptively large bar and grille. From the outside, it had seemed an average-sized restaurant with large, plate-glass windows with navy blue and tan striped awnings. Once inside, however, it had much more depth with a large, rectangular-shaped bar, made of light, polished wood . On one side was the smaller of two large seating areas, plus a game area with a pair of pool tables and a trio of dart boards that she'd have to play while she was in town. To the right was a much larger, family-friendly seating area with tables and booths along the windows. There was even a small dance floor with a juke box in the corner.

TVs were mounted above the bar and on the outside walls, all with various sporting events on them. Families and other locals filled the restaurant for a good meal and whatever game happened to be on. A handful of servers bustled about to take care of all the customers.

Callie's food was served quickly.

"Here you go," said Jo.

"Thank you!" Callie's mouth watered again as she saw her cheeseburger. "Looks like you do a pretty fair business during the week. It's only a Tuesday."

"Yes, we do. Folks like coming out to enjoy the square. It's the heart of the town, really. What brings you to Grant's Crossing?"

Callie started with a smile. "I'm here to check up on my grandfather's childhood home," she said before adding, "And while I'm here, I figure I'd try to get some work done."

"Get some work done? What do you do?"

"I'm a journalist," Callie responded. "But eventually, I want to write a book, so I'm playing around with some ideas while I'm here."

Jo set out a ketchup bottle. "What's your name so I can say *I knew you when?*"

"Callie Thomas," Callie said with a laugh.

"Great to meet you, Callie. And Brockmoor is the house you'll be renovating?"

Callie raised a hand in surprise. "How do you know?"

"Small town," Jo offered a reassuring smile. "Can't wait to see what you do with the place. It's been an eyesore for a while now."

"That's what I hear." Callie grabbed the ketchup for her fries.

"Enjoy your food while it's hot, and let me know if there's anything else you need." Jo placed the check in an empty glass in front of Callie's meal at the bar.

Jo returned a few minutes later. "How is everything?"

"It's good," Callie said, mid-chew as she wiped her mouth with a napkin.

The sound of raucous laughter burst forth from a few tables away, prompting Callie to turn around and look in time to catch six men at a table laughing.

"Ahh. That's just the boys," Jo mused with a smile. "Pay no mind."

"The boys?"

"Yes. The men of GC Fire." She shrugged as she refilled Callie's soda. "I always call them the boys."

Setting down the glass, Jo added, "They all get a bit rowdy from time to time, well, just loud really, in their off time, but considering the work they do, they've earned it. They always pay their tab, tip well, and don't bother the other customers, so it's all good."

"You'll often find them here on their off days, celebrating birthdays, anniversaries, Tuesdays, anything, really." She laughed. "They're all good guys. And if you're ever in a pinch, well?" Jo looked over at them with a big smile and a wave as they all called her name as if cheering, "Not a single one would hesitate to help you out."

Callie turned to look over in their direction just as Derek caught her eye. He nodded and held up his bottle, receiving a nod from her in return before she turned back around.

Kiro caught Derek's gesture and turned around to see who he'd just toasted. "Who's that at the bar?" he asked.

"She looks cute," Tim said, receiving a smack on the arm from the redhead sitting next to him.

"Aren't you dating Vanessa?"

"We're not together at the moment."

"Yeah, Emerson," Steve interjected. "Didn't you hear they broke up?"

"Together, not together." Emerson moved his hands up and down as if weighing his options. "It's so hard to keep track."

"She," Derek answered, "is the person sent to check up on Brockmoor."

"Who?"

"My new landlord," Derek clarified.

"Whaaaa? You're kidding!" Kiro and a couple of other guys craned their heads to get a better look. "Your landlord?"

"Yep." Derek took a drink. "It's true. Well, it's some guy out of town, but Dad said somebody would be scoping the place out for him."

"Wait." Kiro glanced back at Callie and then at Derek. "Isn't she the same girl who fell through the front porch?"

"Yep," Derek acknowledged, taking a drink of beer and glancing in Callie's direction. "She's the one."

"Ha!" Steve laughed. "She's the one," he announced, causing them all to start laughing.

"Like Mitchell ever has just one!" Emerson joked, garnering more laughter.

With a sigh, Derek shook his head and looked down at the table.

Leaning forward, Kiro spoke to his friend in a lower voice. "So are you going to at least talk to her? Because if you're not," Kiro pointed his thumb back in her direction. "I can invite her over to join us."

"Nah," Derek exhaled. "Not this time."

Kiro let out a slow exhale. "That's not like you to pass up on–" Kiro held up a hand in surrender when Derek glared at him. "Okay, then."

"It's nothing." Derek shook his head at Kiro. "I mean, nothing." He took another drink of his beer, unaccustomed to being anything other than one hundred percent sure of himself, especially when it came to women.

"Yeah, Okay." Kiro leaned back in his seat with a smirk.

Derek glanced back up at Callie and took another drink. "It's nothing." He mumbled as if still trying to convince himself it was true.

Chapter 15

New Arrival

CALLIE GLANCED BACK AGAIN AS DEREK'S HEAD TURNED, missing eye contact but still taking a moment to check out what she could see of him from where she sat.

"Why is she gone?" A man at the end of the bar cried out loudly, his words slurred.

Callie's gaze shifted in his direction of the bar before turning back to offer Jo a quizzical look, "Is he okay?"

"That's just Carl," Jo explained while pouring a couple of beers. "His wife left him last year. Broke his heart. So, he comes in here from time to time to forget."

"Oh," Callie acknowledged, throwing a sad glance in his direction.

"He's still not able to deal with it," Jo added. "We've already called his son. He just needs to walk his dad home, that's all."

Just then, a young, college aged kid entered the bar. He walked straight to Carl and spoke softly to him.

"I don't want to go!" Carl sadly cried.

"Come on, Dad," the kid answered. "Let's go home." He gently put his arm around the older man's shoulders and helped him off the stool. He looked up at Jo with an apologetic look. "Sorry, Jo. I'll stop by later to settle up."

"Don't you worry about that, Bryan," Jo said with an understanding tone as she handed him a carry out bag. "You just take care of your dad."

He nodded appreciatively, supporting his dad as he led him out of the bar.

Suddenly, the men of GC Fire pulled out their wallets, each throwing some cash into a pile.

Derek stood up. "Hey Jo," he called out to her. "What's he owe?"

"Right at forty dollars," Jo replied as she cleared his spot at the bar.

Derek turned back around to the table and said something to the guys. He grabbed the pile of cash after a couple more bills were thrown in, straightening them in his hands as he walked up to the bar and handed them all to Jo. "That'll cover him."

"Thanks, boys!" Jo smiled. "Appreciate it."

"That was nice," Callie said.

"Folks do that from time to time," Jo explained. "Times are hard, and he's had it harder than most lately, so they help out when they can. Besides, Bryan's too young to have to go to college and take care of his father."

"I take it that her leaving was unexpected?" Callie asked.

Jo hesitated before shrugging. "Not really." She studied Callie before responding. "He was already a drinker. She'd had enough, and Bryan was almost old enough to move out if he wanted. So, she left, and now Bryan takes care of him."

"That's tough." Callie acknowledged with a nod.

"Yeah. Carl went to school with my husband and older brother, so I have a soft spot for him. So, we just cut him off and call his son or walk him home ourselves when we can instead of calling my younger brother." Jo waved toward the front door. "Speak of the devil."

Callie followed Jo's gaze to find a man in uniform weaving his way through the tables, greeting folks along the way. Talking to nearly everyone, he'd made it as far as the third table before Jo rolled her eyes. "I'd introduce you, but he's going to take forever to get over here."

With a laugh, Callie settled her bill and pulled her messenger bag over her head. On her way out, she stopped to say hello to Derek, who lifted his chin in acknowledgment.

"That was a really nice thing you did earlier for Carl."

"That's what we do in small towns." Derek cynically commented as he stared right at her. "Probably not what you're used to seeing out east." He earned a stern look from Kiro and silence from the rest of the table. "I didn't realize you'd been here long enough to know him on a first-name basis," he added while taking a drink of his beer, earning an unfazed look from Callie.

"Carl's just having a rough go of it, that's all," Kiro said, easing the sudden tension. He stood up. "I'm Kiro."

"Kiro, is it?" She drew out his first name as KEER-oh, like Hero with a K.

"Yeah. That's right."

"Great to meet you." Her face warmed into a smile. "I'm Callie."

Callie motioned between Kiro and Steve. "You two were at the house the other day, weren't you?"

"Yes. We were," Kiro confirmed. "Let me introduce the guys. That's Steve Cook." Kiro pointed to the tattooed man with pierced ears that Callie recognized, who nodded as his name was called. "You know Derek already," he said, giving Derek a stern look, "That's R.J. Emerson with the red hair, then Juan Palacios, but we call him Tank."

"Hello." Tank and Emerson both waved as Kiro introduced them to her.

"Tank? I'm sure there's a story there," Callie said as she acknowledged him by name.

"Oh yeah. We've got lots of stories."

Tank wadded up a napkin and threw it at Kiro. "Watch it, Kiro!"

"And the big guy at the end there is Tim, or," Kiro gave a quick laugh as he tilted his head to Callie, "as we like to call him, Tiny Tim."

All muscle and with a shaved head, Tiny Tim stood to his full height of at least six feet, five inches tall and extended his arms, "And God bless us, everyone!" prompting everyone, even Derek, to laugh.

After waving to each in turn, "Well, it's very nice to meet you all. I just wanted to come over and say hello."

"You're here to check on Brockmoor?"

She threw her hands in the air. "Everybody knows this!"

"It's a small town thing." Kiro quipped.

"If you're checking up on me, Ms. Thomas, no need to worry. I'll be back to the grindstone tomorrow," Derek commented, wearing a blank expression and knowing he needed to get the property lawn mowed, which was his agreement in exchange for low rent. "We indentured servants go out to dinner once in a while."

Callie countered his neutral expression. "Good to know. Thanks." Returning her attention to the rest of the table, she gave a quick wave."Have a great evening, gentlemen!"

"Wow, D." Kiro looked at Derek in disbelief after Callie exited through the front door. "Just ... wow."

Derek was unfazed. "What?"

"You can be such a dick." Kiro grabbed his jacket and rushed out the front door.

"What?" Derek repeated, looking at Steve and the others for support but finding none.

"Kiro's not wrong," Steve responded matter-of-factly before popping another French fry in his mouth.

Derek shrugged and finished off his beer.

Chapter 16

Not Usually

"Hey, Callie," Kiro called out as he rushed out the door. "CALLIE! WAIT UP!"

Callie heard a voice behind her as she started the walk back to Brockmoor, where she'd parked her car. Turning back, she saw Kiro jogging to catch up.

"Hey, Callie. Hold up!" Kiro fell in step. "Where are you headed?"

"Back to the hotel."

"Oh yeah? I'll walk with you then." Only a few inches taller than Callie, Kiro fell into step as he put on his jacket. "Are you staying in Delaware?" he asked, referring to the largest city in the county that shared its name.

"Yes," she replied as they walked down the sidewalk. "Seemed the closest option."

Kiro nodded, then motioned back toward Jo's. "Sorry about that back there."

"About what?"

"Derek's not usually such a jerk. He's just had a few beers."

"Hmm. He drinks a lot, I take it?"

"Yeah." He cringed. "I mean, no. Ugh." He laughed while shaking his head. "I'm not helping, am I?"

"Not really, no." Callie found herself laughing with him. "No need to apologize on his account, but thanks anyway."

"Yeah." Kiro took a few steps before adding, "So Derek mentioned the big city. Where are you from?"

"Originally, Baltimore, Maryland, but now I'm in D.C. How about you?"

"Born and bred right here in Ohio," Kiro said proudly.

"My parents both came to America as teenagers," he explained. "Somehow, they managed to find each other and ended up here in Grant's Crossing. Crazy that both sets of grandparents are from the same city back home," he added as they paused before crossing the street off the square.

"And where's home?" Callie asked as they continued walking.

"Bulgaria. Plovdiv, Bulgaria," he answered. "It's a city right in the center of the country, kind of like Columbus is for Ohio."

"Ahh. The Balkans. Beautiful region of the world." Callie admitted.

"You know it?" Kiro perked up. "Nobody ever knows where Bulgaria is."

"Just barely," she admitted. "I spent a few days relaxing on the Black Sea on my way to Croatia. Do you get to go there often?"

"Only once so far," he answered. "Back in grade school, before Mom and Dad opened the diner."

"So, is Kiro a nickname?"

"Kind of." He waved his hand from side to side. "It's the diminutive for Kiril. My grandmother was a teacher before they immigrated, so she always celebrated Kiril and Methodius Day, which is a holiday for educators. Saint Kiril, or Cyril, in English, is the man who created the Cyrillic alphabet, so I'm named after him."

"Russian uses the Cyrillic alphabet, right?"

"Yeah, but they got it from us Bulgarians." Kiro laughed." I think my grandmother may have been a little disappointed I didn't become a teacher. Can't imagine grading all those papers, though. I'd rather see more action."

"Is that why you're a firefighter?" she asked.

"Yep. Derek and I are the primary paramedic team."

"Ahhh. I see. What does your grandmother think of your being a paramedic rather than a teacher?"

"Well, she's not with us anymore, but I think she liked that I help people," he said with a shrug.

"Growing up, Baba was still a teacher to my sister, Stefi, and me. Made sure we spoke Bulgarian so we wouldn't forget where we came from," he said as Callie smiled.

"Wait. Baba? Like the diner on the square?"

"Yes! That's my parents' place - named after my *baba*." He tipped his head to the side, "which is Bulgarian for grandmother. Have you been?"

"Yes. I was there yesterday morning and again today for lunch." Callie smiled. "The lady who helped me, Anna? I think her name was. She's super nice."

"That's my mom." Kiro's face lit up with a big smile. "She probably had you eating *Mekitsis*. That's her go-to suggestion for new customers."

"That she did." Callie's mouth watered as she reminisced about the delicious Bulgarian donuts. "They were so good, too."

"I'll have to tell her you liked them."

"Oh. She knows," Callie assured him as they came up to Brockmoor. "I may have to get some more tomorrow."

"She'd love that. Before too long, she'll probably try to adopt you, so be ready."

"Oh? What do you mean?" She leaned up against her rental car as Kiro stood on the sidewalk.

"She tends to mother everyone. But, in a good way, I promise." He held his palms out in reassurance. "She became a second mother to Derek when he lost his mom back in high school. She always had him over when his dad was working or was with her at the hospital. Mom just added him to the family, and now she considers him a second son. He became an older brother to Stefi and me." He chuckled. "A really annoying older brother sometimes."

"I have an older brother," Callie acknowledged, still laughing. "So, trust me. I get it. He's a Marine, so he's always getting in the face of anyone who even hints at bothering his little sister." She rolled her eyes before pausing. "It's kind of sweet, actually, like my own personal protector. He's always there for me. But," she quickly caught herself, "don't ever tell him I said any of that. It would go straight to his head!"

"Not a word." He tried but failed to keep a straight face. "Your secret is safe with me."

"Well, I'm gonna head back and check on the guys." Kiro glanced down the street. "Make sure they're not causing any more trouble. Jo's pretty tolerant of us, but we don't want to push our luck. Are you going to be in town for a while?"

"Yeah." Callie gestured toward Brockmoor. "I'm getting things started for my grandpa."

"Oh, good! So, that means you'll be here for the festival then?"

"Festival?"

"Yeah. HomeFest. It's Homecoming weekend at the high school with the big game on Friday night, then a festival on the square Saturday, with a big fireworks display that night."

"Sounds like fun. If I'm still in town, I'll check it out."

"It is, though Derek and some of the guys usually skip out before the fireworks get going. They all served overseas and usually end up at Jo's or someplace to watch a game."

"Combat vets?"

"Yeah. Well, I'm sure I'll see you around. It was great meeting you, Callie!" With a wave, he headed back to the square.

"You, too, Kiro." Callie tossed her bag in the passenger seat, got in the car, and started the engine.

Chapter 17

Fine

"I really hoped the two runs in the seventh would have started our comeback," Emerson said as they exited Jo's after the game.

Steve laughed. "Yeah, well. I'm just happy the Reds didn't sweep the series."

"Who do your Cards play next?"

"Pirates," Steve answered.

As they continued their animated conversation about the baseball game, Derek caught Kiro by the arm. "Hold up, K."

He wanted to talk to Kiro, but the crowded sidewalk denied them the opportunity to talk in private. They said their goodbyes, then crossed the street to the park that made up the square in the center of town.

Kiro turned and crossed his arms across his chest. "What? No woman tonight?"

Derek cringed. "I probably deserved that."

"Probably?"

"Fine. Definitely."

Once away from prying eyes, Derek stuck his hands in his pockets and looked everywhere but directly at Kiro.

"Hey." Derek scraped at the ground with the toe of his shoe as if rubbing out an imaginary cigarette he'd never smoke if his life depended on it. "You were right back there."

Kiro's forehead creased. "Right back where?"

Derek stared up at the tall trees that lined the streets. The early autumn leaves were beginning to show hints of red and yellow when the sun hit them just right.

"Inside," he started. "Back there when you called me a dick."

Kiro stood in obvious annoyance.

"I should probably apologize to her, huh?"

"Might be a good start, D."

"Yeah, well."

"Yeah, well, what?"

"Jesus, K." Derek pulled his hands out of his pockets, raked his fingers through his hair, then immediately put them back in his jeans pockets. "Remember the other day at the station?"

"When?" Kiro prompted him.

"Um, week before last," Derek confirmed. "Chief wanted me to talk to somebody about ... " He trailed off, unable to finish describing how his friends had found him earlier in the week. "About what happened."

Kiro kept his gaze forward. "Tank and I never said anything to–"

"I know," Derek cut him off, distracted by a teenager praising his dog for catching the frisbee he had just tossed. "Chief said he saw Tank cleaning up Joey's ... " He cleared his throat. "Joey's gravesite."

Kiro remained silent.

"And he wanted me to call the doc who ... " He trailed off as if unable to complete his thought out loud.

"So, you're seeing somebody then?"

Derek nodded. "Yeah. A couple of times now."

"That's good, right? Having someone to talk to?" Kiro forced a smile. "I mean, I'm always happy to help–"

"I know you are, and I appreciate it, but I'm going because the chief will bench me otherwise." Derek stared at the trees on the square, swaying in the summer wind. "I think I'm fine."

"But–"

"I'm fine."

"That's just it, D. You're not."

"I don't need this from you, K," Derek warned with a hard stare. "I really don't."

"You haven't been the same," Kiro stated the obvious, but Derek probably needed to hear it. "I mean, you were always cocky, especially about women, but now?" Kiro extended his arms in frustration. "You're just a real asshole sometimes. You never used to be like that."

"Yeah, well, I think we're all a little different, don't you think? Can't you at least grant us that?"

"Sure, but you're taking it personally." Kiro held up a hand. "Hell. You're taking everything personally. And I know why, but dammit. You've got people here, D. You're not alone. You're just acting like it. You're fighting us at every turn." He shook his head. "You have people who love you and who care about how you're doing, and right now, we're all just sitting around waiting for you to be that drunk driver at some car accident that kills a family while getting off without a scratch."

Kiro took a few steps away, then returned. "You think it's bad now? What about when you kill a family with little children? It happens. You know it does. We've both seen it."

"I ... I don't."

"You don't what? Don't want to see what that feels like for something that was actually preventable? Jesus, D. How long do you think you can last?"

"I'm always fine."

"Fine? Fucking fine? You've really set the bar low on that one, because you're not fine. You were face down in the dirt on Joey's grave, for fuck's sake. Do you even remember crashing against the tree? You're lucky it stopped you, so the gravestone wouldn't have to. You think he'd want that?"

When Derek said nothing in return, Kiro kept talking. "I wasn't there, okay? I don't know what it's like to have bullets flying overhead day in and day out. But I know what it's like to treat a critically wounded patient. I know what it's like to do everything in my power to save someone's life. And I know what it's like to do everything in my power to save them yet still fail. You don't have the monopoly on that experience."

Kiro took a deep breath before continuing. "I also know that not everyone can be saved, and I move on. I don't go around playing the martyr because a 9-1-1 call didn't come in fast enough. I don't go around being a dick to all my friends, or … or to complete strangers because I assume they're going to judge me for something. Yeah. I may tell bad jokes," Kiro released a humorless laugh. "But I also know I can't save everyone. I know my limits, and sure, I try to better myself with every call because I do save lives. WE save lives, but Joey's gone, D. I loved him, too. But he's gone."

He drew in a long breath and motioned to both Derek and back to himself. "We're not gone, though. We're still here. And, yeah. I don't have the shared experience you and Tank have, but I've not been so sheltered that I don't see what can go wrong. I see what happens to people who drink too much and drive. I see what happens to people who get alcohol poisoning."

"K–" Derek started.

"No, Derek. No." Kiro poked Derek in the chest. "I do not want to see you kill yourself because you think you killed him. I refuse to believe you didn't do absolutely everything humanly possible over there."

Kiro started to walk away.

"Kiro?"

"What?" he snapped.

Derek opened his mouth, but nothing came out. He dropped his head and stared at the ground.

Kiro stepped back and stood right in front of Derek so he could keep his voice low. He waited for a family to walk by and get out of earshot before he spoke. "D, you're a brother to me. I love you. My family loves you. You know that. And I will always be there for you. You know that, too." Kiro swallowed hard before finishing. "I'm just worried that one day I'll come over and find you passed out beyond the point where I can bring you back." His jaw clenched. He sniffed before tapping his chest. "And you know I'm a damned good medic, too."

Derek must have found a little bit of courage because he knew that wouldn't happen. At least that's what he always told himself. "Kiro, I'm fine."

Kiro scoffed. "Yeah. You keep telling yourself that."

He threw his hands up in the air and left Derek where he stood.

THERAPY 3

Letdown

Doc Majors met Derek at the door and stood back to let him into his office. "Good morning, Derek. Go ahead and have a seat." He held up a folder and wiggled it back and forth. "Need to drop this off, then I'll be right there in a sec."

With a single nod, Derek entered the room, tossed his backpack on the closest end of the couch, and sat down on the farthest. He stretched and let out a yawn. They'd responded to a house fire in the middle of the night, so he hadn't gotten much sleep to speak of at the station.

Scrubbing his hand down his face, he scanned the room and noticed nothing new. Nothing interesting. Of course, he didn't notice anything at all, really.

He never did.

So far, it had been the same thing every time. He arrived at his appointment. He sat down on the couch. He answered questions. He talked about irrelevant stuff, like the house his dad was fixing up. He talked about his latest shift at the fire station.

Blah. Blah. Blah.

There was never anything of note inside the room. By all accounts, the doctor seemed pretty boring, so when Derek entered each session, he saw the same things he always saw. To his right, the couch and chairs where they talked, or rather where he talked and the doc took notes.

In front of him, the desk, some shelves filled with books, and a small fridge.

To his immediate left, a wide cabinet along the wall and finally, in the far corner, the door that led to another small lounge area and a way out. On the boring beige walls were boring pictures, along with the doctor's degrees, in well-polished, boring brown frames.

Boring. Boring. Boring.

The doc worked for the county, so it's not like they had a ton of money to throw into office furnishings.

Overall, the doctor's office was as appealing as a proctology exam.

Derek yawned again. He faced the door through which he'd just entered. "Where is he?" Derek checked his watch and started bouncing his knee in annoyance.

Another yawn.

Leaning back he let his head fall back on the cushion and stared up at the ceiling. It wasn't the most comfortable of positions, so he shifted and slid further down to get comfortable, resting one of his feet on top of his backpack and leaving the other on the floor.

"Ahh... better."

The ceiling looked familiar. He had no idea why a perfectly blasé ceiling would look familiar, but it did. His thoughts wandered back to the military barracks they lived in at Bagram Air Base in Afghanistan. He cocked his head to the side a little bit as he pondered the white ceiling above him.

Without moving his head, he pulled his wrist up so he could check his watch one more time. Stifling another yawn, he dropped his hand back on the couch. Growing tired after a long night, his lids drew heavy. The doc wasn't back yet, so Derek didn't bother to fight it. He closed his eyes. "If the doc wants to talk, he can wake me up."

Afghanistan - Two years earlier

Joey wasn't breathing.

"FUCK!" Derek called out as he let go of Joey's hand and started chest compressions.

"Don't leave me, Joey," Derek's voice cracked as he called out to him, desperate to keep his best friend alive.

Joey's lifeless eyes stared upwards, but Derek didn't stop. "Don't go, Joey," he begged. "Please," his last word came out as a raspy whisper.

"Doc. He's gone." Jonesy reached out to try to stop him from giving chest compressions.

"No!" Derek shoved him backward as he continued compressions. "Come on, Joey," he pleaded, "Come back."

***

"SERGEANT!" Doc Majors called out.

Strong hands gripped Derek's shoulders as his eyes shot open. He'd grown accustomed to being called by his first name, so hearing someone call him by rank triggered an instant snap to attention.

He was back in the doctor's office. He sat up to get his bearings. Couch. Door. Cabinet. In the distance, the door to the lounge. To his right, the wall and the window. In front of him was a very concerned Doc Majors, shaking him awake. The doctor's hands were squeezing his shoulders.

Derek tried to shrug loose of his hold but couldn't free himself. "Let me go," he snapped.

Still leaning over him, the doc held up his hands and stepped back. "Okay." He reached down to gather the documents he dropped when he rushed into the room.

Still disoriented, Derek's eyes darted around the rest of the room while he worked to catch his breath.

Meanwhile, the doctor exchanged the collected documents with his usual clipboard and notebook. Without a word, he grabbed a bottle of water out of the refrigerator and sat down in the cushioned chair opposite Derek. He offered the bottle to Derek.

Eyeing the doctor warily, Derek accepted it and slowly unscrewed the lid while scanning the room. He took a slow drink as his eyes confirmed he was back at Grant's Crossing, in the boring doctor's office.

"Where were you just now?"

"Where was I... what?"

"You were yelling," Doc Majors explained. "Where were you?"

Derek held the bottle to his lips. "Nowhere." He took a drink.

"Didn't sound like nowhere."

Anger flashed across Derek's face as his brows drew together. "The fuck? What do you mean 'it didn't sound like nowhere?'" Derek dropped back into the cushions with a huff. "Shit. I dozed off. It happens. It was a long shift and I'm tired. Aren't I allowed to lie down and rest?"

"Okay then. Tell me about Joey."

"No."

"This is not the first time you've mentioned his name." Doc Majors waited patiently, but after a minute or two, he broke the silence to prompt Derek in his usual calm voice. "Who is Joey to you, Derek?"

Derek scrubbed his face with his hands, then stared back at the doctor for a few moments. "Someone I let down."

Chapter 18

Follow Up

"Good morning!" A middle-aged, round lady with short, blond hair happily called out from behind the reception desk as Callie entered via the Emergency Department entrance.

"Hi. I called earlier and was told I could get a tetanus shot?"

"Yes, who's your primary care physician?"

"Oh. She's back in D.C., but I called Urgent Care and they said I could just come in. It's been a while." She held up her hand, which was down to only a band-aid. "Cut my hand, a few days ago on an old porch."

"Ahh. Come on back, ma'am."

Callie ignored being called ma'am. "Thank you."

A few minutes later, having received a necessary shot in the arm, Callie was heading toward the door when she heard a swoosh of the emergency department's doors. Standing to the side, she observed doctors surrounding a patient who was brought in on a gurney.

" ... male, early forties, fell off the roof. Positive LOC. GCS eleven with movement in the extremities. Pressure is ninety-two over sixty. Heart rate 104. Sixteen-gauge in both arms."

Callie didn't know what any of the abbreviations meant, but she recognized Derek's voice. Turning, she caught sight of him just as he and Kiro disappeared behind a set of double doors. With a silent prayer for the man who was wheeled in, she walked outside past their ambulance to her car. She glanced up at the overcast sky, worried that it might start raining at any moment.

A text alert sounded.. Reaching into the outside pocket of her messenger bag, Callie pulled out her phone to read it.

Marc: Call Me

Callie's heart jumped in her throat as she hurriedly dialed her brother's number, feeling a shiver of concern as soon as his voice came through the phone.

"Hi, CAT," Marc said, calling her by her initials.

She responded in kind and leaned against her car. "Hey, MAT. Is everything okay?"

"Grandpa took a fall."

She brought her hand to her mouth.

"He's doing okay, but he's really frail. They're going to keep him in the hospital for a few days to make sure, but I thought you'd want to know."

"Should I come home?"

"No. He's going to be okay, all things considered. He's been asking about you and wonders how you like the house."

"I did a walk-through." Callie laughed. "Needs a ton of work, but it's what he expected, I think. I didn't, but I think he did."

Callie updated her brother on the tour she took. "I'll bring the quotes back. I may stay in town for a couple more days and finish my story. Besides, there's some festival or something tomorrow night, so I may walk down for that, then come home on Sunday."

"He really is okay, CAT, but ... he's just not as strong as he used to be."

"Yeah. I know." She sniffed. "I hate it, but I know."

Derek and Kiro emerged from the hospital ER and stowed the gurney back inside the ambulance before heading around to the front to climb into the driver's seat.

Derek caught sight of Callie as he opened the driver's side door, pausing as he looked over to see her on the phone, slouching by her car, looking down.

"Something's up," he said to Kiro, who was already back inside the ambulance. "Be right back."

Kiro nodded and looked in the direction Derek was headed.

Derek walked up to her, concern prominent in his features. "Callie? Are you alright?"

She lifted her gaze and forced a smile, dropping her hand off her forehead and placing her phone back in her pocket in her messenger bag. "Yeah. All good, thanks. You?"

"Uh-huh," he said in disbelief, but didn't press for more detail. It's not as if they knew each other well at all, and he doesn't like to share much about his personal life, either. "I'm good. We just brought someone in." He motioned back at the ER with his thumb.

"Yes." She sniffed. "I saw you come in. A guy fell or something?"

"Yeah."

"I hope he's alright."

"He will be."

They looked at each other during an uncomfortable moment of silence.

"What are you doing at the hospital?"

"Following your advice."

Derek furrowed his brow.

She held up and wiggled the fingers on her injured hand. "Tetanus shot."

"Ahh. Good."

Callie glanced to her left after hearing a police siren in the distance.

"Look. I've uh ... got to go," Callie motioned toward her car just as Derek nodded his head toward the ambulance and added that he should get back.

"Glad you're okay," he muttered.

"Yeah," she agreed as she opened her car door and paused before tossing her messenger bag inside.

"Hey. I'm sorry about the other day. At Jo's, I mean." He dropped his gaze to the ground and kicked at a rock, struggling to find the words.

"It's fine."

"I didn't mean to be such an ass." He huffed out a laugh. "Okay. Maybe I did because I am. I'm just used to having the whole place to myself and ... "

"Kiro said you were in the Army?" she asked, relieving him of his painfully awkward apology. "And you were deployed overseas?"

Derek met her gaze. "Yeah. I was with the 3/75."

She tilted her head to the side. "What's the Three-Seven-Five?"

"Rangers. Spent most of my time in Afghanistan. With Tank, actually, until he got injured."

"My brother was there with the Marines."

"Where?"

"Korengal Valley, among other places. A few places in Iraq. too. He's stationed in D.C. now, so it's good to have him home."

"Korengal? That was a tough spot."

Callie's expression softened. "I imagine they all were."

"True that."

A call came through Derek's radio. "Dispatch to GC Medic."

Not taking his eyes off Callie, Derek put his hand over the small black box hanging over his shoulder. "GC Medic. Go ahead."

"Construction accident. 1732 Mason Ave. Twenty-seven-year-old male. Possible puncture wound."

"Copy that. Medic en route."

"Gotta run." He took a few steps backward, then turned with a wave.

"Bye." She waved to his back as he jogged back to the ambulance.

"Idiot." He ran his hand through his hair, berating himself yet again as he climbed into the driver's seat.

"Jesus, D." Kiro laughed, clearly amused. "Even from here, that looked awkward."

"Yeah," Derek mumbled as he fumbled with his seatbelt before flipping on the lights and sirens and pulling away from the hospital.

Chapter 19

Small Town Life

Derek was slowly adjusting to having someone else spend time around Brockmoor and its carriage house.

Callie wasn't going to stick around for long on this particular visit, so the façade he put up of having to look the part of someone who had their life together would soon be able to tumble down.

Or so he thought.

On the afternoon of the HomeFest, the sun made a valiant, yet unsuccessful, attempt to break through the clouds just as Callie pulled her rental car into the drive at Brockmoor.

Derek and Abe were laughing inside the lower level of the carriage house, converted into a workshop for the renovations, when Callie arrived. Dressed in his paramedic uniform, Derek appeared as if he were about to go on shift at the Fire Station.

Callie shut off the engine and joined them. "Good afternoon, gentlemen."

Receiving greetings from both Derek and Abe as they were still laughing, she set her bag down on one of the tables. "What's so funny?"

Derek looked at her with a big smile. "I was just sharing some of the questions we had from all the elementary school kids earlier this week."

"Do you visit schools? Or do they visit you?"

"We do both, actually, but this week the third graders from Grant's Crossing Elementary toured the fire and police stations as part of their safety week."

Callie leaned back against the workbench. "Oh yeah? That sounds like fun. Now, I'm curious."

Derek chuckled. "First responder fun, so the kids got to be firefighters and policemen."

"No paramedics?"

He shrugged. "We don't have the cool hats. I mean, we have the gear, but since we typically don't run into fires or climb the ladder truck to pull cats out of trees." He shrugged. "Kids don't think we're nearly as cool."

Callie laughed. "Well, that's a shame. What kinds of questions do you typically get?"

"Same ones we'll get at the festival today. You should stop by."

"Any teachers ask about a calendar?" Abe asked.

Derek rolled his eyes. "Ugh. Yes. Never fails. Some teacher inevitably asks about calendars and then goes on and on about how they'd like to see us without our shirts."

Callie cocked a brow and lifted her shoulder. "And what'd you tell them?"

Abe stifled a laugh as Derek sighed and stared at her, stunned. "What do you mean? What did we tell them? We're in Ohio, not Australia."

"Well, it's not as if the Aussies have the monopoly on calendars."

Placing her hand on her chest, Callie attempted to be helpful. "I've got a lot of connections, so I'm sure I could get you some extra sales in D.C."

Abe could no longer contain his laughter, followed soon after by Callie.

"Really, Dad?"

Motioning toward Callie while catching his breath, "Son, she's just trying to help."

"This is what I've been reduced to?" Derek's straight face finally broke. He held his hands up and backed down the drive toward the street. "Fine. I can tell when I'm outnumbered." He pointed toward his dad. "I hope your missing drill turns up." He checked his watch. "I've gotta go. Steve and I are supposed to take over in a bit."

Callie and Abe gave him a wave as he disappeared down the sidewalk.

"It's a rough life my son leads, huh?"

"Definitely," Callie agreed while looking in the direction Derek just headed. "Still. Might make for a good fundraiser. I mean, I'd buy one."

"You would?"

"Of course!"

Abe laughed again. "Not sure if the guys would enjoy that."

"Don't know about the guys, but the rest of us sure would."

Abe threw her a sideways glance.

"What?" She gave him her best innocent look, blinking a few extra times for effect. Callie laughed. "But did I hear you right a minute ago? Something about a missing drill?"

"Yes," Abe said. "A couple of tools have been misplaced. Probably weren't signed back in at our main location. For Brockmoor, we'll eventually move everything back on site since we're keeping this as our workshop." Abe used his hands to unroll the blueprints, placing a hammer and a few wrenches in the corners to hold them open. "Now, what do you say we take a last look at the plans so you can get to the festival?"

Chapter 20

HomeFest

Derek and Steve were just finishing their two-hour festival shift, answering any and all questions from kids and adults alike who wanted to stop by and learn more about the Grant's Crossing Fire Department without having to see it firsthand while in the middle of an actual emergency.

While Derek was indifferent to being in the spotlight for a Q&A session with the general public, Steve was eating it up. He especially reveled in the ability to talk to all the schoolchildren with their silly questions that typically came out of nowhere.

Steve was covered in tattoos and had multiple body piercings, including more that Derek probably didn't care to know about. He had the potential to be outwardly intimidating, but with little kids? He was a natural. Derek was okay, but he'd rather hit on their moms and aunts instead. Maybe he'd call Robyn. She was always a sure thing.

The sound of laughter drew his attention from one of the vendor stalls. In between shelves of autumn-colored ceramic mugs, bowls, and plates in deep reds, browns, and oranges, Derek caught a flash of brown hair.

Callie.

She was laughing with the vendor about who knows what, but damn if her smile didn't light up her whole face. Derek's lip curled up. He hadn't seen it yet directed toward him, but he wanted to see that smile close up.

Steve turned to Derek as the most recent kids left to play carnival games on the opposite side of the square. "So, what's the deal with your new landlord?"

For a moment, the crowd cleared so Derek could take in her shapely profile. Even in khakis, a blue shirt, and a tan jacket, she looked sexy as hell.

Steve smacked Derek's arm when he didn't answer. "Hey, Mitchell."

"Hmm?" Derek lost sight of her when she disappeared into another vendor stall. "What?"

"Have you hooked up with her yet?"

Derek finally acknowledged Steve. "Hooked up? Who are you talking about?"

Steve shook his head and chuckled. "Who were you just looking at over there?"

"Nobody."

"Nobody?" Steve stepped around Derek to take in the scene around the arts and crafts vendor area along Adams Street. After a few seconds, he grinned. "Isn't that the chick at the house? What's her name again? Carrie? Cathy?"

"Callie," Derek corrected him.

"That's right." Steve raised his hand in a quick wave, earning him a quick elbow to the ribs. "Nobody."

"That's enough."

"You should invite her to join us for dinner. Maybe you'll get lucky."

"Nah." Derek motioned toward some kids heading their way. "I probably won't see her tonight. Pretty sure she doesn't like me, anyway."

"Too bad."

"What?" Derek shot a glare at Steve. "Why?"

Steve smiled at the approaching kids. "Because she's heading this way."

"Shi ... shoot," Derek caught himself just in time for three grade-school kids to arrive and start bombarding them with questions.

Out of the corner of his eye, Derek caught Callie walking past the sheriff's cruiser before the boy and two girls started asking questions.

"Does a dog live in the firehouse?" the boy asked.

"No. We don't have a dog living at the firehouse."

"Does fire hurt?" the girl inquired.

"Yes, it does."

"Why is the truck red?"

"So people can see it coming."

"Why are the sirens loud?"

"So people can hear us coming."

"How long is the fire hose?"

"100 or 200 feet long."

The young boy tilted his head to the side in confusion. "Don't you know?"

Derek laughed. "We have both."

"How old do you have to be to join?"

"Eighteen."

"Can we try on a helmet?"

"Sure!"

Derek and Steve both grabbed a helmet for the kids to try. Placing them on top of a young boy and a young girl. It was enormous on the girl whose head disappeared the moment she put it on.

"Why do you wear such a big helmet?" She lifted her head, but the helmet fell forward and covered her whole face. She pushed the brim back up, raising her chin so she could see out from under it.

Steve smiled. "It's big, so it fits our heads, but it's also shaped the way it is, so it protects your eyes and the back of your neck."

He grabbed a jacket hanging on the side of the truck and wrapped it around the girl's narrow shoulders. It covered her almost to her knees.

"This is the turnout jacket that we wear inside the fires."

"This keeps you from getting burned?" She looked down at the huge jacket she was trying on. She extended her arms, which weren't even close to reaching the end of the long sleeves.

"It does a really good job of it, yes."

"Wow. It's heavy."

"Yes. Now add the pants and boots and a tank of oxygen on your back, and it gets really heavy."

"You have to be strong to be a fireman!"

"That we do," he said, removing the turnout jacket and hanging it back on the side of the truck.

Taking back the helmets, Steve and Derek set them on the truck as they waved goodbye to the group of kids.

A slightly older boy walked up and started to ask questions, though a bit less cute and more on the gruesome side. "Have you ever been burned?"

"Sure. I burned my hand once while cooking dinner at the firehouse." Steve laughed.

"Dinner still tasted alright, all things considered," Derek added, smiling over at Callie, who leaned against a nearby street sign, observing their interaction with interest.

"Yeah, but have you ever seen someone get burned?"

Nodding their heads, they gave serious looks and answered honestly. "Yes, we have."

"Where's your ambulance?"

"Back at the station."

"What happens when someone dies in the ambulance?"

"You can't die in an ambulance."

That surprised the kid, who scrunched up his face at Steve. "Huh?"

"It's true."

"Ever see someone get blown up?"

Derek flinched at the question, so Steve quickly stepped up. "Are you going to watch the fireworks tonight?"

"Yeah. But ... "

Steve leaned forward to look the kid in the eye. "There are going to be firefighters there to make sure explosions don't happen."

Disappointed that he didn't get any gory details, the boy skulked away, passing a little girl about three or four years old who was crying inconsolably in her father's arms.

"I don't suppose you could take a look at her hand, could you?" the father asked while approaching the truck. "She scraped it on one of the tables, and it looks like she has a splinter. I only have Band-Aids on me."

"Sure! Have a seat." Derek pointed to the side of the truck as the father sat down with his daughter on his lap. Reaching inside to grab his kit, Derek put on some gloves to take a look at her hand.

"Hi. What's your name?" Derek smiled at her.

She hesitated, still crying.

"It's okay," her dad reassured her. "You can tell him. He's going to make your hand feel better."

"Kensi," a small voice answered in between sniffs.

"Kensi? That's a great name." Derek smiled as he started cleaning off her hand. "Well, Kensi, my name's Derek, and I'm going to take care of your hand so you can go back and play, okay?"

She sniffed, tears still falling. "Okay."

Her hand seemed tiny by comparison as Derek took a look at it. "Yeah. Definitely a splinter."

She sniffed, but the tears were slowing down.

He made quick work of removing it from her hand. "There. It's out. See? It's all gone."

Callie smiled from a distance as Derek calmed the little girl whose teary eyes watched his every move. He carefully cleaned her little hand and placed a Band-Aid on it.

"There. Feel better?"

The beginnings of a small smile began to appear on Kensi's face.

"I'll take that as a yes." Derek grinned as he stood up and took off one of his gloves.

"What do you say, Kensi?" Her father prompted her.

She whispered a thank you.

"You're welcome."

Her dad extended his hand to shake hands with Derek. "Thanks a lot."

"Happy to help!"

Standing up, he grabbed her hand, "Come on, Kensi. Let's go."

She stopped long enough to turn around and give Derek a shy wave.

"Bye," she squeaked.

Derek waved back with a big smile. "Bye, Kensi!"

Seeing a break in the action, Callie walked up to say hello to Derek and Steve. "Saving the day, I see."

"I wish they were all that easy."

Callie pointed toward the sheriff's cruiser. "The sheriff had some fun questions, but he almost had to arrest a little boy for picking on his little sister. It was close, but he was able to talk him down."

Steve laughed. "Man, if brothers got arrested every time they picked on little brothers and sisters, we'd all be in jail!"

"And then all the little brothers and sisters would be in charge." Callie grinned as Derek and Steve both raised their eyebrows in response. "I think we're on to something here!"

"Hey guys." Kiro's arrival was well-timed. "Hey, Callie," Kiro greeted Callie with a hug before Tank arrived right on his heels.

"Been busy?"

Steve ran down the afternoon, "Just the usual. Lots of little kids with questions. Had one kid looking for horror stories, and so far, no calendar requests."

"Oh. Add one paramedic call." Derek added.

Tank paused. "Nothing serious, I hope."

"Little girl had a splinter."

"Ahh." Tank's lips curled into a warm smile. "Good thing you were here, then."

Derek clasped his hands together. "Alright, K? Tank? Are you both good to go?"

"Yeah. We're good," Tank answered. "Have fun!"

Steve elbowed Derek and gave a less-than-subtle head nod toward Callie.

Derek glared at him, but quickly put on a smile. "Hey, Cal. Steve and I are going to wander around and then get some dinner. Care to join us?"

"Sure!"

Kiro and Tank exchanged amused expressions at Derek's question as the trio walked away. "Cal?" Tank asked.

Whatever Kiro was going to say next fell to the wayside when more children descended with a barrage of questions.

Wandering in the park at the square, Callie, Steve, and Derek passed small groups of families and friends sitting at the tables that had been added around the Carousel stage.

"Those kids loved you back there, you know," Callie said as they strolled past tables of people laughing and enjoying their dinners. "They looked so cute wearing helmets that were way too big for them."

"They always have fun, especially when there's not a real fire going on, and it's not scary," Derek answered as they paused to survey the various food trucks.

"And when they see us at our real size, without all the added gear," Steve added.

"True that," Derek agreed.

"Do you always have someone asking about the gruesome stuff?"

"There's always some kid obsessed with that sort of thing. Not really the thing we want to dwell on," Steve added.

Callie nodded. "I don't blame you. But why did you tell him you can't die in an ambulance?"

"Because you can't," Steve answered as they checked out a food truck offering Greek food. "Though it's more a legal distinction, really. As paramedics, we can pronounce someone dead at the scene, but once a patient is in the rig, they can only be pronounced dead by a doctor."

Derek continued the explanation, "And since there's usually no doctor in an ambulance and doctors and nurses have to first make an attempt at life-saving measures in the emergency department, a person can't legally die in an ambulance."

"Wow. I never knew that."

They walked past a stage where a band was setting up for an acoustic set. There were plenty of tables set up for festival-goers.

"This might be a good place to end up for dinner later." Steve pointed toward the stage. "Tara will like it if we can actually hear each other."

Chapter 21

Hustled

A POP SOUNDED IN THE DISTANCE. CALLIE'S HEAD SNAPPED UP before turning left and right. "What was that?"

"What was what?" Derek exchanged a confused look with Steve.

Another pop sounded not too far from them.

Callie stopped. "There. I just heard it again."

"Balloon darts." Steve pointed toward one of the games as they passed the stage onto the west side of the square, where all the carnival games were located.

Ahead of them were colorful tents with games people could play to win all sorts of prizes, including a wide variety of stuffed animals. Lighting up the entire street were strings upon strings of bright faerie lights, contributing to the party-like atmosphere. Above the source of the popping sounds they'd heard was a whole slew of stuffed dogs hanging over a large rectangular pegboard covered in balloons. People in front were throwing darts at them, trying to win a prize.

They approached the booth, but waited while a girl threw two darts and missed.

Callie tilted her head in Derek's direction while keeping her eye on the girl who'd just missed her third shot. "How is she missing those?"

"No idea. I should show them how it's done."

"We should," Callie agreed.

"We?" Derek smirked. "I can definitely beat you at that."

Steve grinned, "Sounds like a challenge."

"Yes. It does." Callie turned to face Derek. "Loser buys dinner?"

"You're on." A cocky laugh escaped his lips. "Should I tell you what I want now? Or do you want me to wait until after?"

Callie responded with a confident smile and stepped up to the counter. She pointed toward the prizes. "They have stuffed Dalmatians."

"The firehouse does need a mascot," Steve added.

"I'll get one for you," Callie offered.

They were greeted by a young, twenty-something man with dark hair pulled back in a man-bun.

"Hello! Care to try your luck at the balloon darts? You can buy two or four darts. Pop two balloons, and you'll get a small stuffed animal. Pop four balloons for a large stuffed animal."

"Like the Dalmatian, I plan to win?"

"Yes, but you'll have to hit four balloons for that, ma'am. How many would you like?"

She turned a wry look at Derek. "He called me ma'am."

He shook his head but answered the man behind the counter. "We'll both take four." Derek smacked down the cash for both of them. Looking over at Callie. "Figured I'd get yours since you'll be getting dinner anyway."

"Uh-huh. Right. You want to go first?"

He extended his hand. "Ladies first."

"Oh no. You laid down the challenge. Let's see what you've got."

He narrowed his eyes and met her gaze. "Alright. We'll take turns."

"Agreed."

Derek shot first and popped a red balloon, offering a smug look as he held up one finger. "There's one."

Callie followed, popping a green balloon. "One."

"Even K could make that shot," Derek scoffed.

Steve laughed. "Trash talking already?"

"Trash talking?" Confused, Callie directed her gaze to Steve, who turned deadly serious.

"Oh yeah. Kiro's lousy at darts." Steve said as Derek nodded in solemn agreement.

"Yep," Derek agreed. "He is."

"Ahh."

Derek and Callie both popped yellow balloons with their second shots.

"That's two. At least you can walk away with a stuffed gorilla while I get your mascot." Callie boasted as Derek rolled his eyes and took out a blue balloon before Callie took out another yellow one.

"Last one," Steve called out while rubbing his hands together in anticipation. "The pressure is on."

Derek took a shot and narrowly missed a red balloon. "Dammit!" He glared at Steve, whose shoulders already shook with laughter.

"Don't worry. I'll get it." Callie eyed the red balloon he missed. "Didn't I see a food truck back there with Greek food? A gyro sounds really good right about now."

Callie threw and popped it with her last dart.

"Shit." Derek's hands went to his waist as he dropped his chin to his chest.

Steve laughed again. "Was she even looking when she threw that?"

The carnival worker handed Callie a stuffed Dalmatian. "Congratulations."

"Why, thank you!"

"Sir? What color gorilla would you like?"

Frustrated at losing, Derek shook his head at Callie. "You decide, Cal."

Callie gave a sugary, sweet smile. "He'll take the green, please."

The man handed Derek a green stuffed gorilla.

"Uh, thanks."

He looked at his stuffed animal, then over at Callie's Dalmatian, and shook his head. "Can't believe you pulled that off!"

"Pulled that off?" she scoffed. "That was pure skill, thank you very much."

"Luck is more like it."

"Says the man who just lost. Still." She took pity on him. "You are the one who works at a fire station. Care to trade?"

"Yeah?" His expression turned as hopeful as a kid being told he can open a Christmas present on Christmas Eve.

"Sure. Steve just said you guys needed a mascot. And it's already been established today that as a paramedic, you're far less cool than the men who run into fires, so I don't want your self-esteem to take too much of a hit."

Derek's expression dropped as Steve doubled over in laughter.

"You have got to keep her around, man."

Callie somehow managed to keep a straight face throughout their exchange.

Derek finally laughed as he handed over his green gorilla. "Give me the damned dog!"

Stuffed animal exchange complete, the three wandered in the direction of the gyro truck, which wasn't far from where Kiro and Tank were talking to a couple of children.

"D, you won a Dalmatian! Nice," Kiro said upon their approach.

Callie cleared her throat, shooting Derek a look that demanded an explanation.

Looking a tad sheepish, Derek said, "Uh, Cal won it for us."

Having joined Kiro and Tank, Emerson stepped over and took it from Derek, patting Callie on the shoulder. He checked it out before setting it on the driver's seat of their truck. "Thanks, Callie!"

"You're welcome!" Callie and Steve both laughed at the exchange.

"Hey, Mitchell," Steve called out. "Callie. You should get a picture with your prizes. Grab our mascot."

Callie handed Steve her phone for the picture as Derek reached up to grab the Dalmatian off the seat. Posing in front of the truck, he put his arm around Callie's shoulders as she put hers around his waist, feeling unexpected sparks from his touch.

Holding the green gorilla next to the Dalmatian, they smiled for the camera. Steve started snapping a few candid shots as Kiro leaned in from the other side of Callie, adding goofy poses for fun. Tank placed a fire helmet on Callie's head as he joined in for a few pictures before Steve backed in for the requisite group selfie.

Hearing some laughter, they turned as Kiro and Tank walked over to a couple of families with small children who started bombarding them with all sorts of questions.

Steve spoke first, "Ready to grab some food?"

Still standing arm in arm, Derek and Callie turned toward each other and nodded.

"Yes!" They said to each other as Derek dropped his arm to put the Dalmatian back in the driver's seat.

Callie felt cooler at the loss of his touch. He turned back to grab the helmet off Callie's head and set it down next to the stuffed Dalmatian.

Steve handed Callie's phone back to her before he greeted a tall redhead with a kiss.

"Tara, this is Callie Thomas. Callie, this is my fiancée, Tara Bailey. She owns the bookstore on the other side of the square."

"Very nice to meet you, Tara." Callie extended her hand. "I've already been in your shop a couple of times since I've been in town."

"Glad to hear it! I thought you looked familiar. It's good to officially meet you." She turned to Steve. "Are Nick and Logan coming?"

"They're meeting us later for the fireworks," Steve answered.

"So, we're going to watch them this year?" Tara laughed as Steve pulled her in to drop a kiss on her temple.

"I'll show you some fireworks, Sugar." He cleared his throat. "But let's get some food first," Steve announced, grabbing Tara's hand while recounting how Derek had lost a bet to Callie and had to buy her dinner.

Picking up dinner from the Greek food truck Callie had mentioned, the four of them settled into a table near the acoustic stage so they had a fighting chance of hearing each other.

"Where did you learn to throw darts, Callie?" Steve unwrapped his gyro.

"I was on an intramural team back at GW."

"On a team?" Derek eyed her with suspicion before stuffing a pair of fries in his mouth.

"Mmhmm," Callie responded as she took a bite of her gyro.

"What's GW?" Steve took a drink.

"Sorry." She wiped her lips with a napkin. "George Washington University, in D.C. There was an intramural darts team in my dorm."

Tara snorted a laugh but nodded to Callie in admiration. "That's awesome."

"Mitchell Hall, actually." Callie gave a nod to Derek, having lived in a dorm with his namesake. "Though it's now a freshman dorm, I think."

Steve agreed. "Mitchell? I think you just got hustled."

"What? No!" In her attempt to appear offended at the accusation, Callie couldn't keep a straight face. "I didn't hustle him, but since you brought it up," she grinned as she held her soda up as if to toast Derek. "Thanks for dinner!"

Derek gave her a sideways glare that morphed into a reluctant smile. "Well, you didn't exactly disclose that you were a pro, but you're welcome."

"Hardly a pro. You were so confident. I didn't want to dash your hopes, at least not until after you missed, anyway."

"Yeah. Yeah. Yeah." Resigned to being the center of a friendly joke, Derek shook his head as he popped the last of his gyro in his mouth.

Tara leaned across the table toward Callie. "You sound like an old married couple. How long have you two been dating?"

Callie's eyes went wide. "What? Huh? Oh. We're not dating. We just met."

Tara smiled as the next song started. "Uh-huh. Sure."

After an hour of conversation and good music, the sun had finally dipped below the horizon, darkening the sky with stars shining between the fast-moving clouds.

"Fireworks are going to start up soon." Steve watched people starting to head toward the river.

Derek tensed up at the mention of fireworks.

"Tara and I are going to stick around for the last of the music before heading down. Are you guys going?"

"I need to go back soon since I have to catch a flight out tomorrow."

Derek sprang up. "I'll walk you back."

Callie said her goodbyes and then departed with Derek for Brockmoor.

Tara leaned into Steve. "She said they weren't dating."

He wrapped his arms around her as they watched them walk away, "Not yet, maybe."

Chapter 22

We All Need Help Sometimes

"Thanks for staying with us!" Sierra, the turquoise-eye-shadowed hotel clerk, called out the next morning as Callie stepped out of the front lobby with a quick wave.

Loading her bags into her rental car, she made one last trip into Grant's Crossing to pick up some paperwork that she'd forgotten at the carriage house before she flew back to D.C. for a few weeks.

She pulled into the drive at Brockmoor next to an SUV she didn't recognize. Stepping out of her car, she saw Kiro standing outside the carriage house door, looking up at Derek's apartment with his phone to his ear. His backpack was sitting on the ground by his feet. He reached up and rang the bell again as Callie stepped out of her car.

"Hi, Kiro. Everything okay?"

"I don't know," he answered as he redialed his phone. "Derek didn't make it to breakfast this morning, and now I can't get through to him. He's not answering his phone. His truck's still here, so I'm hoping he's home, but he changed the code, so I can't get in."

"Yeah - I changed the code, but I can let you in. I have to run up to my apartment anyway."

"Yours?" He appeared surprised. "So you're moving in then?" He reached down for his backpack and slung it over one shoulder.

"Yeah. I can work remotely." She turned the key to the door and walked inside, holding the door for Kiro to follow. "Besides, there's no point in paying for a hotel if I'm going to be spending more time here."

"Makes sense."

"I'm just here a few minutes before I head to the airport, but let me know if you need anything." Callie walked the length of the hallway to her door as Kiro pounded on Derek's door.

"D! Are you there?"

Callie walked inside her apartment to collect her folder off the counter while listening to Kiro call out. As she locked her door, she heard what sounded like empty bottles crashing onto the floor. She turned, worried about what may have happened.

"Shit!"

His tone was more frustrated than surprised.

She walked back into the hall to find Derek's apartment door open. Pushing the door open to see inside, she took in the scene with empty beer bottles on the counter, the coffee table, and the floor. Derek was passed out on the couch, wearing only his boxers, his knees spread wide and his arms resting haphazardly on the cushions. In one was a bottle, and in the other, the stuffed gorilla she'd forgotten to take back after dinner the night before. His head was tilted against the back of the couch, facing the ceiling.

"Come on, D! Talk to me." Kiro leaned over the couch and held his head up, gently slapping the side of Derek's face a few times to get a reaction out of him. Callie heard him moan again as Kiro moved the bottle resting in the crook of his arm to the floor and took his pulse, apparently relieved by the result.

"Hi, K," Derek moaned. His eyes lifted slightly, then fell shut again as his head plopped back with a groan.

Kiro closed his eyes and exhaled in frustration.

She stood in the doorway while Kiro took great care to gently reposition Derek on the couch so he was lying on his side. He then placed a pillow under his head before tucking his arms closer to his body so they were on the couch instead of hanging off the edge of the cushions. Looking around, Kiro reached for the blanket on the back of the oversized chair and spread it over his friend.

He pulled the blanket over Derek's shoulder, resting his hand there for a few seconds. He had just started taking inventory of the room when he noticed Callie, visibly saddened by the scene on display before her.

"Is he going to be okay?"

"Eventually." Kiro pressed his lips together as he started grabbing bottles and carrying them to the kitchen trash can, dropping them slowly so as not to startle Derek. "He's just not been the same since he came back."

"No veteran is," Callie added.

"Fair." Kiro dropped a few more bottles in the trash can before disappearing into the bedroom and reappearing with a small trash can that he placed on the floor next to the couch for when Derek might need it. "Callie?" He dropped a couple of small towels on the coffee table.

"Yes?"

"He wouldn't want you to see him like this." He picked up another bottle, "but since you have ... " Derek shifted on the couch, the movement diverting Kiro's eyes in that direction. Raising his head back up to meet Callie's gaze, Kiro continued. "Can you please keep it between us? Somehow, it hasn't managed to get out that this sometimes happens, and ... for his sake, I don't want it to."

That this sometimes happens.

"He doesn't need to be the next Carl," he added.

Her heart sank hearing Kiro's words, thinking back to the care Carl's son took every time he received a call to take him home from Jo's. Callie blinked a few times and nodded. "Yes. Of course."

"And Callie?" he called out again.

She offered an understanding smile. "We all need help sometimes, Kiro." She took a few seconds to look back at Derek, sleeping on his couch. She reached into her bag and grabbed her business card. She wrote on it, hesitated, wrote some more, then held it up for Kiro to see.

"My cell is on here, along with the new code. Will you let me know later how he's doing? Even just a text letting me know he's okay?" She paused for a moment and then placed it on top of the small table near the door.

With a glance back at Kiro in time to see him nod, she turned and exited the carriage house.

Kiro adjusted the thermostat and flipped the switch for the fireplace to heat the room. He sat on the coffee table just as Derek leaned over and emptied his stomach into the trash can Kiro had placed there.

"I feel terrible," Derek mumbled before he retched again.

With a towel at the ready, Kiro put one hand on Derek's shoulder and another on his forehead as he heaved. "Please stop doing this, D."

THERAPY 4
Monday Morning Quarterback

THE LAST TIME YOU WERE HERE, WE TALKED ABOUT JOEY," Doc Majors started. "You said you let him down."

Derek played with the zipper on his backpack that he'd set down on the floor between his legs. "You don't waste any time, do you, Doc?"

"We've got an hour unless you'd like to take a few minutes first to exchange pleasantries?"

Derek may have been annoyed, but he understood snark. He sighed and then responded after a few moments of silence. "Yeah. I let him down."

Doc Majors nodded. "Okay. Is that what you dream about?"

"Yes."

"How often?"

Derek leaned back on the couch and closed his eyes. "Every damned night." He took a few deep breaths before sitting back up and resting his forearms on his knees. He wiped his face with his hand, pausing to rub his scruffy chin with his fingers. "I can't stop reliving it."

"Reliving what?"

"What I did." Derek spread his fingers wide. "What I didn't do."

He stared out the window for a minute before directing his gaze back at the beige, Berber carpet. "What I could have done. What I should have done."

"It's easy to be a Monday morning quarterback."

"I guess so."

"Want to talk about it?"

"No."

"Okay." A black lab appeared from behind the desk and nudged the doctor's hand. Without any other acknowledgement, the doctor started petting the dog's head. "What do you want to talk about then?"

Derek shrugged but stared at the dog, who seemed satisfied with the attention and lay down on the floor by the doctor.

"What do you do to deal with it?"

"I escape," Derek answered, intrigued by the dog.

"How do you escape?"

"I grab a beer and put on a game."

"How many beers?"

"No idea. I don't keep count. Too many? Not enough? What's it matter?"

"How else do you deal with it?"

"Women." Derek shrugs.

"Women," he repeated.

"Yeah? I drink and I fuck women."

"When's the last time you actually dated a woman?"

"What does that matter? I don't do relationships."

"Let's see." Doc Majors flipped through a couple of pages, then recited Derek's work history. "You enlisted right after 9/11 when you were nineteen, almost twenty. You got out roughly two years ago, which makes you just shy of thirty-six now." The doctor turned his attention from the papers back to Derek. "Did you ever date anyone there?"

"Kaitlyn Sutters."

"Kaitlyn Sutters? And who's that?"

"She is someone I dated from high school through a couple of years into my enlistment."

"What happened?"

"What happened is, I got a letter from her as soon as I arrived at Bagram that it was over. And since then? I hook up with any woman who will let me."

"Condoms?"

"Always. Seriously, Doc, I'm in it to get off, not to start a family."

"So you're not seeking a relationship with any of them?"

Derek scoffed. "No way."

"How does it work for you? Do you just walk up to someone, ask if they want to hook up, and go from there?"

"More or less." Derek's lips curled up. "Though I've got a bit more finesse, but women call me, too. Don't need to put that much effort into things."

"And what if they say no?"

"Not a problem."

"What do you mean by that?"

"I mean, if they say no, they say no. Plenty of other women I can call." Derek grinned. "Like I said before: I'm in it to get off. I'm not in it to hurt anyone."

"What about hurting yourself?"

Derek dropped his gaze to avoid making eye contact. "I'm fine."

"Are you?"

"I'm fine." Derek thought back to his conversation with the chief, where he gave the same response. "Although, I haven't been on a date in about two weeks."

The doctor arched his brows and smiled. "A whole two weeks?"

"I fuck women, remember."

"I remember," Doc Majors said. "How often do you normally go out with them?"

"Once or twice a week at least. Or they come over."

"Come over?" He scribbled something on his clipboard. "And this is on a date? Do you cook dinner? Watch a movie?"

It took a minute for Derek's laughter to calm down enough to where he could talk. "Cook dinner? Yeah, no. I don't do that. She'll come over. We'll do our thing. She'll leave. Or, I'll leave, depending on where we hook up."

"Hook up."

"Yeah." Derek laughed again. "I, uh, don't *date* date anyone."

"And does that help you forget?"

Derek met his gaze with a smirk. "For a while."

"So you don't cook then?"

"No. I cook." Derek stretched out on the couch. "Hell. I'm the best damn cook at the station."

"But you don't cook for any of the women you date."

"No."

"Why not?"

"That would imply I want them to stay."

"So, they never spend the night?"

"Only by accident."

"What do you mean?"

"If I pass out."

"Pass out?"

"Meh. Fall asleep, I mean."

"Mmhmm."

"It's only happened once or twice," Derek explained. "Usually they're gone or I'm gone."

"Does anyone ever see you?"

"What do you mean?"

"Do you meet these women out in public? Anyone ever see you take one home?"

"I'm sure people know. I mean, it's not as if there's a person in town who's never been to Jo's."

"Anyone say no lately?"

"Not lately."

"Anyone *not* fall for your finesse?"

Derek shifted uncomfortably.

"Anyone walk away?" The doctor pushed. "Any woman you talk to that doesn't result in falling straight into bed?"

Derek stared at the dog.

"Derek?"

"Yeah," he croaked out. "One."

"Hmm." The doctor wrote some more notes. "You mentioned before that your house was being renovated?"

"Not my house," Derek corrected him. "I live in a carriage house apartment. One of them, anyway."

"One of them?"

"There are two apartments. Though the carriage house is more of an oversized garage. Workshop on the ground floor. Two apartments upstairs."

"That's right." He petted his dog for a few moments. "And there's a new owner? Is the owner on-site?"

"She's going to be in town, I think, to oversee the reno work, but it might not start for a while."

"And what are your thoughts on that?"

"I don't have any."

"Have you met her? Have you talked to her?"

Derek's lips curled up. "She's kind of cold."

"Yet thinking of her makes you smile?"

"Well," Derek shrugged again. "She's really hot." He tapped above his eyebrow. "She has a scar right above her eye. But she's definitely standoffish."

"Standoffish," Doc Majors repeated. "How so? Did you approach her?"

"Maybe I did the first couple of times we met."

"A couple of times?"

"Yeah."

"Tell me about it."

"The first time was when she walked into the diner, so I checked her out."

"Checked her out?"

"You keep repeating me."

"Mmhmm."

Derek exhaled. "Well, yeah. Like I said. She's hot and well, that's when I noticed the scar."

"And the next time?"

"The next time, she was at the house." Derek held up his hand. "She, uh, cut herself. Cut her hand, so I took care of it. Patched it up."

"So, did you introduce yourself while she was there?"

"No." Derek furrowed his brow. "She didn't want to be called ma'am. Um. Then there was the third time inside the house when Dad gave her the tour. That's when I learned she was the new owner."

"She didn't introduce herself either?"

"No."

"Is that why you consider her standoffish?"

"Maybe."

"Okay. So you didn't officially exchange names until the third time?"

"Yeah. Dad was showing her around her new house. I went upstairs and saw her." Derek stared into space for a few moments, then shook his head. "Whatever."

"What do you mean by whatever?"

"I don't know. I wasn't expecting to see her. I probably sounded like an idiot. In fact, I know I did."

"How do you know?"

"My dad said as much." He laughed. "He finished showing her the house, and after she left, he told me that I'd sounded like I'd just discovered girls."

"So you're attracted to her then."

"She's a woman, and she's hot, so yeah."

"Yet you viewed her as an object."

"What?"

"The first time you saw her, you viewed her as an object."

"Huh? No."

"And then you viewed her as a patient."

"Well, yeah. Her hand was bleeding."

"It wasn't until the third time, when names were exchanged, that you saw her as a person, as a woman."

"She's not an object. She's not easy ...," he explained. "Women are usually an easy catch for me. I kind of want to get to know *her*. It's just ... "

When Derek didn't finish his sentence, Doc Majors spoke up. "Just what?"

"Nothing."

Derek stared back at the carpet before focusing on the chocolate lab on the floor. "I won't be good enough," he whispered. "I wasn't good enough."

"Would you consider cooking for her?"

Derek considered this for a moment, then slowly shook his head. He rested his forearm over his eyes. "I don't know. She ... she saw me."

"When you met, you mean?"

"No. Not there. She ... saw me after."

"After what?"

Derek swallowed hard and licked his lips. "After a bender."

"What did you say to her?"

"Nothing."

"Why nothing?"

"I didn't know she was there."

"What do you mean?"

"I was," Derek avoided eye contact and exhaled loudly. "passed out on the couch."

"She found you like that?"

"No. K did."

"K?"

"Kiro." Derek swallowed again. "The other paramedic I work with. He takes care of me when ..."

"When?" The doctor let his question trail off.

"When I drink."

"Sounds like a good friend," the doc offered.

Derek nodded slowly, taking a moment to stare out the office window. It was overcast, and raindrops started appearing on the plate glass.

"Derek?"

"The best."

"And how often do you need to drink?"

"I can't. I can't sleep without it."

"Yet when you do try to sleep, you have nightmares."

"Yeah." Derek felt something cold against his fingers. He turned to find the doctor's dog nudging his hand. He leaned forward and slowly started petting it. No sooner did he rest his feet back on the floor than the dog rested her head on his knee. Derek scratched behind her ears, forgetting everything else in favor of focusing his attention on the cute lab lavishing him with attention. "How'd you get your dog in here with you?"

"Sadie's my service dog."

Derek stayed his hand to make eye contact with the doctor. "Service dog?"

"Yes."

"What's she trained for?"

"PTSD."

Chapter 23

A Friendship Emerges

Two years and three months after Joey Parker died

November 2016

Derek's blue Silverado appeared in the driveway as Callie rounded the corner of the house with her empty coffee cup from Cafe Mocha on the square. She waved while attempting to take in the final drops of the remaining, now-cold liquid.

"Hi, Callie," Derek greeted her. "I heard you were back in town."

He opened the back door and reached inside.

"Hey, Derek. More groceries?"

"Yeah. Mind getting the door?" Derek called out to Callie as she turned to see his arms full of groceries.

"Sure. Need help carrying anything?"

"No thanks. Just the door."

"I'm going to start expecting a tip for all this door opening I'm doing." Callie's eyes widened at all the food he carried in as he walked through the door. "Whoa. Feeding the whole neighborhood, I see."

He laughed. "Nah, just K and Dad tomorrow, though I still have to figure out something for tonight. Was just running low on a few things."

"A few things?" she asked, following him up the stairs.

"Yeah." He tilted his head to the side. "Do you like to cook?"

She started laughing as he set the bags in front of his door and grabbed his key. Realizing he was serious, she cleared her throat. "Um. No. Nothing complicated, anyway."

"Define complicated." He turned the key and opened his door before reaching back down for his bags.

She blinked a few times. "Anything with more than four ingredients?"

His brow furrowed, and his mouth opened, then shut again. "Please tell me you eat more than mac and cheese or burgers from Jo's."

She placed her hands on her hips and threw out an indignant stare. "I do. I eat crab cakes."

He grinned in excitement. "You can make crab cakes?"

"No. I can eat crab cakes. Then, I do the dishes after my friend makes them."

"Right." He laughed. "And what's for dinner tonight?"

"Don't know. Depends on how far I go on my run. Probably carry out?"

He poured every ounce of mock disappointment into his exhale. "Callie. Callie. Callie."

"What?"

"Need to work on your food intake."

"My food intake?"

"Yeah. I love Jo's for dinner, too, but I still like to mix things up."

"How did you ...?" Callie cut off her own answer since she was indeed planning on hitting up Jo's for dinner.

Dammit. He had a good point.

"What were you going to order?"

She avoided eye contact, looking a tad sheepish before she mumbled. "Grilled turkey and Swiss with seasoned fries." Ugh.

Only her second time in town, and she was already memorizing the menu.

"I can teach you how to make that," he informed her matter-of-factly.

Feeling brazen, she narrowed her eyes. "Fine. Okay then." She followed him into his apartment. "What do you recommend I have for dinner?"

"Depends. What are your plans for the rest of the day?" Seems Derek was feeling brazen, too.

She lifted a shoulder. "Go for a run. Get some writing in. Watch a movie."

He studied her for a moment. "I'm thinking chicken creole would be good for you."

Her eyebrows shot up. "Chicken creole? Sounds fancy."

"It's not."

"How many ingredients?"

"More than four."

"Yep. Fancy."

"Dinner's at seven." His tone was playful, as was the mischievous smile that lit up his face. "And if you really want, you can do the dishes."

She considered his offer for a minute and then nodded. "That's fair. Seven it is." She did an about-face to exit his apartment. He peeked around the door frame.

"Bring a movie," he called out as he retreated inside his apartment.

Derek caught a glimpse of Callie in her running clothes as she jogged back into the drive around an hour before dinner. His lips curled up at the skin-tight black running pants she wore. They didn't leave much to the imagination.

Derek opened the oven to check on dinner just as he heard a knock at the door. He double-checked his appearance and made sure his comfortable navy blue button-down shirt was tucked into the well-worn pair of jeans before answering.

"It's open," he called out, standing over a pan of food on the stove.

She opened the door and peeked inside. "Hi."

He glanced toward the door to find Callie in a pair of form-fitting black leggings and an oversized George Washington University Alumni sweatshirt. She didn't wear much in terms of makeup, but she didn't really need any, either. Her hair was mostly pulled up in a messy bun he'd love to let down. "Come on in."

She entered his apartment and dropped her bag on his oversized chair. She took a surreptitious peek at the food on the stove. "That smells good."

"Thanks." He stirred the chicken in its red sauce. "Should be ready in a few minutes."

"Want help with anything?"

"I'm good, thanks." He paused and added a last-second dash of salt and pepper. "Probably safe to assume you're not a vegetarian, but you're not gluten-free or anything, are you? No peanut or wheat allergies?"

"Nope. All good."

"I mean, I can get a paramedic here pretty fast if you have an allergic reaction to anything."

She laughed. "You've thought of everything."

He stirred the contents of the pan around a little bit. "Well, the guys would never let me hear the end of it if I sent you into anaphylactic shock."

She leaned against the island in his kitchen. "No offense, but I hope I never need your services."

"None taken." He turned off the burner and rotated the pan so the handle didn't point out. "How was your run?"

"It was good, thanks."

"Yeah? Where'd you go?"

"I headed east for a couple of miles, went south for a bit, and then doubled back. It's been a great way to learn the town."

He reached into the cabinet for a couple of plates and set them on the counter. "Five miles, huh?"

"More or less."

"Mind putting these on the table?" He passed the silverware and napkins to Callie. "Have you gone across the river yet?"

She set their places on the small, rectangular table. "No. I've mostly stayed in town so far."

"Good. Probably best to have someone with you if you go near the industrial buildings. Not the safest of places, but a lap around them also makes for a good five-mile run." He grabbed a couple of glasses. "Water, okay? Otherwise, it's beer or pop."

"Beer or what?"

He turned to discover she was already halfway back toward the table. "I have Coke and Diet Coke - pop - if you want."

"Oh. Soda. Yes, please."

He held up a bottle. "Want a glass?"

"Bottle's fine, thanks." She took the bottle offered to her. "Sorry. I'm still not used to hearing people call it pop. Back when I was on assignment in Africa, people referred to it as a cool drink or they'd just ask for a Fanta."

He chuckled. "Welcome to the Midwest."

He dished out the food, setting one down in front of Callie, before placing his own on the table. "Here you go. Hope you like it."

She studied her dish of white rice covered with chicken and vegetables. The scent of garlic and other delicious spices flooded her nostrils. "This smells great. Much better than anything I can make."

"Well, yeah," Derek said, stabbing a piece of chicken on his plate. "It's definitely better than tuna casserole."

"I like tuna casserole." She shot him a stern look as she moved some of the food around on her plate to discover tomatoes, onions, bell peppers, and celery. "You were right. More than four ingredients."

He motioned with his fork. "It's even better when you actually eat it."

With only the slightest hesitation, Callie scooped a bit of rice and chicken onto her fork and slipped it between her lips. She closed her eyes to enjoy the explosion of flavor that instantly greeted her taste buds. "Mmm. This is delicious." She enjoyed a second bite. "Don't tell Jo because I'd probably be banned, but this was infinitely better than what I would have ordered from there tonight."

A smile tugged at his lips as she chewed. "Your secret is safe with me."

"Wow. I expected it to have more heat."

Derek's lips turned down in a thoughtful frown. "Nah. This is more comfort food than anything. Doesn't have much of a kick to it."

Callie finished chewing another bite. "I like it. It's really good."

"Thanks."

"I don't eat a lot of home-cooked food back in D.C., unless I'm over at my friend's place. She's married to a chef. In fact, I'll be there this weekend when I'm back."

"For crab cakes?"

Callie's eyes widened in excitement at the thought, her fork poised in front of her mouth. "Oh, I hope so."

Derek laughed.

"You mentioned dinner for Kiro and your dad before. Do you get together with them often?" Callie asked after a few minutes of eating in companionable silence.

"About once a week or so. We've been doing that for a while now."

"That's nice."

"Mmhmm," he answered while taking a sip of water, willing his leg to stop bouncing. "How about you? Do you get together with your family often?"

She paused long enough to finish chewing. "As often as I can, though I travel a lot for my job. I've stayed in the country for the last year or so–"

"In country?" Derek asked between bites.

"Yes. I've spent a lot of time in Africa and along the Mediterranean."

"That makes sense. Kiro said you'd been to Bulgaria before."

"Took a trip up the coast when I was working out of Istanbul." She smiled. "I've been lucky to have seen so much of the world. Anyway, being home in the States allowed me to see more of my grandfather."

"Dad said your grandfather was the owner."

Callie washed down a bite with a sip of her Diet Coke. "He is, yes, but his great-grandfather originally built it."

"His grandfather?" Derek asked.

"Great-grandfather," Callie corrected him. When she finished eating, she stood up and took her plate out to the kitchen.

"So, your great great-great-grandfather built the house?"

Callie stared up at the ceiling, then narrowed her eyes as if calculating the exact relationship. "I think so, yes."

"Wow. Your family's been here as long as ours."

"Oh, I wouldn't say that," she said, leaning against the counter. "They moved away when he was a teenager back in the 1940s or 1950s, I think." She turned back to face the sink. "Anyway, I brought some popcorn and a movie to watch. Hope you like black and white movies."

He took the change of subject as a good time to clear the table. "Sounds great. Which one?"

"Laura," she answered as she rinsed the plates off for the dishwasher. "It's a film noir with Gene Tierney and Vincent Price. A murder mystery."

"Ever see the Maltese Falcon?"

Her face lit up with excitement. "I love that one. You can't go wrong with Humphrey Bogart and Mary Astor. Maybe I can bring that next time."

He smiled at the thought of a next time. "Sounds good. I'll start thinking about the menu. Let me know if you have any requests."

"I will."

Derek brought his dishes to the sink. "You really don't have to do the dishes. I can get those later."

"You sure? I don't mind. I mean, it's only fair."

"Positive."

"Well, I'm about done, so I can leave them for you next time." She placed the dishes in the dishwasher. She grabbed the dishcloth and handed it to him. "Here. You get the table. I'll be done in a sec."

Not wanting to argue, Derek cleaned off the table and put the food away. Once she started the dishwasher, she wiped down the counters.

"There. See? No time at all."

"Thank you."

"You're welcome." She dried off her hands with a towel. "Thank you for the delicious dinner."

"Anytime."

"Anytime, huh? Careful. I may take you up on that." Her smile never faded as she looked up at him and met his gaze; his smile was just as wide.

He stood close to her. Their eyes locked as his green eyes turned gray and, for a brief moment, started to darken. His eyes dropped to her lips.

Callie raised her eyebrows and grinned. "So, shall we start the movie?" His eyes snapped back up to hers as she rushed to the couch and plopped down with her feet tucked under her legs.

"Yeah." He swallowed and shook his head with a smile. "On my way."

Chapter 24

Climbing Helps

"I appreciate you helping to make sure my furniture deliveries can be taken inside for me so it's here when I'm spending more time in Ohio. There shouldn't be too–"

Callie's phone buzzed with a text alert just as she and Abe were finalizing some details about the house.

"Son of a …!"

"Everything okay?"

"Bad news on the bedside tables I wanted. Their driver broke down, but they say I can pick them up this week." Callie brushed a wisp of hair off her face. "I'm going back tomorrow, so I'd have to get them today."

"Can't they push back the delivery?"

"Yes, but not for another few weeks at least because they're going on vacation. It's a mom-and-pop shop, and they close down every year at this time or something. They close at 4 pm." Callie turned when Derek pulled his truck into the driveway and cut the engine.

"Perfect timing. Derek," Abe called out as Derek stepped out of the truck. "Come here, Son."

"What's up, Dad?" Derek smiled at Callie. "Hi, Callie."

Callie gave him a half-wave as she reread the message.

"Do you have anything going on today? Callie needs to pick up a couple of end tables this afternoon."

She looked up from her phone. "A headboard and a couple of bedside tables. Maybe a few other things? I mean, I can always try to pick it up myself."

He started laughing. "No."

Callie startled. "No? What do you mean, no?"

"It won't work with your rental car. You'll need a truck."

"Well, not to state the obvious, but I don't have a truck. I may have to make two trips. They can't deliver for a while, and I want to get it in there before I go back to D.C."

"I do."

"What?" Callie's mouth dropped open. "I ... I can't take your truck."

Derek scoffed. "Of course not. Nobody touches my truck. No, I'll drive you there."

"Oh," Callie breathed out. "I didn't mean ... wait. What?"

"I'll drive."

Abe coughed to mask his amusement and pointed his thumb toward the makeshift construction office inside the carriage house. "I'll be in the workshop."

"You're going to drive me all the way down to Columbus to pick up my furniture?"

"Why not?" Derek pointed toward the carriage house. "I just need to take my stuff inside, but I can take you down."

"Really?" Callie's face lit up. "I'd appreciate that. Thanks!"

"Need anything from inside before we leave?"

"No thanks. I'm good," Callie said as she waited by the passenger side door of his Silverado.

Before Derek walked around to the driver's side, he caught her hesitating. "What's wrong?"

"You said nobody touches your truck." She looked up and blinked. "How do I get in if I can't touch it?"

Not bothering to conceal his laughter as he walked around, "Smart ass." He opened the door and held out his hand. "Your carriage, madame."

"Thank you, sir!" She smiled sweetly as she took his hand to step up before stopping short. "Seriously, how do you get into this thing?" Her eyes darted around for a step or a handle to help her get inside the truck, much higher off the ground than she anticipated.

"Climbing helps."

"Climbing. Right. Got it."

It was anything but graceful, but by grabbing the seat with one hand and the top of the door with the other, she clambered into the passenger seat. Derek shook his head and closed the door.

On his way around, Derek exchanged a few words with his father that made Abe laugh. He opened the door and effortlessly slipped into the driver's seat.

Callie looked at him, mouth agape. "You made that look so easy. How'd you do that?"

He looked over at her while turning the ignition. "Height helps," he told her as he nonchalantly put the truck in gear.

She opened her mouth as if to say more, but responded with a single word. "Right."

Putting his hand behind her seat, he chuckled and turned his head for a view out the back window to start backing out of the drive. "Where are we heading?"

"Oh." Callie grabbed her phone to pull up the confirmation email. "Dublin Road ... near Trabue Road?"

Braking while still in the driveway, he held out his hand. "May I?"

She handed him her phone so he could confirm its location.

"Oh, okay. Yeah, I know where that is. Dad has to go down there sometimes."

"Do you have a pickup appointment?" he asked as they drove through town.

"No. Just have to be there by 4 pm."

"Good. Plenty of time to make a stop on the way."

"A stop?"

"Yeah. It's on the way."

"What kind of stop?"

"You'll see."

"Will it take long?"

"Cal!"

"What?"

He shot her a stern look while stopping at the intersection. "Trust me, would you?"

"Okay."

About forty-five minutes later, he pulled his truck into a tiny parking lot off Hayden Run Road, big enough to hold nine, maybe ten cars, tops. Nestled between the stoplight at a busy intersection with a house on the corner and the bridge going over the Scioto River, it seemed little more than an enlarged shoulder off the side of the road.

"Okay. This is it."

"This is what?"

"Our stop."

"There's nothing here."

He laughed until she started to open the door.

"Wait," he cautioned as he climbed out of the truck and stepped around to her side. He opened her door and offered his hand to help her get out.

"Thanks." She took his hand and stepped down. "Saved me from having to rappel down."

"You're welcome." He smiled back as he shut the door and locked the truck.

"Getting out is definitely easier than getting in."

Derek laughed. "Be glad I never added lifts."

"Added what?"

"Never mind."

Callie turned her head right and left, up and down, within the tiny parking area boxed in by beautiful, dense, tree-filled woods on one side and the road on the other. "So what is this place?"

"You'll see."

Callie scanned the paved area with room for a handful of cars. "It's just a parking lot. Is there something behind the trees?"

"Would you stop being a journalist for five minutes?"

She warmed up when he placed his hand on the small of her back for a moment, leading her to a small opening in the trees just past the last parked car. "But–"

"No buts. Just wait. I'll show you."

Unseen from the road was a long wooden staircase leading deep into a large, wooded gully.

The heat from his touch still lingered in her mind as they slowly descended the steep, wooden steps leading to a boardwalk that wound around and disappeared into the woods.

Callie paused to scan the area before continuing down the stairs. "How far down does this go? It's beautiful here."

"Not far. That's the Scioto River over there through the trees," Derek said, pointing to his left.

Once down the steep stairs, Callie could hear the cars on the road above but couldn't see anything except bits and pieces of the sky through the canopy above and a small creek that paralleled the long, wooden walkway. In the distance, she could almost hear rushing water. She stopped.

"Is that a waterfall, I hear?"

Derek smiled and nodded as they strolled. "Before she got sick,

Mom would bring me down here after a rough game or a tough week at school or when Lainee wouldn't leave me alone."

"Lainee?"

"Alayne. Lainee. My little sister. She would never leave me alone."

"Yeah." She giggled. "We little sisters are good at that."

"Yeah. Really annoying sometimes."

Callie grinned as she nodded in agreement. "Only if we're doing it right!"

Shaking his head, Derek reminisced. "Mom brought me here to give us mother and son time together. She always found a way to spend time with each of us so we'd never feel left out, you know?"

Callie's lips curled up into a smile as he spoke.

He paused his story long enough to exchange hellos with an approaching couple as they strolled by.

"After a bad week or a game loss, we'd come down here and just talk," Derek reminisced. "No matter what was going on at school or with my friends, she was always interested. And she always listened as if what I had to say was the most important thing in the world to her."

He stopped and gave a half-shrug. "I know she did the same for Lainee, too. She was really good about that."

He cleared his throat before continuing down the path. "Anyway, the first time we came here was after I had a fight with another boy in grade school, Joey Parker." He smiled as he said his name.

"He was a scrawny kid, always tagging along. Always alone, too." They took a few more steps along the path. "He'd play with Tank and me at the park. We couldn't have been more than ten, and at the time, I was pretty scrawny, too. One day, when we were playing on the slide, I saw two boys picking on Lainee. She was just playing on the swing. They were yelling and pushing her, so I charged after them to get them to leave her alone. Turns out, Joey was running right behind me the whole time to stick up for her, too." He scoffed. "I ended up with a bloody nose. He ended up with a shiner and a busted lip."

Derek looked at Callie to find her eyebrows raised in surprise. He shrugged. "What? We were boys."

Callie shook her head and chuckled. "What about the other boys?"

"Pretty sure they looked about as bad as we did. Nothing like getting full-named at a park full of kids."

"Oh, wow. Bet everyone stopped playing when that happened."

Derek laughed. "Oh yeah. They did, but the two boys ran off as soon as they figured out it wasn't their name that was called."

They passed another couple on the boardwalk. "After the fight, Mom told me that sometimes you have to look really hard to find something good in a person, something special, because it wasn't always apparent. She said I shouldn't take anything for granted, either, not even the scrawny kid who always followed me around. Needless to say, she made me go to his house and apologize for involving him in the fight."

"Wow," Callie said softly. "So what happened?"

"I went over. I apologized. Then, we discovered we both liked comic books and hit it off. We became best friends after that."

Callie smiled up at him before turning her gaze back to the wooded path ahead of them.

He stopped walking again. "You see, Joey was an only child who was essentially raising himself since his single mom had to work two jobs just to pay the bills. He pretty much lived on PB&J sandwiches since that was all he could make by himself.

"He had a lot of dinners at our place after that. It's like Mom told me, not everyone has it easy, but if you don't give up, you'll find something wonderful where you least expect it."

"My grandpa says something similar," Callie said. "He tells us that if we give something our all, anything is possible." She smiled, then blinked away a tear. "He's not been well lately."

"I'm sorry to hear that."

"Thanks," she whispered, but then she perked up. "He's still with us, but his body just doesn't want to cooperate anymore."

"Yeah. That's gotta be tough."

"It is." Callie's face lit up. "But he's sharp as a tack and has the greatest stories."

"Enjoy that as long as you can." Derek remained quiet for a few more steps until the boardwalk opened up. "This is where she brought me." Derek motioned with his arm to reveal a big waterfall.

Chapter 25

Hayden Falls

Callie's mouth opened as she took in the view, making a slow, 360-degree turn. "This is beautiful!" Surrounded by a small, horseshoe-shaped cliff directly in front of the wooden walkway was a pool of water being fed by the large waterfall and leading out via a small creek to the Scioto River. "I would never have expected this in the middle of the city."

"Mom was right. Something wonderful right where you least expect it." He smiled down at Callie before looking back up at the waterfall.

"I think the real reason Mom always brought me here was that she knew I had a temper, and the sound of the water would sometimes be the only thing that could calm me down. To this day, I love it when it rains."

"So what is Joey Parker up to these days?"

Derek tensed. His smile disappeared, and his eyes went distant. He took a deep breath, held it for a moment, and exhaled slowly.

"After 9/11, Tank, Joey, and I enlisted in the Army. Thirteen years later, Tank had already been back a few years, but Joey and I were on another deployment to Afghanistan. We were on our way back from meeting with some tribal elders when we were ambushed.

We took heavy fire from insurgents when Joey was shot. He'd been hit, but he was still okay."

Derek leaned forward and rested his arms on the edge of the railing around the boardwalk and stared blankly at the waterfall as he talked. "A few seconds later, an RPG hit overhead, and the blast tossed us both back. It took me a few seconds to get my bearings, but when I looked over, one of the other men was stunned, and another was already gone. Joey was bleeding from everywhere. I did what I could, but his internal injuries were just too severe."

Callie put her hand on the back of his wrist while he talked. He turned his hand and laced his fingers in hers.

Staring at their hands, he said, "I got to him pretty fast, but it was too late. No matter what I tried, I couldn't save him." Derek's voice shook as he spoke. "He died holding my hand and calling out for his mom." He sniffed and looked up at the sky as he remembered his friend. "She'd been dead for two years."

Staring ahead, he shrugged and squeezed her hand while trying to collect himself, wondering why the words were pouring out of him.

"From fifth grade on, we did everything together. We were inseparable. When we got back to base, I stayed by his body, wondering what else I could have done. What could I have done differently to have saved him?" Derek exhaled and remained silent a moment or two while he held himself together. "He had no other family. I was his designated contact in lieu of a next of kin. So, I was granted emergency leave to escort him home. He had just turned thirty-three a few weeks earlier." Derek released a humorless laugh. "He'd even been promoted on his birthday. We finally held the same rank."

He cleared his throat as he stared back at the water. "By the time I was back from leave, I'd pretty much lost motivation. Ended up back at Fort Benning until my enlistment expired a few months later. Didn't see the point of re-upping. I'd loved serving up to that point, but without Joey, I was done. Thirteen years was enough."

He glanced over at Callie before staring down at the water. "Anyway, he's buried next to his mom at the cemetery back home."

"I'm so sorry."

Still listening to the sound of the water, he looked back over at Callie, whose golden-brown eyes were fixed on his with unwavering attention. Their eyes locked, and neither one could bring themselves to look away from the other.

"I don't know why I just told you about Joey. I don't really talk about him anymore."

Unable to break their gaze, he was connected to her in a way he hadn't felt with any woman or anyone really since he'd returned to civilian life. He reached out and gently pushed some hair behind her ears and caressed her cheek as she looked up at him, not pulling away.

Looking down at her lips, he hesitated before he leaned in. Then he closed his eyes and pressed his mouth against hers. Gently. Softly.

The second his lips touched hers, the tension flowed right out of him, replaced instead with a longing he hadn't experienced before. Sure, he'd been with other women, plenty of them, but they'd never made him truly *feel*. They were just a quick escape from reality for a few minutes before he sent them home.

No. This was different. He wanted more, and he never wanted more. This was hunger and a raw need for a woman he barely knew. As soon as she opened her lips to deepen the kiss, he reached his hand around to the back of her head to hold her closer. Callie's hands reached up to his chest and began to loop her arms behind his neck.

"ROCKY! NO! GET BACK HERE!"

A young voice cried out, causing them to jump apart, cutting short their tender moment.

A big, excited German Shepherd ran right up to Derek and Callie, wagging its tail and bouncing around for attention.

"SORRY!" A kid yelled as he hurried over to grab the leash that had been pulled out of his hands. "Don't worry. He won't hurt you. Got away from me. Sorry, sir. Sorry, ma'am." He grabbed the leash and ran toward his parents with his dog in tow.

Willing her heart rate to slow down, Callie took a step back, reading Derek's expression.

He chuckled. "He called you ma'am."

"Yeah," she muttered, forcing a brief smile as she pressed her hands together, already missing his touch. "He did. Um ... maybe we should go?"

He blinked a couple of times and recovered as if locking his vulnerable side away. He forced a smile and nodded. "Yeah. Let's go."

They returned to the truck in silence. After helping her climb in a bit more gracefully this time, they traveled the rest of the way to pick up her furniture.

With everything secured in the back of the truck, they drove home, listening to Derek's country music the entire way. He hadn't said a word since they'd made the pick up and started the trip back to Grant's Crossing.

The tension that now existed between them was palpable, but Callie couldn't help but wonder what would have been had they not been interrupted. She rubbed her hands together and stared out the window, thinking about when they'd held hands at the waterfall.

Thinking about the feel of his hand caressing her face. And when his lips touched hers.

It had been a long time since she'd felt butterflies over a man, not since her time on assignment with Rafi, back in Africa.

Derek, though. He was different, tortured.

The truck stopped moving, pulling Callie back into the present as they arrived back at Brockmoor.

Kiro bounced up from where he'd been leaning up against the carriage house with his hands in his jacket pockets, one foot propped against the wall.

"Been here long?" Derek opened the back of the truck as Kiro approached.

"Nope. Just a few minutes."

"How's it going, Callie?"

"Great, Kiro. Thanks. Did you just happen to be here?"

"I texted him after we got everything loaded," Derek said as he and Kiro started unloading her furniture.

"Oh. Thank you."

"Cal, if you want to get the doors for us, we'll get these upstairs for you."

"Yep!" Callie jogged over to unlock and hold open the door as they brought the tables inside and carried them up the stairs, waiting for her to get the apartment door open. Once she did, they went back down for the headboard and moved it all inside.

"Thanks, guys!" Callie stepped into the hall and locked her apartment door.

"Are you staying in Grant's Crossing now?" Kiro asked.

"Yes, but probably not until after the new year."

"I'll walk you down." Derek unlocked his door so Kiro could go inside. "I'll be back in a minute, K."

Kiro slid into Derek's apartment, letting the door close while Derek walked Callie out to her car.

Derek stood by Callie's rental car for a moment after she opened the door and took a deep breath. "Cal, I'm sorry about earlier. I didn't mean ... I just ... " Derek stumbled over his words.

"Don't be sorry."

"But–"

"Derek, it's alright." She smiled up at him. "We're good."

Their eyes were locked when she put her hand on his face to lean up and kiss him on the cheek.

"I won't be back until December, so happy Thanksgiving." She tossed her messenger bag onto the passenger seat and climbed in.

———

Watching through the window, Kiro smiled. "About time, D."

THERAPY 5
A Big Step

Derek usually enjoyed a good rainstorm, but the relentless tapping of the rain on the windows grated on his nerves during his regular post-shift therapy session with Doc Majors.

The doc was running through his usual start-of-session questions. *How are you? How was your shift? Et cetera, et cetera,* when Derek's impatience got the better of him.

"I talked to someone about Joey," Derek blurted out as he sat upright on the couch.

"Oh yeah?" Doc answered with genuine surprise.

Derek rubbed his hands together but nodded in the affirmative.

"That's great, Derek. What did you talk about? Joey as a friend? Or as a comrade in arms?"

"Yeah. Joey. How we'd been friends since we were kids." Derek almost smiled. "How we met." His expression dropped. "How he died."

"Who did you talk to? A friend? Family?"

Derek leaned forward and clasped his hands with his elbows on his legs. He drew in a breath before responding. "My landlord."

"The annoying one?"

Derek flashed a sheepish expression. "She's not so annoying."

"That's really good, Derek. That's a big step." Doc Majors' proud expression didn't go unnoticed. "What prompted you to open up to her?"

"I took her into Columbus to pick up some furniture she'd ordered."

Derek started rambling about how most of her furniture had been delivered, but these had to be picked up before the doc paused him. "And how did you feel afterward?"

"Relieved? Sad. Happy. Conflicted." Derek drew in a long breath. "But mostly relieved. Someone else knows."

Chapter 26

Brockmoor

Two years and four months after Joey Parker died

"IS SHE FURNISHING BOTH OF OUR APARTMENTS?" DEREK signed the paperwork for yet another delivery driver and stared at the boxes that now took up at least one-third of the workshop area in the ground level of the carriage house. What used to be for horses and then the horseless carriage was now full of the furniture Callie Thomas had ordered for the apartment she planned to stay in once they started work on her grandfather's home.

"She's taking the two-bedroom apartment upstairs, so she'll need more furniture than you," Abe answered nonchalantly while flipping through papers on his clipboard. "She's also starting from scratch. Based on the state of the interior of the house itself, not much will be able to be saved and used in the interim."

Brockmoor was one of the larger Queen Anne Victorian homes that had been built after the fire of 1905 that took out half of downtown and seven lives by the wealthier residents of Grant's Crossing. Named after a married couple who both perished in the fire, Brockmoor had already been added to the National Register of Historic Places. According to Abe, the commemorative plaque indicating its addition had been lost. They hoped to eventually find it within the house itself, but it was probably long gone and would have to be replaced once the home was renovated.

"She's furnishing it, so she doesn't have to pay for a hotel in Delaware." Abe squeezed Derek's shoulder. "Can't blame her for wanting to be comfortable or not wanting to unpack every time she comes out. Once we start working on the house, she'll want to be out here to check on things."

"And that doesn't bother you at all?"

Abe furrowed his brow and shook his head. "Not at all."

Derek stared at his father. "Do you plan on lugging all this upstairs?"

"Oh no." Abe set his clipboard on the table and leaned back with a smirk. "That's why I have people working for me. I figure you can rustle up a few friends to get it all up there."

"Me?"

"Mmhmm," Abe confirmed.

Derek knew he wasn't going to win that argument, so he nodded in resignation. "Right. And when are you planning on scheduling the demo?"

"Oh, not for a while yet. After the holidays, sometime."

"And I can't talk you into taking at least one box upstairs?"

Abe checked his watch. "Nope. I have plans." He made a beeline for his truck, leaving Derek alone to close up the garage-turned-workshop.

Derek extended his arms. "Plans? What plans?"

"Goodnight, son. See you tomorrow."

The word tomorrow was a bit clipped since Abe shut the driver's side door mid-sentence. Derek was stunned as his dad backed out of the large drive and onto Adams Street with a quick wave from inside the cab.

Derek turned to the large number of boxes and exhaled. He could take some up himself, but he'd need an extra set of hands for the rest. Nothing a home-cooked meal for Kiro and Steve couldn't take care of.

"Oh, that was good," Kiro exclaimed, pushing his dish away from the edge of the table. "I tell you what. If you ever open up a restaurant, you'd give my parents some serious competition."

Steve agreed. "Anytime you need help with anything, I'm happy to lift some boxes in exchange for a great home-cooked meal. Tara makes a good casserole, and I can make ... well ... I can't really make anything, but this was amazing."

Derek laughed. "I could probably make red beans and rice in my sleep, but I appreciate your help and am happy to make it again, anytime. Oh, and I made extra cornbread if you want to take some home with you."

"Excellent." Kiro finished off his glass of Coke. "Celeste loves your cornbread."

"I can teach you how to make it, you know."

"Nah, I'm good with my grandma's recipes, not all this Cajun stuff you make."

"Ha!" Derek couldn't resist mocking his friend. "Heaven forbid you add actual spice to anything."

"What?" Steve asked. "Kiro's cooking is good."

"It is, yes, but Tank and I always have to add hot sauce to it. Speaking of which," Derek added. "I should probably pick up more for the station since we're running low."

"There's more to life than hot sauce, you know," Kiro quipped. He carried his dirty dishes to the kitchen.

"You just can't handle the heat."

"Celeste would say otherwise!"

Steve laughed as he checked his phone. He cleared the rest of the table and helped Kiro clean up. "Do you need anything else tonight, Mitchell?"

"Nah. I'm all good, thanks." Derek stood and exchanged a half-handshake, half-hug with Steve, who did the same with Kiro. "See you both later."

Kiro sat back down at the table. "So, what's the deal with you and Callie?"

"What do you mean? There's no deal."

"We came over to carry a few boxes upstairs, and before we knew it, you had us putting everything together and setting up her apartment." Kiro leaned back and stretched his arm over the back of the chair next to him.

Derek scoffed. "We left plenty of boxes for her to unpack. We just put together a few pieces of furniture, that's all."

"Uh-huh. Right." Kiro shot his friend a dubious look. "And what were you saying about decorating the place?"

"I'm not going to decorate the place."

Kiro didn't say a word in response.

"What?" Derek shrugged. "She just needs a few pieces of Ohio in there."

"Does she even like the Bengals? Heck, she's probably a Ravens fan or something. Worse, she could be a Pittsburgh fan." Kiro faked an exaggerated shudder.

"Yeah, but if she's going to be staying here, she needs to blend in with the locals."

Kiro rolled his eyes, but couldn't stop laughing at Derek's ridiculous ideas.

"Dad said she'd be here late next week, so we'll know soon enough what she thinks."

Chapter 27

Back in Town

CALLIE STEPPED OFF THE PLANE AT JOHN GLENN International Airport and started heading for the baggage claim with her messenger bag and pulling a carry-on bag behind her. She was greeted by a friendly face as she stepped off the escalator.

"Callie!" Abe greeted her with a big smile. "Good to see you, dear!"

She couldn't help but smile and greeted him warmly with a kiss on the cheek and a hug, which he was happy to return.

"Thanks for picking me up. Sorry for the sudden change of plans. My assignment got moved up so I wanted to take care of a few things in Ohio before I had to head out again."

"My pleasure. How was your flight?" He asked as they walked toward the conveyer belt to wait for her checked-in bags.

"Nice and uneventful. Just the way I like them."

"Good. Good. And, how was home?"

"Nice. It was good to be back in D.C."

They waited a few minutes as the lights came on and luggage started coming up the conveyor belt.

After a couple of minutes, Callie spotted her suitcases and grabbed them off the belt when they came around.

Abe took one and pulled it to the truck as they headed underground to the elevator. "We're just across the way, a couple of levels up."

Stepping off the elevator in the garage, they started walking down the aisle when she saw Derek's truck parked in a spot.

"That's not your truck," she observed as he pulled the keys out of his pocket.

"No." He stowed her bags underneath the cover and closed the tailgate. "Mine is filled with too many tools to drive down here, so I borrowed Derek's."

Callie's jaw dropped. "He actually lets you touch his truck?"

"Benefits of being the family patriarch," he admitted, causing Callie to laugh. "Besides, he's on shift today, so he doesn't need it."

With her luggage secured, they opened their respective doors before Callie stopped again.

"Whoa! This is new," she exclaimed at the extra step to get in his truck.

"Yeah. He added running boards while you were gone."

Callie smiled as she climbed into the truck. "Oh, wow. Much easier."

Abe put the car in gear and backed out. They rode in silence as he exited the lot and entered the freeway to work their way around Columbus for the one-hour drive back up to Grant's Crossing.

Callie eyed the cloud-filled sky. "What a dreary day."

"Welcome to Ohio." Abe laughed. "You start appreciating sunny days this time of year. They tend to be fewer and farther between."

"Great day to try out the fireplace, curled up on the couch with a good book."

Considering she started from scratch, Callie was relieved to learn that all the furniture deliveries she'd planned during her absence arrived as expected.

"I appreciate all your help with the deliveries, Abe. Thank you"

"My pleasure. Derek and his friends did most of the heavy lifting, but I was happy to open a few doors. The furniture is all assembled, and Derek added a few of his own decorative touches."

Callie burst out laughing as soon as they walked inside her apartment. The first new decoration of note was the Ohio State Buckeyes blanket, carefully placed on the back of her couch. On her empty bookshelves, she discovered a Columbus Blue Jackets hockey puck had been angled just so, tilted up so the logo faced out. The ticking of a Cincinnati Bengals clock that hung on the wall in the kitchen drew her attention.

"Bengals? What was he thinking?"

"Apparently," Abe did his best to get his answer out between laughs, "he thought it a good idea for you to be a local. I'm pretty sure that clock has been hanging in his bedroom since he was in middle school. Don't be surprised if you find stadium cups in the cabinet."

Callie walked over and opened the cabinets. Sure enough, there were stadium cups from Ohio State, the Blue Jackets, Columbus Clippers, Columbus Crew, and even the Toledo Mudhens. A Cincinnati Reds coffee mug sat alone on the shelf above.

She held up a cup with a yellow and black logo. "Columbus Crew. That's MLS, right?" she asked, referring to the professional soccer league.

"Yes." Abe nodded. "Mapfre Stadium, near the fairgrounds, though they're trying to get a new stadium downtown."

She picked up the Clippers cup. "And the Clippers?"

"AAA baseball team. Farm team for the Cleveland Indians," Abe explained. "They've got a great stadium in the Arena District. Games are a lot of fun."

"Well, at least they're American League," She countered as she put it back on the shelf. When she turned, she saw Abe's confused expression. "I'm an Orioles fan."

"Ahh."

Callie sighed. "He and I are going to have a serious discussion about his team choices."

Callie woke up after her first night's sleep in her new apartment, feeling well-rested. It had been a while since she woke up in something other than a hotel room when traveling. While she hadn't planned on spending much time in the Midwest, she was grateful to have her own place. The first thing she did to celebrate was establish a morning routine, so she headed outside for a little exercise.

It was a crisp fall morning, with carved pumpkins still on many front porches in the neighborhood. Though still overcast like the day before, it was a lovely day for a long run. Since she needed to learn her new town, she used her morning runs to get the lay of the land.

Today, she would head north, further away from the square with which she was the most familiar. Having mostly stayed in residential areas and crossing paths with a handful of other runners along the way, she got about six and a half miles in by the time she returned to Brockmoor an hour or so later.

Turning into the drive, a red hatchback was now parked next to where Abe had parked Derek's truck the day before. Callie didn't think anything of it since Abe had said a handful of people would occasionally be around to check on things for the house.

She didn't know if Derek would be home yet since she had no idea of his work schedule. She just knew he worked for a solid day and came home after, assuming he wasn't delayed with a fire someplace.

She raised her hand to plug in the security code when an

attractive, long-haired blond woman exited through the carriage house door, startling her into taking a step back.

Without stopping, the woman looked at Callie with a suggestive smile. "Guess you're next!"

"What?" Callie took a few seconds to collect herself, then caught the door before it closed. Stunned, she turned back to see the woman climb into her car and drive away.

"Huh," she muttered as she stepped inside and let the door close behind her.

"Robyn, did you forget someth–?"

Callie had just rounded the corner at the top of the stairs when she crashed into an unexpected, solid wall.

Only walls don't typically have a smattering of hair on them.

Or muscles.

They also don't catch you by the shoulders.

When Callie looked up, she was face-to-face with Derek Mitchell.

Literally.

"Uh. Cal. Hi. I didn't know you were back."

His hands didn't move off her shoulders.

Callie's eyebrows shot up as she realized her hands were pressed against his bare chest. "Oh."

Snapping her hands back, she took a step back, but couldn't help herself from looking at him from head to toe, not at all failing to notice the amazing job he did to stay in shape.

That chest.

Wow.

If ever a man were meant to be objectified, it would be right here. Right now.

Those legs. Those legs covered only by a pair of boxers. And that's when it hit her that he'd just been with another woman.

"Oh!" Her eyes opened wide as she tried to collect herself,

taking every ounce of energy she could muster to pull her gaze up to his face rather than the rest of him.

"Hi Derek. Yeah. Uh. Got back yesterday. Going out?"

"Huh?" He glanced down at his current state of dress. Stifling a laugh, he flubbed his way through an apology. "Oh. Um. Sorry."

"Right." She held her hands out, trying to maintain distance as she slid by him, walking almost backward toward her door. Despite everything, she couldn't avoid taking another look at his chest since it was right in her line of sight. "See you later."

She turned and scurried down the hall, fighting the urge to look back, no matter how much she wanted to. Fumbling with the keys, she unlocked the door to her apartment and hastily shut the door behind her.

Inside, she turned and leaned her back against the door. Glancing up at the ceiling, she closed her eyes and exhaled through her mouth.

Derek ducked inside his own apartment and ran his hands through his hair. "Idiot."

Chapter 28

On the Edge

Derek jerked awake with a sudden inhale as he sat up on the couch. He wiped his face with his hand as he glanced outside to see that night had fallen.

"Shit." He started to stand up, but fell back down on the couch with an audible groan. He could have counted the four or five empty bottles sitting on the coffee table had his eyes been able to focus.

"I must have been more tired than I thought."

Making more of an effort, he blinked his eyes a few times, stood back up, and staggered over to the island in the kitchen to catch himself. Looking down, he saw he still had a bottle in his hand. He held it up and drained the last of the liquid inside, then let it fall into his trash can, where it landed with a high-pitched crash into the other bottles already residing there.

Thoughts of greeting Callie in his boxers earlier in the day, right after Robyn had left, added to his existing headache. He could apologize to her later.

He stumbled back through his bedroom, holding onto the walls as he went until he worked his way into the bathroom. Barely getting his jeans unfastened in time, he relieved himself before wandering back out and collapsing on his bed.

The sun disappeared behind the trees outside the living room window as Callie hit send on her latest article to her editor. A door slammed down the hallway just as she closed her laptop.

BANG! BANG! BANG!

Her head snapped toward her front door. "Derek?" She wondered out loud, knowing he was the only person other than Abe with a key to the outside door of the carriage house.

"CAL! I'M SORRY, CAL."

She closed her eyes and let out a strong exhale. "Derek." She set her glasses down on the table. Shaking her head, she stood up and walked over to the door.

BANG! BANG! BANG!

The pounding continued as Callie unlocked the deadbolt and chain. No sooner did she turn the doorknob than a very drunk Derek fell on her, wrapping his arms around her tightly, giving her nowhere to move but backward.

"Cal."

"Derek. Stand up," she grunted, but his weight was too much and it forced her back inside her apartment. Hearing something fall to the floor, Callie stepped back and nearly stumbled as her foot rolled on a bottle that Derek must have dropped when he barged inside.

"I'm sorry!"

"Sorry for what? Ugh." She looked over her shoulder as he continued apologizing. His grip didn't lighten up, either, so she could barely move with an extra couple hundred or so pounds of weight pushing against her. Forced backward, she did her best to guide him toward her couch. It took some doing, and it wasn't pretty, but she managed to get him there. Of course, he landed on her, so she now had to extricate herself from underneath him. Were he sober, she might have enjoyed her current position, but since he most definitely was not, she wasn't having it.

His arms wrapped around her the way sheets wrapped a person like a mummy after a hot summer's night of tossing and turning. "Derek. Get. Off. Me. Ugh!" She struggled to wriggle herself out from underneath him and grunted as she landed on her butt with a thud. "Ouch."

She stood up to find Derek face down on her couch. At least he was fully dressed this time. He just wasn't moving. Nor was he apologizing. She wasn't even sure he was breathing. "Oh shit." She pushed his shoulder back to find his mouth partly open and his eyes closed. "Derek?" She shook his shoulders a little bit. "DEREK?"

Worry overtook anger as she climbed to her knees beside the couch. "Derek? Please say something." She observed him very closely to determine that he was still breathing and breathed a silent prayer of thanks. "Please tell me you're just passed out and not something worse. Derek?" She called his name again and received no response. Shaking his shoulders again, "Derek, please," she pleaded. "I don't know what to do."

Running back to the kitchen, she grabbed her phone and dialed Kiro's number.

***

His face hovering over hers, Kiro leaned in and kissed Celeste like it was going out of style, releasing her lips only when they were both out of breath before kissing her again.

And again.

He pulled the covers back over them and whispered, "I love you."

Her eyes were still closed, but she smiled. "Mmm."

"I'll assume that means, 'I love you, too, Kiro.'" His lips curled up in a smile as he lowered his lids and leaned in again, this time pressing his lips against her chin. Or, 'you're amazing, Kiro.'"

"Mmhmm," Celeste responded, still smiling.

His lips brushed her neck and shoulder as he slid his hand down her curvy body before reaching around to grab her hip and pull her against him. "Or even, I'm ready for another round, Kiro."

Her arms reached around as she leaned in to kiss him. "I'm definitely ready for that." She grinned as he shifted his body on top of hers, smiling mischievously as he pulled the blankets over his head.

"Good."

His phone rang as his head dropped to kiss her collarbone. Letting out a groan, he didn't stop kissing her as his arm appeared from beneath the blankets, fumbling to turn off the ringer. He pushed the phone back on the nightstand, where it teetered on the edge before falling to its final resting place inside his shoe.

His lips had just worked their way down to her stomach when Celeste's phone rang. He exhaled. "Tomorrow, I'm throwing our phones into the river."

"Ignore it, baby," she moaned. "Don't stop."

It stopped ringing just before Kiro's started to ring again. He poked his head out of the covers and gave her a quick kiss on the lips. "I'll make it quick."

Her smile was full of mischief. "But you're never quick."

"That's why you love me." He kissed her lips and reached over the side of the bed to get his phone out of his shoe. "Yeah," he growled as he moved back on top of Celeste, leaning in for another kiss.

"Callie?" He stopped short and leaned on his side. "Callie? What's wrong?"

Celeste perked up with concern.

"Whoa. Whoa. Slow down." He sat up. "Tell me what happened." He listened for a minute. "And where is he now?" he asked. "The couch? Good. Make sure he's on his side. Can you do that?"

He waited until she came back on the phone to confirm he was lying on his side. "Now make sure there's a small pillow under his head. That'll help keep his airway open. Let me know when that's done."

Celeste was sitting up by this time, the covers pulled up over her chest. "Is it Derek?"

Kiro held the phone away from his face. "Yeah. Came into her apartment, drunk as hell. Now he's passed out on her couch."

"Poor girl." She leaned against his chest as he wrapped his free arm around her shoulder to hold her close.

"Okay, good. Now, I need you to take his pulse for me if you can. Just on his wrist, below the thumb. Can you feel it? Good. Count it for ten seconds and let me know what the number is."

He waited for her to get the number, then did the math in his head. "Okay. Sounds about right. That's low but not overly worrisome." He closed his eyes and breathed a sigh of relief. "His body just needs to work through it now. He'll sleep it off, but will probably be sick when he wakes up. You may want to have a small trash can or a bucket nearby. Keep him warm, too, so if you haven't already, cover him up and get a fire going."

He listened while Callie's voice came through the line.

"He'll be dehydrated, so if he's awake, try to get some water in him, but small sips. Just a little at a time, or he won't keep it down." He paused as she spoke. "Are you okay? Do you need me to come over?"

He gave Celeste another squeeze and a quick kiss on the top of her head as he listened to Callie talk. "Okay, good. Just keep me posted. I'll come over in the morning and help get some nutrients in him."

Kiro shook his head. "I know. I know." He looked up and

blinked, heartbroken at her description of Derek in his current state. "Call me if you need me. Day or night, okay?"

He nodded as he listened. "Alright. Yeah. You're welcome. Goodnight."

Kiro ended the call and stared at the phone in his lap.

"Is he okay?"

Kiro took a deep breath and released a slow exhale. "I don't know if he's going to make it, Celeste." His face contorted with the painful thought that his friend seemed to be getting worse. "It's been over two years, and he's still on the edge of breaking."

"I know, baby. I know." She wrapped her arms around him as he set the phone on the nightstand and lay back down, pulling her toward him. "You can only do so much."

"I really hoped she was what he needed. He is doing better since she's been around. It's just that when anything happens, he hits the fucking bottle."

Celeste rested her head on his chest as Kiro held her tight.

"I don't know what I can do to keep him from self-destructing."

"He's got to want to pull himself back. You know that."

Kiro kissed the top of her head, then stared at the ceiling as Celeste drifted off to sleep in his arms.

Chapter 29

So Sorry

Callie was relieved he would be okay and could sleep it off, but she couldn't understand how Derek could do this to himself again. The more she thought about it, the sadder she became that someone with seemingly so much going for him could deliberately go down into such a dark place. Of course, as soon as she thought that, she thought that maybe it wasn't deliberate.

Surprisingly, Derek mattered to her, and she couldn't leave him to his own devices. Not in his current condition. How he could be so self-destructive, she couldn't imagine.

Callie set him up with a small glass of water on the end table, covered him with a blanket, and got a fire going in the fireplace. She was also sure to bring a bathroom trash can out just in case he needed it. She hoped he wouldn't, but she remembered how Kiro had done the same thing, so she prepared herself for the inevitable. This also included having a couple of hand towels and washcloths at the ready.

Grabbing her laptop off the kitchen table, she moved into her oversized chair and went back to work, keeping him in her sight the entire time she worked until she heard a groan and what sounded like a name. Joey, maybe?

"Derek?" she called out, seeing his eyes flutter open a little bit. He was disoriented and looked around to get his bearings, but didn't try to sit up.

"Derek?" she called out again, her voice still gentle. She could see him looking around, trying to find the source of the voice that had called his name. He didn't seem able to focus, so he closed his eyes again to go back to sleep. His face was pale, drained of all color, as if he had a bad flu, not a shitload of beer in him.

"Help me, D."

His weak voice called out in the dark. "Joey?"

Derek shifted on the couch and opened his eyes. The apartment was dark, save for the glow of the fireplace. A bit queasy, Derek groaned as he tried to prop himself up on his elbow and look around to get his bearings. Moving as little as possible, he squinted his eyes and looked over to see Callie asleep. Curled up in her oversized chair, she had fallen asleep. From underneath a throw blanket, her hand was hanging down over the side, just above the book she'd been reading, her place long lost as it had landed on the floor upside down and closed.

He didn't remember how he'd gotten there, but he could figure that out later because whatever he had consumed the day before wasn't going to stay down much longer.

With his hand on his stomach, he dry heaved at first but looked down just in time to see a small trash can there. He barely registered his own relief at having something in which to catch yesterday's dinner of beer, something he'd enjoyed with a side of more beer.

The sound of his retching roused Callie from her sleep as she sprang up to see Derek hunched over the side of the couch. She scrunched her face at what he was doing, and was grateful Kiro had suggested she have a trash can at the ready. Of course, she'd brought one from the second bathroom as well, in case he needed another. With a sigh, she stood up to grab one of the towels and take it to the kitchen, where she soaked it in cold water.

When she returned, he was still face down in the trash bin. She sat on the ottoman and held the cool towel against his forehead when he sat back up. She also handed him another towel that he used to wipe his mouth. He looked at her, pale, sick, his expression a mix of embarrassment and shame. That look lasted a few seconds before he dropped back down to repeat the process. She closed her eyes and tried her best not to look, knowing it would trigger her own sensitive gag reflexes.

She could be mad at him later.

And she would be, but right now, he was in no condition to hear a lecture anyway, not that she knew what she wanted to say to him. It was one thing to have a misunderstanding or an argument, but if his way of dealing with life was to get so incredibly drunk that he couldn't get through the night without emptying his stomach, that seemed the bigger issue. He needed something more, something she wasn't qualified to provide.

He pulled himself back up and closed his eyes as he slouched back and let his knees fall over the side of the couch. He leaned forward, resting his forearms arms on his knees. His head dropped down as if he were going to retch again. She could hear him swallow hard as if he were trying to keep down anything left in his stomach. After a few deep breaths and a few more swallows, he looked up, his eyes watering either from emotion or being sick, probably the latter. He whispered, "I'm so sorry." Then he went back to staring at the floor.

"Oh, Derek," she whispered. "Here." She placed the folded, wet towel on his knee and grabbed the trash can, putting the empty one in front of him, just in case. Standing up, she took it to the bathroom to empty and clean it out, all while trying not to look or get a whiff of the contents so as not to get sick herself.

She had no idea how long it took him to get over something like this, but she could at least help him through it. Back in the living room, she placed the cleaned trash can next to the other one. She felt him grab her hand weakly as she stood back up. "I'm getting you some water, hon. I'll be right back." His head still faced the floor as he reluctantly let go. When she returned, she sat down on the ottoman again in front of him and offered him the glass. "Here. Take a sip."

His hands fumbled for the glass, so she maintained a grip on it as he took a sip. Not saying a word, he just looked toward her without actually making eye contact. Callie pulled it back as he tried to take a big gulp. He was clearly dehydrated. "Take it slow."

His eyes were red and watery as he used both hands to try to grip her hands on the glass she knew he couldn't hold up on his own.

"Thank you," he croaked, glancing at Callie, who pressed her lips together with a nod. Then he looked slightly panicked and croaked, "Oh shit. I'm not done."

"What?" she asked as he plunged his head back down to get sick again. His knees fell to the floor as he knelt over the trash can.

"Oh." She set the water on the coffee table and rubbed circles on his back as he heaved. She made sure to look away to keep her own stomach in check while holding his hair off his forehead.

After a couple more dry heaves, he stayed bent over. Callie gently wiped his forehead with the damp towel, praying he was done. He grabbed it from her, used it to wipe his face, and handed it back to her. Then he slowly fell back on his haunches and lifted his head enough to rest it on her leg. She watched him reach his arms around her.

"I'm sorry, Cal," he cried in a whisper. "I'm so sorry."

She looked up at the ceiling and blinked her eyes to will away any heartbreak she felt at his wretched state. With her hand still on his back, she didn't know what else to do but comb her fingers through his hair. "Shh. It's okay," she whispered back. "I've got you."

After a few minutes, she leaned in. "Derek?" He lifted his head a little bit with a moan. "Come on. I need you to stand up so I can get you to bed, okay?"

He met her gaze through his bloodshot eyes and nodded. He tried to say "Okay," but no sound came out. He stood up slowly, unsteady on his feet. She wrapped her arms around his waist to help support him as best she could, despite the height difference. Stumbling their way down the hall, they made it just shy of her second bedroom, where she'd already turned back the sheets and bedspread.

She directed him first to the bathroom. "Here," she said as she unpackaged a new toothbrush and put some toothpaste on it. "Brush your teeth first. You'll thank me in the morning." He looked zombie-like as he halfheartedly brushed his teeth. "Spit," she instructed. He leaned over and spit into the sink. She turned on the water. "Now rinse." He lowered his hand to bring some water to his mouth and spit it out again, wiping his mouth with the back of his hand before noticing she had a towel at the ready.

He wiped off his mouth and hands and dropped the towel on the counter. She led him into the bedroom, where she eased him onto the bed, collapsing on it with him. She stood back up to unbutton his shirt, which needed to be washed. She dropped it on the floor and pulled off the t-shirt he had on underneath. She then knelt down to untie his shoes, removing those along with his socks, before reaching up to pull out his belt. He just watched her in silence as she unzipped his jeans.

He didn't say a word. He just watched her, not caring that a tear occasionally dropped down his cheek.

"I need you to stand for a minute." He hesitated until what she said registered.

She grabbed his hands. "Come on. Stand up for me, please." He let her help him up so she could pull down his jeans, leaving him in his boxers. "Now sit back down," she gently ordered as he eased back down on the bed, still watching as he reached out to touch her hair while she carefully removed his jeans from each leg and dropped them onto the pile of his clothes.

Any other time, she'd enjoy taking a man's clothes off, but all that remained was evidence of how truly broken he was.

And her heart broke right along with him.

"Okay, hon. Let's get you under the covers."

With her help, he pulled his legs onto the bed as she pulled the covers up and eased him down so his head rested on the pillow. She touched his face with her hand and smiled. "I'll be right back," she told him as she scooped up his clothes and left the room.

She returned with a fresh glass of water and the newly cleaned waste basket. She placed the water on the nightstand and sat down on the edge of the bed. He was almost asleep as she brushed his hair off his face with her fingers.

He opened his eyes and looked up at her, almost frightened, looking like the shell of the strong man she knew him to be. "Cal ..." he croaked while trying to raise his hand to touch her face.

Callie smiled and grabbed his hand, gently placing it on his chest. "I know." She caressed his face with the back of her fingers as his eyes closed and his head fell to the side. For a few minutes, she sat there, combing her fingers through his hair until his breathing evened out. Once he was asleep, she pulled the blanket up to his shoulders. On her way out, she paused long enough to take in the broken man who lay sleeping before her. It didn't exactly play out as a romantic moment of a girl's dreams, but she could save that for another day.

She closed the door behind her, her smile dropping as she turned off the light.

Chapter 30

Don't Know How

ABE AND HIS CREW WERE ALREADY AT WORK ON THE HOUSE when Kiro arrived, backpack in tow. He did his best to stay under the radar, knowing his friend was up there, hungover. Fortunately, he was over often enough to get by with the usual greetings on his way in.

"How is he?" Kiro asked as he hugged Callie after stepping inside the carriage house.

"He's sleeping," she replied. "Has been since about 4 am or so, though I heard him get up at least once after that."

About an hour or two after getting him in bed, she heard him get up and make it to the bathroom. Not sure if he was sick again or just relieving himself ... or both, since she'd heard the toilet flush a couple of times. He made it back to bed on his own without incident, something she knew because she'd checked in on him to make sure he was under the covers.

"And how are you?" he asked as they climbed the stairs to her apartment.

"I've slept better," she exhaled with a half smile.

"I'm sure."

"You want some coffee?" she offered as she closed her apartment door behind them.

"Yeah. Please."

"Milk or sugar?"

"Black is fine." He grabbed the mug she had set down in front of him.

"How often does he do this, Kiro? I need to know."

Before speaking, he took a sip of his coffee. He didn't want to have this conversation, but she deserved an explanation.

"He's been better the last several months. It's been a few weeks since the last time." Figuring honesty was the best policy, he laid it all out for her. "It used to be every few days. We'd be on shift. Then, he'd come home and would go on a bender that night, waking up in a stupor the next morning. He'd be fine by the time we'd go out that night, probably have a few more beers before going to bed, and then he'd be fine again for shift the following morning. He's always on time, and he never makes mistakes on the job."

"And how long has this been going on?" Her face was sad at the thought of his going through that over and over again.

Telling her the truth would only serve to betray his friend. He took a deep breath, before meeting Callie's gaze. "Since he got back," he mumbled.

"SINCE HE GOT BACK?"

Kiro snapped back when she yelled.

"My god, Kiro. That's been over two years. And you've been helping him hide it all this time?"

"Hide it? I've been *helping* him all this time," he answered roughly.

"Helping him?" Her voice rose higher. "How? You haven't been helping. You've been enabling him."

"What the hell am I supposed to do?" Kiro snapped, pushing his coffee back on the counter. He pressed his lips together in an effort to calm down. "He has to work, Callie and it hasn't affected his job. Not yet, anyway."

"It's affected *him!*" She held up her hands. "It's not as if he's going to be able to keep this up indefinitely, you know. I'm no medic, but even I know that."

"I DON'T KNOW HOW!" Kiro's raised voice - and exasperated expression - stunned Callie. "OKAY?" He glared at her and lowered his voice a decibel or two, but still looked like a man at the end of his rope. "Is that what you want to hear?" he pleaded. "I don't know how to help him. I've tried talking to him. I've tried getting Tank to talk to him. His dad. His sister. My mom. Anyone he cares about. Nobody can get through to him. I CAN'T DO IT!" Kiro backed up and held out his arms in defeat.

"I can't do it." His voice became lower. Softer. Heartbroken. "But I can do my best to keep him alive." He backed up and put his hands on his hips, staring down at the floor. Looking back up, he added, "At least I think I can. He's been my friend since I was in middle school. He's like a big brother to me." His voice cracked. "I just ... I don't know how to make him want to stop. I really don't."

He walked closer to the window, watching Abe's crew go in and out of the house. His mind drifted to what Celeste told him the night before, so he repeated it. "He has to want to pull himself back."

He turned back to Callie, who hadn't left the kitchen, still shaking from his outburst. "I can't do that for him. And I don't know how to get him to want to do that for himself. I just ... I don't know how to help. I'm not enough."

He walked back to the living room, where he'd dropped his backpack. Picking it up, he took a few steps toward the hallway leading to the bedrooms. He stopped and turned around. "He likes you, you know."

Callie looked up from the counter and met his gaze with a nod. "I know." She shrugged. "He might not remember it, but he started to say something before he passed out." She shook her head. "I don't know what he was trying to say, really."

Kiro smiled. "That's alright."

Callie called out before he took another step.

"Kiro?"

"Yeah?" He looked over his shoulder.

"I don't know how to help him either."

"Yeah, you do."

Her brow furrowed at his response. "How?" she whispered.

"Be his friend."

"Kiro ..."

He slung his pack over his shoulder and disappeared around the corner.

Chapter 31

Heart to Heart

It was raining again by the time Kiro left. With the drop in temperature, it was sure to change to snowfall before too long. Callie kept the fire going and adjusted the thermostat a bit to compensate. It was going to be a cold day and night.

"Cal."

Jumping at the sound of her name, she brought her hand to her heart as she looked up to see Derek standing at her bedroom door. His hair was wet from the shower he'd just taken, and he was wearing the clothing she'd washed for him while he was sleeping. His bloodshot eyes betrayed just how tired he was.

"Derek." Sitting in the middle of her bed, she closed her laptop and placed it on her nightstand. It was the middle of the day, but without lights on, the overcast sky outside darkened the room. It was just light enough to see each other.

"Thanks for washing these for me." He motioned to his clothes, but didn't move away from the door as if unsure how to proceed.

"You're welcome."

"Kiro helped me out. Got some nutrients in me," he offered despite her not asking for an update.

"Good."

A few moments of awkward silence passed until Callie patted her bed. "Here. Have a seat."

"Thanks."

He slouched down on the bed next to where she sat cross-legged. They sat in silence for a couple of minutes, listening to the rain pouring down outside. He'd become far more withdrawn than his usual outgoing self.

"How are you feeling?" When he didn't respond, she placed her hand on his leg. "Derek?"

Taking her hand in his, he lifted his head enough to glance over with a slight nod. "I've been better."

She squeezed his hand as he squeezed back. Without a word, they held hands in silence until Derek turned toward Callie.

"I should never have done that." He dropped his head. The patter of rain grew louder as it turned to sleet.

"What? Get drunk?"

Derek winced, but remained calm.

"Or pound on my door so loud I could have heard you back in D.C.?"

"I was thinking the latter ... and passing out on your couch." He cleared his throat. "But you could probably make a good argument for the former as well."

"Derek." Callie hesitated to ask the question she wanted to ask, but only he could answer for her. "May I ask you something?"

He tensed up. "Why am I a drunk?"

"Kind of. Yeah. Why do you do that to yourself?"

"I don't know, Cal. I really don't know," he whispered. His eyes were closed as he sniffed. "I think it's ... I don't know," he shuddered a breath and paused before continuing. "I think it's the only thing I can do to forget."

"Does it ever work?"

"Not really, no."

Callie exhaled, surprised by his honest response.

"It's temporary," he added. "At best, because I still hear him. In my head. His last words. Asking if I'm still there. Calling out for his dead mother. Asking me to tell his fiancé, Logan, that he loved him." Derek sniffed. "And I told him no. He could do it himself."

"What are you trying to forget?"

"That I couldn't save Joey." His eyes met hers, nearly panicking at the thought. "I can't get his voice out of my head, asking me to help him."

"Have you ever tried to stop? Stop drinking, I mean?"

"No. I ... " His Adam's apple bobbed up and down before he continued. "This is my life, my new life since my discharge. I'm just not good at this."

"Not good at what?"

"Relationships. Not that this is one. I mean relationships of any kind, friendships ..."

She chuckled. "They're not supposed to be easy, Derek."

"I get that, but I've just never–"

"Never what?"

He let out a sigh. "I've never really been in one."

Callie pulled back. "What do you mean?"

"It means I just turned thirty-five, and I'm just now in my first real relationship." He leaned back into her. "At least, it could be, a friendship at least if you want. Every other woman, well ..." He exhaled again.

"I mean, high school doesn't count, and the girl I was dating after high school dumped me during my first deployment, so that went to shit. And it's not like there were any women Rangers, though they're allowed in as of earlier this year," he added. "And since I've been back, I never go beyond a date or two. If even that long." His expression turned sheepish.

"I just hook up and never attempt to get to know them. I don't want to, really, but," he released a humorless laugh. "I could really use a friend right about now. I may not deserve you, after all I've already put you through."

Callie smiled. "Yes."

Derek finally made eye contact, and a hint of hope sparkled in his eye. "Yes, what?"

"Yes. I'll be your friend. I mean," She shrugged. "I feel like I've already been through an on-the-job interview."

Derek laughed. "I don't know. It's probably safe to say you've earned a rather hefty signing bonus."

"Yeah, well. You can cook for me."

"And you can still do the dishes. But when my Bengals take on your Ravens–"

Callie chuckled. "Now. Now. None of that."

Derek hedged a moment, then smirked. "I'll have to cook here since you have the bigger TV."

"Takes a secure man to admit that."

Derek breathed out a laugh. "Yeah. I guess."

"It's quiet," Callie whispered. Out the window, wispy snowflakes floated down on the street behind the carriage house. "It's snowing."

Christmas was still a few weeks away, but maybe Grant's Crossing would see snow for the holidays this year.

"Cal?"

"Yes?"

"I'm broken." Derek dropped his head on her shoulder. "And I don't know how to fix myself."

She wrapped her arms around him and rubbed circles on his back. "It's okay."

"No. It's not. But ..." She didn't know how long she held him there, but when he pulled back, he looked her in the eyes and pleaded. "Don't give up on me?" His eyes were filled with desperation. "Please?"

THERAPY 6

Disqualification

"Good morning, Derek. Have a seat." Doc Majors closed the door behind Derek, then grabbed his clipboard off his desk. He cleared his throat and sat down in his usual chair for today's session. "How are you doing?"

Derek rolled his eyes, tossed his backpack on the floor, shed his coat, scarf, and hat, then plopped on the couch. He rubbed his arms to warm up while making note of a few Christmas decorations on the doctor's bookshelves. "I'm fine."

"How was–"

"My shift was fine. Yes, I've been eating. I've been sleeping the same as always, which is not at all. That about sum it up for you?"

"Sums 'em up great. Guess you've done my work for me. Thanks." Doc Majors dropped the clipboard on the coffee table and leaned back in his seat. He raised his brows in question. "Still want me to tell you what to do?"

"No. My Dad's got that covered, thanks."

"How so?"

Derek exhaled and shook his head. Then he scrubbed his face with his hands, spending a few extra seconds to scratch the scruff he didn't bother to shave off after showering at the end of his shift.

"He and I have dinner at least once a week, during the week. And with Kiro or Tank, though it's usually just Kiro since Tank has a family."

"Don't you drink when you have dinner with them?"

"Not really. I mean, I just start later, but I think it's his way of checking in on me."

"Derek."

Derek met the doctor's gaze.

"If and when you decide–"

Derek rolled his eyes. "Shit. Come on, Doc. This is getting old. Can't you just be done with this? Give me something so I can sleep and be done with it?"

Doc Majors sat back. "Yeah. I can."

Derek slapped his knees. "About fucking time."

"But before I do, let me ask you this."

Derek threw his arms up in frustration and released a loud exhale. "What!"

The doctor leaned forward and set his clipboard on the coffee table, ignoring Derek's momentary frustration. "What do you do when you get off shift?"

"Huh?"

"What do you do when you get off shift?" he repeated. "What's your routine?"

"My routine? I go home. No. Wait. I eat something first. K and I," he held out his hand. "KIRO and I, and sometimes Steve, we have breakfast at the diner."

"And then you go home."

"And then I go home."

"And then you start drinking. "

No response from Derek.

"And then you start drinking."

Derek nodded slowly. "It helps me forget."

"Right," the doctor confirmed. "At, say, 9 am? 10 am? Between breakfast and lunch, right?"

"No. I usually sleep through lunch." Derek lifted his gaze. "Are you going to give me something or what?"

"It's not that easy, Derek, and I think you know that."

"But you said–"

"It's not so simple."

Derek closed his eyes for a moment and shook his head without responding.

"Look. I've already filled out the forms. They just need your signature."

"Signature for what? What forms?"

The doctor met Derek's gaze.

"I don't need one for meds," Derek said, confused. "I just need a scrip."

"I'm not giving you a prescription."

"What the fuck! Then why the fuck do you need my signature?" Derek scoffed, getting angrier by the second. His voice grew louder with each subsequent word. "Is this some sort of pledge thing? Like saving myself for marriage or some shit? Because it's a bit too late for that, Doc."

"No."

Derek leaned back and folded his arms. His heart was beating harder and harder. "In other words, you're making shit up."

"What do you know about Post Traumatic Stress Disorder, Derek?"

"I don't have PTSD, Doc." Derek shot a quick glance at the doctor and then back out the window, all while fidgeting with his fingernails.

"Have you been assessed before?"

"Assessed?" He stared at the doctor's service dog, Sadie, dutifully sitting next to the doctor's chair.

"I don't have your full medical records, just what you released from the Fire Department," Doc Majors explained. "Have you ever been diagnosed by any other doctors?"

"What? No." Derek's breath shortened. "Why would I be? It's not like I can get a VA appointment anyway. It takes months."

"Because it might help you."

Derek's arms shot out. "I don't need help, Doc. Fuck. I just need something to help me sleep."

"Right. And why is that?"

Derek stared out the window.

Doc Majors released an audible sigh but spoke gently. "When was the last time you slept through the night, Derek?"

Still no answer from Derek, so the doctor continued.

"How about this? When's the last time you slept a full eight hours?"

Not receiving an answer, the doctor tried again. "Derek? When's the last night you got a decent night's sleep and actually felt rested afterward?"

"I don't know," Derek finally mumbled.

"What was that?"

Derek shook his head. He glanced back through the windows to see if any birds were outside on the fire escape railing.

"I didn't hear you."

Derek started rubbing his hands together. He stared toward the door in the far corner. He could make a run for it.

The doctor turned his gaze to the same corner, then back to Derek. "Go. You'll beat me to the door. Without my blades, I'm not nearly as fast as I used to be. Are you?"

Derek shot a panicked look at the doctor but immediately turned away. The door? The window? Derek's heart was about to burst out of his chest.

"I'll ask you again, Derek."

"No." Derek quickly wiped a tear escaping down his cheek with the palm of his hand.

"No, what?"

"Don't ask me again." He shook his head as he spoke.

"Derek? When was the last time you slept?"

"Are you still here, D?"

"Stop it." Derek couldn't shake the sound of Joey's voice out of his head.

"When, Derek?" Doc Majors insisted.

"I don't fucking know, okay?"

"I think you do."

Derek raked his fingers through his hair. He held his fingers in front of his face and rubbed the tips with his thumbs. They were damp. "Fuck."

"Tell Logan, I love him, D."

"Derek?"

"Don't leave me, Joey," Derek mumbled. Snatching up a pillow and clutching it against his chest. He choked back a sob as he rocked back and forth.

"How long has it been?"

"Don't."

"Derek?"

Derek threw it past the doctor's large, wooden desk. It knocked a wooden plaque off the shelf. It landed on the floor, unharmed, thanks to the soft carpet below. "SINCE AUGUST 15, 2014, OKAY?"

The doctor showed no outward reaction to Derek's outburst. He'd read Derek's file. It had all the dates, including the date of Joey Parker's death on August 17, 2014. He wasn't unaccustomed to his patients showing their emotions, so his calm demeanor remained unchanged. "August 15–"

"YES, DOC. AUGUST 15, 2014. That's the last time I slept through the fucking night, okay? August 15, 2014." He held his palms up, staring at them as if they'd failed him. He rubbed his fingers with his thumbs briefly, then clenched his fists. "That's the last night before I had his blood ... " He choked back a sob and sniffed. "When I ... when I had his ... his blood on my hands. I couldn't." Derek's head collapsed into his hands, and his shoulders shook. Tears began to fall. "I couldn't stop it." He managed to get out between sobs. "I tried."

Doc Majors handed Derek a box of tissues, then gave him the time he needed to pull himself together.

"I don't know how else to keep this up," Derek confessed, his voice little more than a whisper. "I've tried, but I can't do this."

"Can't do what?"

Derek kept his gaze aimed at the floor. "Live with the fact that I killed him."

"Killed who? Joey Parker?"

Derek's head snapped up at the familiarity of those words. He scrubbed his face with his hand and sniffed. Then, he used his sleeve to wipe the tears off his face. He opened his mouth, but unable to speak, he merely nodded.

"Okay," Doc Majors said with an understanding smile. "I can help you with this. We can work with this."

"Finally." Derek sniffed, then angrily wiped his eyes with the palms of his hands. He rubbed them against his jeans. Collecting himself, he stared at the doctor. So, how can you help me?"

"I'm going to start with an official diagnosis."

"What?"

"You have PTSD, Derek."

"Doc, I–"

The doctor raised a hand to cut Derek off. "Like it or not, you have PTSD, which is what my diagnosis to the VA will state."

"But I don't have ..." Derek trailed off, resigned to accepting the inevitable.

"You have nightmares reliving your last mission over and over again," the doctor began. "You become irritable with even the slightest provocation. You respond in anger over simple situations or requests. You've become more and more dependent on depressants, namely alcohol."

Derek's gaze dropped to the floor.

"You haven't had any sort of romantic relationship that has lasted more than an hour or two since you enlisted."

The doctor wasn't wrong, but Derek opened his mouth to speak anyway. He closed it when the doctor cocked a brow.

"You couldn't stand being in this room the first time you visited."

Derek sniffed again. "In fairness, I can't stand being in this room any time I visit, Doc."

Doc Majors chuckled. "Fair enough, but you have a visceral reaction to being in this room, to being asked about Joey. Just a while ago, you contemplated escaping."

Derek dropped his gaze again, not wanting to admit he still wanted to escape.

The doctor exhaled before speaking again. "It's PTSD, Derek. You have PTSD."

Derek didn't respond.

"And I can help you with that. Based on my experience and with what you're experiencing, I'm confident you'll be eligible for at least seventy percent disability."

"Disability? I need to work."

"I feel like I can make a good argument for one hundred percent, but we'll tamp down on those expectations until after I submit the paperwork. You'll still be able to work. You wouldn't be the only first responder on disability from the military to also work in the civilian world."

"What does that mean?"

"It means you could use some help, and I'm going to make sure you get it."

"Oh."

"I also think you're potentially an excellent candidate for a service dog, which will help lessen the effects of PTSD and help you sleep."

Derek's attention shifted to the doctor's dog, Sadie, taking up her usual spot at his feet. He stared at her while the doctor continued.

"A service dog will help you handle the anxiety, the restlessness, the lack of sleep. And a service dog will help you live without being overpowered by it all."

Derek lifted his gaze but shifted it back and forth between the doctor and his faithful and well-trained service dog lying on the floor between his legs. "Wait. You said potentially. What do you mean by that?"

The doctor took a moment to scratch Sadie's head before she rested it back on her front paws. Then, he leaned forward, clasped his hands together, and rested his forearms on his knees. "I'll go ahead and get the ball rolling on the disability paperwork, but we need to talk about the process needed to qualify for a service animal."

"Qualify?"

"There's an application process."

"Okay. So I fill out a few forms, right?"

"Kind of."

A crease formed between his brows. "Kind of?"

The doctor bobbed his head from side to side. "You have to meet all the qualifications."

"Great. What are they?"

"You have to have been honorably discharged."

Derek started to perk up. "Done."

Doc Majors listed the necessary qualifications, counting on his fingers along the way. "You have to have a verifiable diagnosis of service-related PTSD, which I'm taking care of. No felony convictions. US residency. Stable living situation, i.e., you have a job and a place to live. You'll have to take three weeks off to learn how to work with your dog."

"Easy. I'll sign now." Derek actually smiled in anticipation. "When do I go?"

"Well, there's a waiting period."

"Okay. Fine." Derek shrugged. "So I have to wait a little bit. I just need to submit an application, right?"

"It's not that easy, Derek."

"Jesus, Doc. What's not that easy? I've got everything you said I needed. I can fill out a few forms."

"Yeah. Those are the easy ones."

"What do you mean?"

Doc Majors' expression turned somber. "There's one more condition that you don't yet meet."

"What condition do I not ..." Derek's heart dropped when the realization hit him right in the chest.

"It's your drinking, Derek." The doctor looked him right in the eyes. "Your drinking disqualifies you."

Chapter 32

Not Alone

Derek sat in his truck in his friend's driveway, but couldn't bring himself to cut the engine. The pouring rain lacked its usual calming effect, making it more difficult to decide whether or not he wanted to climb out of his warm, dry truck cab and knock on his friend's door.

A child's bike had been left outside the garage door. He stared at it, tapping his fingers to the rhythm of the wipers, which squeaked as they fought a losing battle against the never-ending deluge of water laying siege to the windshield. He'd have to replace those soon.

Ten minutes later, he still sat inside his truck. He was sure Tank had seen him there through the window, but he didn't push him to come inside.

Earlier in the day, the doctor said something out loud that Derek didn't want to hear: that his drinking held him back. The thought of ridding himself of a crutch he'd been using since he was discharged scared him. Hearing it in today's session was a kick in the gut that he wasn't yet ready to face.

He wasn't ready to face his friend, either, but after everything they'd been through together in the Army, he was the one person he could open up to and be honest.

"Shit." Derek finally cut the engine and jumped out. He jogged to the front door, snatching up the small bike on the way. He leaned it against the wall and knocked.

He couldn't help but smile at the stomping of excited little feet and excited voices that were loud enough to hear through the door. A minute later, the door opened to reveal one of the kindest and happiest people Derek knew, Tank's wife, Araceli. Her smile could light up an entire room, a stark contrast to the darkness he'd been living in. Flanked by two of her children and holding her youngest toddler, she wasted no time greeting Derek with a one-armed hug. "Hi, Derek. So good to see you. Come on in out of the cold. I'll get Juan for you."

Their two boys, Daniel and Diego, each grabbed a leg, then let go while talking a mile a minute about some new game they were playing. "Tio Derek!" Rocio, now in third grade, practically tackled him with an energetic hug. A laugh escaped his lips as he reciprocated her joyful embrace.

Tank gently herded his children to the family room. And with the chaos under control, he greeted Derek with a hug. "I saw you outside when you pulled up."

"Couldn't decide if I wanted to come in or not."

"I figured you would when you were ready."

"Yeah."

Tank motioned for Derek to join him in the small office in the front of the house. Derek sat in the loveseat in front of the window while Tank sat in a wingback chair in front of some bookshelves. "What's troubling you?"

"I went to see the shrink again today."

"You usually go after shift, right?"

"I do," Derek confirmed. "I just had a tough session."

Tank nodded in understanding. "Did it help?"

"I don't know." Derek relayed some of his latest visit to the doctor.

"Reliving Joey's death couldn't have been easy."

Tank was right, but Derek couldn't bring himself to respond right away.

Shit. This was hard.

"There's uh, something else."

Tank leaned forward, resting his forearms on his knees. "Tell me."

Derek cleared his throat and kept his eyes down, unsure if he wanted to say this aloud for the first time. "He, uh ... he said I have PTSD."

Tank didn't appear surprised. "That makes sense, I guess."

"Huh?"

"Well, think about it, Doc. The things we've seen? You especially." Tank motioned toward Derek. "You've seen us at our worst. You still do. So I don't doubt you see it in your nightmares. Add to that your drinking, your one-night stands?"

"Have me all figured out, do you?"

Tank breathed out a friendly laugh. "Come on. You're pretty much an open book. But, all things considered, considering what you've seen firsthand? Yes. It makes sense."

Derek took a moment to consider his friend's words. "He's helping me apply for disability."

"That's great."

"Great? Not sure if I'll still be able to work though."

"Yes. You will," Tank assured him. "I know several first responders on disability, including some for PTSD, who do their job very well."

"There's something else."

Tank arched a brow. And leaned against the back of his chair. "What's that?"

"He wants me to get a service dog."

"Really?"

Derek nodded. "Yeah. Says it'll help me sleep better and it'll help me not turn to beer as much or some shit like that."

"That's great. I'm happy for you. How long will that take to get one?"

"There's a wait list. It'll take a while, but ..." Derek trailed off.

"But, what?"

Derek swallowed. "I don't exactly qualify."

Tank's forehead creased. "I don't understand. What do you mean?"

"I can't get on the waiting list because of my ..." Derek was afraid to make eye contact, not that Tank wouldn't be able to figure it out on his own.

And that's when the light bulb went off. "Because of your drinking."

"Yeah," Derek begrudgingly confirmed. "It could be as long as a year or more on the waitlist, but right now? It's the only thing that helps me forget and—"

"But the drinking is what may lose you your job."

Derek shrank into himself, but met Tank's gaze. "You see the problem."

Tank squeezed Derek's shoulder. "You won't go through anything alone, Doc. Whatever you decide. You won't go through it alone."

Chapter 33

Catwalk

ACROSS THE SCIOTO RIVER, THE SUN PEEKED THROUGH THE clouds, bringing the hope of warmth on a crisp, mid-December morning. GC Fire trucks pulled up to Red Storley, the largest and most prominent building in the abandoned industrial complex on the far side of town. Two police cars with lights flashing were already parked outside, with a few onlookers being held at bay by a uniformed officer just outside the large entrance to the warehouse.

Getting out at what would be the last call of their shift, Derek and Kiro grabbed the gurney and their go bags out of the back of the ambulance to have them at the ready, just in case.

"Why did she leave us?" a weak voice cried from inside the warehouse.

Inside, they were greeted by Sheriff Andrew Strager, who coordinated the efforts of the police officers in conjunction with Chief Travis. He pointed to the catwalk about forty feet above the ground. Directly over some abandoned machinery surrounded by large pieces of waste metal was an unsteady, inebriated Carl Reynolds. If the bottle he waved were an indicator, he was already about three sheets to the wind.

A uniformed police officer stood on a nearby platform, trying to talk him down, unable to close the distance thanks to a rusted-out section of the catwalk that probably wouldn't support the weight of a second person.

Chief Travis was already assessing the situation, figuring out how best to get Carl down safely. Because of so much abandoned machinery, they couldn't drive the fire engine inside and rescue him with the ladder. "If he falls from that, it'll be ugly."

The sheriff nodded in solemn agreement as Kiro and Derek approached.

Chief gave orders to Tank and the others to start clearing a path up and work to shore up the catwalk to get Carl down if he couldn't be coaxed to the platform where the deputy stood.

"How long's he been up there, Drew?" Derek asked.

"About twenty minutes so far. Garrett was on patrol when he thought he heard someone yelling. He came in when he saw Carl up there, crying and waving the bottle around, so he's trying to talk him down now. Called you in to help while Chris went to find Bryan."

"Garrett?" Kiro narrowed his gaze to the officer on the platform. "That's Emerson's brother up there?"

"Mmhmm," Drew confirmed.

The catwalk was directly above a large, semi-vertical, rusted-out metal filler. Shaped like an oversized funnel, it leaned away from the catwalk over a large rectangular structure. Like the catwalk, the corroded funnel was dangerously close to collapsing. The attached access ladder had already started to peel away from the top and was hanging over the machinery base with metal supports sticking out at all angles.

"WHY?!" Carl yelled again, crying as he did, taking a healthy drink from the bottle he was holding. "Why is she gone?"

"He's been yelling about his wife the whole time. Garrett's staying up top to keep Carl focused and balanced while he tries to talk him down."

"Shit."

"Yep."

A creaking sound echoed throughout the building as the rusty catwalk shifted. Carl had taken a small step toward the platform. Everyone drew a collective breath as Carl quickly stepped backward on the catwalk, leaning back over the railing, narrowly catching himself to regain his balance. The policeman calling out to Carl didn't move an inch, not wanting any additional movement to cause it to collapse.

Sirens grew louder as another police cruiser pulled up. The three men looked over to see Bryan Reynolds jumping out of the car, running inside, and looking up at his dad.

"Dad," Bryan called out. Not getting his father's attention, he yelled again, louder. "DAD!"

"BRYAN!" Carl waved and then stumbled, barely catching himself on the rail. "I didn't mean for her to leave us."

"I KNOW, DAD," Bryan yelled with all the confidence he could muster. "I KNOW. IT'S OKAY."

"I miss her, Bryan!"

"I MISS HER TOO, DAD!"

Looking around for a way to help, Bryan called out. "DAD. CAN YOU COME DOWN? WE CAN TALK ABOUT IT."

"I can't. I can't bring her back!" Carl took another drink and almost lost his balance again as he leaned his head back for the drink. He narrowly caught himself as the bottle fell below him.

The firefighters scattered as the bottle bounced off the metal debris and shattered on the concrete floor.

Frantically looking around, Bryan saw the stairs on the other side and darted toward them before an officer could stop him. "DAD! I'M COMING UP."

Watching the scene unfold, the sheriff, Kiro, and Derek stood poised to jump in should there be a need, a need they hoped would never arise.

"Don't move, Carl," Derek mumbled as he watched intently.

Kiro nodded in silent encouragement.

Tank was leading the firefighters to secure the catwalk so they could safely get to Carl. The other end was still attached, but to get up would require two straight ladders that were set up and held in place by other firefighters. At the same time, others were working to clear out some of the industrial junk that blocked the entrance and prevented the ladder truck from entering the building.

Suddenly, a loud screech filled the air, followed by a deafening crash. Carl's bloodcurdling scream rang out from above.

"DAD!" Bryan yelled out in fear, held back by the police officer on the platform, who struggled to pull them both down the stairs when the catwalk gave way and crashed to the ground.

"WATCH OUT!" Tank yelled at the firefighters to distance themselves from the flying debris.

Carl's panicked screams grew weaker while scrap metal pieces flew into the air before settling back down in a large pile. He'd grabbed hold of the ladder, which dangled precariously off the large funnel.

POP.

Kiro's eyes widened. "Oh, shit."

"Hold on, Carl," Derek countered.

Another POP.

Another scream.

Carl held on as best he could, but his weight was more than the rusty ladder could bear. The funnel started to sway, and Carl groaned in fear each time it did, nervously focusing on the shards of metallic scrap metal that lay in wait, a good twenty-five feet below him.

POP.

Each pop was a rivet that gave way, drawing Carl closer to inevitable, serious injury, if not worse.

POP.

The firefighters resumed their work to clear the doorway so they could get the ladder truck inside, as Carl was still too high for their straight ladders.

Like the low rumble of a distant storm, a creaking sound grew louder as the ladder gave way, causing the funnel to tip over.

A loud crack filled the air as the funnel finally succumbed to decades of neglect. Carl's shrieks of terror filled the air as he fell. The base of the funnel slowed his fall, but there was no way he could stop himself from sliding down and falling off the edge onto the now upside-down catwalk that was precariously perched atop the large pile of jagged scrap metal and discarded machine parts.

"DAD!" Bryan yelled at the top of his lungs. "DAD!"

Just as he landed, the once grand funnel swayed back and forth before finally tipping over on its side and stopping with a gentle tap against the far wall of the factory. An ignominious end to what was once the largest source of farm equipment in the state.

All the firefighters sprang into action before the dust had a chance to settle. They stopped working to clear the entrance for the truck, shifting their priority from prevention to recovery. "Tim, get the straight ladder over there," Tank ordered. "Emerson, grab the Stokes."

"Got it," Emerson replied before running to the truck to retrieve the Stokes basket to safely move Carl from the wreckage to the ambulance.

Steve and Tim joined Tank, who was already clearing the debris to reach where Carl now lay. A faint, guttural groan emanated from within the pile of scrap metal and machinery parts.

"I hear him," Tank called out. "We're coming, Carl."

Derek and Kiro rushed closer to the scene and waited as the other men freed him.

"I see him!" Tank reached down with a nod to Tim to help.

Garrett and Bryan made it to the bottom of the stairs just as the firefighters caught their first glimpse of Carl's broken body.

"Get me up there!" Derek yelled as Emerson set up a ladder for Derek to use.

Derek grabbed his kit and climbed the ladder to pass up a neck brace for them to put on Carl as they lay him on a backboard.

"DAD!"

"Get him out!" Sheriff Strager called over to Garrett, who started to force Bryan away from the scene. A second officer helped get him out as Bryan yelled, "NO! I'M NOT LEAVING MY DAD! DAD!"

"GET HIM OUT OF HERE!" Sheriff Strager yelled again, turning back to direct his deputies and watch the firefighters work.

"DAD!" Bryan yelled as the two officers struggled but finally got him outside the building and by a squad car.

Chapter 34

———————

Damage is Done

"Careful, men," Tank called out while they moved Carl to a waiting backboard. "Careful."

Standing on the top of the ladder gave Derek his first view of Carl as they pulled him from the debris pile. At first glance, there were multiple bone fractures and numerous lacerations, spilling blood out from various points on his body.

"Set him down," Derek instructed as they set Carl in the Stokes basket directly in front of him.

Initial inspection revealed a lacerated brachial artery, which Derek quickly tied off with a tourniquet to stop the bleeding before checking the rest of Carl's injuries. Carl coughed, sending blood all over his chin as he gasped for air.

With his feet planted on the ladder rung, Derek leaned over Carl, stabilizing him while the other men hooked up the ropes to lower the basket to the gurney, which could then be wheeled to the ambulance.

"Okay," Tank said. "He's hooked up. Ready when you are, Doc."

"Not yet."

Carl had compound fractures to both legs and one arm, but the worry was with the chest. He couldn't breathe. He couldn't inhale.

"Tension pneumo," Derek muttered while checking Carl's chest. He reached into his bag for a needle catheter, which he expertly stuck between Carl's ribs. Pulling out the needle, Derek could hear the air release, allowing the lung to expand so Carl could breathe again. Fractures could wait until they were inside the ambulance.

"Okay. Go."

Derek grabbed his bag and quickly descended the ladder. Kiro edged the gurney closer while the firefighters gently lowered Carl down to meet it.

"Steve! I'll need you in the rig with me," Derek called out while securing Carl onto the gurney and rushing him to the ambulance. Steve jumped in the back to assist.

"What do you think, D? Grant or OSU Med?" Kiro asked as he shut the door and drove away from the scene.

"Grant," Derek called as they secured Carl in the back of the rig.

Sirens and lights on, Derek and Steve worked on Carl in the back as Kiro raced the ambulance to Grant Medical Center, one of Columbus's Level One trauma centers. He and Steve just had to keep Carl alive for the long drive.

And that was with flashing lights and sirens.

Hooking Carl up to oxygen and double-checking the catheter was still in place in Carl's chest, they made sure the tourniquet still held before working on the other injuries. Derek hooked up the saline IV while Steve set up air splints for the arm and leg fractures.

Working his best to stop the bleeding that came from everywhere, Derek started with the deepest lacerations, as there were so many cuts from all the metal debris that crashed around Carl.

"Are you still here, D?"

Derek blinked a couple of times after hearing Joey's voice in his head.

"Not now, Joey. Not now," Derek muttered.

"What was that?" Steve asked, securing his first brace onto Carl's leg.

"Nothing."

Hearing Carl cough, Derek looked down to see he'd passed out. Checking his air and finding nothing. He sprang into action. "He stopped breathing. I'm going to intubate."

Sitting behind him, Derek started to insert the breathing tube down Carl's throat and into his lungs to help him breathe. "There's a lot of blood. I can't visualize it." he muttered in frustration. "There." He pulled out the stylet. "I'm in."

Derek put his stethoscope in his ears and listened to Carl's chest for breathing. "Got it." He taped the tube sticking out of Carl's mouth to keep it in place and attached the oxygen mask to feed air into his lungs.

Carl's eyes opened as he started getting oxygen again. "Welcome back, Carl," Derek said as he worked, noting the fear in his eyes as he did.

Carl lost consciousness again about halfway there as the heart monitor went flat.

"D? Help me."

"Shit," Derek said, standing up. "Get the oxygen." He instructed Steve as they traded places inside the ambulance. Steve took over, feeding air into Carl's lungs as Derek started chest compressions.

"How far out are we, K?"

"Twelve minutes."

"Drive faster!"

The monitor beeped, and Derek paused the compressions momentarily.

"He's back," Steve announced.

With Carl back, they resumed administering aid so he'd be ready for treatment in the emergency department.

About two minutes out, Carl flatlined again.

"Shit!" Derek resumed chest compressions as Steve administered oxygen to Carl.

Sirens blaring, Kiro pulled up to the hospital. Running around to the back of the ambulance, he opened the door to find Derek giving chest compressions to Carl, still flatlined for a second time.

Pausing only long enough to get him out of the ambulance, Derek continued compressions, riding the gurney, and relaying his numerous injuries and stats to the doctors as Steve continued the oxygen. Kiro and others from the hospital pushed Carl inside to a trauma bay.

Transferring him to the bed inside the bay, Kiro pulled their gurney out of the way while doctors and nurses took over. Steve and Derek stood down and got out of the way, feeling deflated, knowing the medical professionals had their work cut out for them.

"DAD!" Bryan yelled as he ran into the Emergency Department toward the bay where they were working on his father. Derek's head turned as Bryan ran in front of him and rushed into the trauma bay. Garrett, the uniformed officer, followed closely behind, nodding to the paramedics.

"Get him back!" the doctor barked, turning his attention back to Carl and giving rapid-fire instructions to the nurses.

"Let them work, Bryan," Garrett said calmly as he reached out and pulled Bryan back as Derek, Kiro, and Steve watched.

"Dad!" Bryan cried out again, his shoulders dropping.

Another slow minute ticked by. The monitor started beeping. "He's back. Let's get him to the OR."

Kiro and Steve rolled the gurney to the ambulance while Derek paused a moment to look back into the trauma bay. Just at that moment, Bryan turned and made eye contact with Derek through the glass. Bryan's expression said it all: bloodshot eyes, cheeks wet from the tears, slumped shoulders from worry and exhaustion, over a now life-threatening injury.

It was hard enough that Bryan was a barely-nineteen year old kid who had to parent his own dad by making sure the family bills were paid. Hard enough, he was a kid responsible for taking his dad home when he drank too much at Jo's. But now his youth was laid bare as a kid who was crushed by seeing his dad lying helpless in a hospital bed.

Frozen in place like a deer in headlights, Derek could only stare at the devastation the fall had wreaked on Carl's body. Bryan's head dropped and his crying took over as Garrett offered words of comfort.

As Derek met Bryan's gaze, he wondered what it was like to have a family member so hell-bent on self-destruction. Did his father and sister think the same about him as Bryan thought of his father? He was sure he wasn't the same as Carl. Derek held down a job. He paid his bills. When he drank, it was in private.

Usually.

"Come on, D."

Oblivious to Kiro's call, Derek still stared blankly into the trauma bay.

Someone grabbed Derek's arm. "D!"

Startled, Derek slowly turned to face Kiro.

"Come on!" Kiro urged him on, exchanging a concerned look with Steve, who went ahead and pushed the gurney through the automatic doors as Kiro extended his arm to grab Derek's shoulder. "Let's go."

Still in a daze, Derek accompanied Kiro and Steve back to the ambulance.

"They'll take good care of him," Kiro assured him.

Derek opened the door and stared at the used bandages, wrappers, and gloves that were strewn all over the blood-drenched ambulance floor, silent remnants of their valiant effort to save Carl's life.

"It's amazing he even made it inside the rig," Steve added. "Much less all the way to the hospital." He patted Derek on the back. "You did that. You got him there."

"Yeah." Derek grudgingly agreed as he climbed into the back and settled himself in the captain's chair.

Finally taking off his gloves as Kiro closed the ambulance doors, Derek let them fall to the floor, a devastating reminder of how close they came to losing Carl.

Chapter 35

Breakdown

On the return trip to Grant's Crossing from downtown Columbus, Derek leaned back and closed his eyes, barely registering the lighthearted conversation Kiro and Steve were having up front.

"Tara wants me to take her to this Turkish restaurant I haven't yet tried," Steve said. "I think it's down on Riverside or someplace?"

"Yes, Cafe Istanbul. Celeste and I have talked about going back there. They've got great kebabs."

"Great kebabs? Really?"

"Hey! Don't knock 'em 'til you try 'em." Kiro changed back out of the faster-moving vehicle lane after passing the Bethel Road exit on 315. "Why don't we all go this weekend and make a night of it?"

"Good idea," Steve agreed as he pulled out his phone and opened his texting app. "I'll run it by Tara. Wait, how formal? Will it count as a dress-up date? Tara's always looking for an excuse to wear a dress."

"It's a nicer casual place."

"Good. She'll love that."

Derek's thoughts wandered while the guys up front planned their double date. With Carl's accident dominating his thoughts, he still couldn't come down from the adrenaline-fueled high that held his body and mind hostage. Out of character for him, he second-guessed everything he did for Carl, both at the scene and in the rig. Did he miss any bleeders? Could he have prevented him from coding on the way to the hospital?

Carl usually got drunk at Jo's. What prompted him to wander around Storley and climb up on a catwalk?

Would that be him someday, waving a bottle of liquor while precariously balanced atop a pile of abandoned machinery?

And when he became the town drunk, would the paramedics be able to save him?

The more he replayed his treatment of Carl's injuries in his mind, the more his chest tightened. And the more he envisioned the bottom of the downward spiral he'd been traveling since he returned to civilian life, toward the world of what could be.

What would probably be.

"Tell Logan I love him, D."

His breathing quickened.

What should have been.

He gasped for breath and rubbed his knuckles against his chest. "Don't go, Joey."

Kiro tilted his head just enough to call back, yet still kept his eyes on the road. "You alright back there, D?"

"I wasn't there for him, D."

Until Kiro called back to him, he hadn't realized he'd said Joey's name out loud. He swallowed, but responded with a cough that, hopefully, was enough to convey that he was. "Yeah."

Kiro laughed at something Steve said, but Derek could no longer make out the conversation.

What could he have done this morning to ensure a better outcome for Carl? Why did it remind him so much of Joey?

After the RPG hit, Joey couldn't breathe just like Carl couldn't breathe after his fall.

Joey lost both his legs at the ankles. Carl had compound fractures in both of his legs.

Derek's thoughts raced, placing him both in an abandoned building and also on that swelteringly hot day on that mountain in Afghanistan.

Joey was covered in lacerations and had all sorts of internal trauma. Carl was covered in lacerations and had a collapsed lung.

They'd exited the freeway and were now traveling past deserted cornfields.

Derek could barely get the slightest bit of air with each breath he attempted.

"I can't breathe. I can't breathe." He pounded on the wall behind Kiro and Steve. "STOP! Kiro. I can't breathe. Stop!"

"What was that?" They had just passed through downtown Delaware and couldn't yet pull over. "Steve, I can't see what's going on," Kiro said, tilting his head while still keeping his eyes on the road. "Is he okay back there?"

Steve turned around and frowned at the scene before him. Derek was hunched over in his seat. His white knuckles clenched the edge of the tiny counter next to the gurney by the captain's chair. His other hand clasped his chest, and his shoulders moved up and down as he struggled for air.

"Better pull over."

Kiro pulled the ambulance onto the shoulder of the road. He was barely stopped before Steve jumped out and raced to the back to open the door. No sooner had Steve pulled the doors wide open than Derek flew past him.

"Joey. Can't ... breathe," Derek muttered as he jumped out the back and wandered off the side of the road, leaving Kiro and Steve staring at his back. He ended up a good ten yards into a frost-covered, long-ago-harvested cornfield.

"What did he say?" Steve asked without turning toward Kiro.

"Don't know, but." Kiro turned to Steve as his eyes shot wide open. "Oh shit." Kiro started toward Derek. "Steve. Get on the radio and get Tank here. Now."

Steve clicked the radio to call back to the station. "Tank? Need you here. Mitchell needs help." He gave the location so they could be found on the side of the road. Fortunately, they weren't too far out of Grant's Crossing. Tank would arrive pretty soon.

"D? Are you okay?" Kiro asked on his way to catch up to Derek, who was now bent over, propping himself up with his hands on his knees, gasping for air.

"Can't breathe. Can't ... "

"Jesus, D. What's wrong?" Kiro placed his hands on Derek's shoulder and back and spoke calmly. "Derek. Breathe in. It's okay. You're okay."

After a few minutes of trying to calm Derek, he still couldn't catch his breath.

Sirens sounded in the distance.

"Derek. Breathe."

He took a few minutes to catch his breath, though it remained erratic at best, no matter how hard he tried.

"No. I tried. I tried." He struggled for air in between each word as the siren drew closer.

"Tried what?" Kiro asked.

Tank brought the entire fire engine. The siren stopped when the engine pulled off the side of the road across from the ambulance. Tank jumped out and ran toward the field, stopping as he drew close enough to where Derek held on by a thread.

The movement caught Kiro's attention. The rest of the firefighters headed toward them. Tank turned and caught Steve's attention. "Keep them back."

"I tried to save him," Derek exclaimed, practically hyperventilating. "I tried ..."

"He keeps saying he tried to save him," a confused Kiro said to

Tank, then returned his attention to Derek. "Breathe, D. Just breathe."

Tank closed his eyes for a moment. When they reopened, he squeezed Kiro's shoulder. "Steve," Tank called out.

"Yeah?"

"Take the men back to quarters. You, too, Kiro. You're about due for a rotation, anyway and that'll let the engine stay in service."

"No," Kiro said resolutely. "I'm staying."

"No. You're going."

Kiro stood his ground. "No."

Tank stared at a determined Kiro and nodded his approval. Turning back to Steve, "We'll come back in the rig."

Steve extended his arms to send the other men back, much like he would a crowd of onlookers at a house fire. "Give him space, men, back in the truck." Steve may still have been the newest firefighter, but he was not to be trifled with, and they all responded by immediately obeying.

Emerson shook his head. "I never thought I'd see the day when Der–."

"That's enough, Emerson," Steve snapped, getting in his face. "You will not utter a single word about this to anyone, do you understand me? Not a word. Not. To. Anyone."

Stunned at Steve's sudden admonishment, Emerson backed up a step and held his hands up in surrender. "No. I won't. We're all family here, Steve."

"Good." Steve patted him on the back. "Come on now. Back to quarters." Steve took one last look at where Tank and Kiro were consoling a broken paramedic and fellow veteran who had just dropped to his knees in the lifeless cornfield.

"It's okay, Doc. We've got you," Tank said as tears poured down Derek's cheeks. He knelt next to Derek with his hand on his back to steady him.

"I couldn't ... " Derek couldn't catch his breath enough to talk. "I couldn't ... " He struggled so much he started hyperventilating, throwing him into a full-blown panic attack.

"Breathe, D," Kiro said from the other side of him. Tank backed up a bit as Kiro took over. "Feel my hand on your back. Take a breath, D. You've got this. You're okay."

"I'm not ... I'm not ... Oh no." Derek's stomach seized up, and he lurched forward. As soon as his hands hit the ground, he emptied his stomach.

Lifting his gaze, Kiro and Tank shared a helpless look as Derek retched onto the dry, brown husks, crumbling in the frozen field. All the while, Kiro kept a hand on Derek's back and another on his forehead.

Derek spit a couple of times before wiping his mouth with the back of his hands and swatting Kiro's hand off his forehead. "Dammit, Joey," he yelled into the air, still crying. "You were supposed to come home. We were all supposed to come home."

"Doc," Tank said calmly. "He–"

"I'm so tired. I tried to bring him back, Tank," Derek pleaded with his arm extended toward Tank. "You've got to believe me. You have to believe me."

Tank grabbed Derek's hand and knelt closer to him. "I believe you, Doc. I do."

"I tried to save him, but ... but he was bleeding out, his feet were gone. I didn't even know where they were. There was blood everywhere." Derek spoke a mile a minute, gesturing all around him as if they were back on that mountainside in Afghanistan after the RPG hit.

"Doc. Doc. Slow down." Tank tried to calm him. "It's okay."

As if Tank had never spoken, Derek kept describing the scene after the blast.

Derek sniffed, and his eyes went wide. "His shoulder was shattered, and that wasn't even the one that had been shot a few minutes earlier. I couldn't keep all of him inside."

"Come on, D," Kiro started as Tank stopped him.

"No, Kiro. He's okay. I mean, let him get it out. He hasn't let it out yet. He's been holding this in for too long."

Derek sobbed, but continued what amounted to a confession. "I tried so hard. He couldn't breathe. And then he wanted me to tell Logan that he loved him, and ... and ... " He turned to Tank as if begging for forgiveness. "I couldn't even tell him I would. I couldn't even do that much. I told him he could tell Logan himself." Derek smacked the heel of his hand against his forehead three times. "Stupid. Stupid. Stupid."

Tank grabbed Derek's wrist to keep him from hitting himself again.

"I kept trying to stop the bleeding, then he stopped breathing. Then I gave him compressions, but he would just bleed out more. And then ... and then ... " Derek tried to breathe in a shuddered breath, but he was on the verge of hyperventilating again.

"Breathe, D. Breathe," Kiro instructed at the same time Tank said, "It's okay, Doc. Let it out."

Derek calmed for a second or two, but resumed talking. "He started calling for his mom." Derek wailed. "His eyes glazed over, and part of me deep down knew he was gone, but I refused to believe it. I couldn't believe it." He reached for Tank and started speaking so fast. "I'm sorry, Tank. I promised to take care of him. All he needed was to be barely alive like you were," Derek said, referring to Tank's own injuries that nearly took his life.

"Just enough alive so we could get him back." He wiped his nose again with the back of his hand. "But I couldn't even do that much. Ninety-two. Ninety-two fucking percent. If they had a pulse, they made it. I needed to find his pulse. I needed to save him. I was desperate to find it."

Derek was on his knees and fell back, so he sat on his heels. He held his palm against his forehead as if he'd just had an epiphany. "Oh shit. Oh shit. Logan. I totally fucked him over by not doing my fucking job. I ruined his life, Tank. I tried."

He turned to Kiro as if finally realizing he was there, too. "I really tried, K. I mean, Rass had the IV. I made Jonesy hold the bandage on his torso. His kidney was probably already beyond saving." His breathing quickened as he shook his head from side to side. "I tried to save him."

"It's okay, Doc," Tank said, grabbing Derek's shoulders.

"I tried to save him. I tried. " Derek collapsed against Tank, who held him while he sobbed. "Oh my god. He was going to die anyway, wasn't he?" Derek pulled back for one last look at Tank before dropping his head back on Tank's shoulder.

"Yeah, Doc. He was," Tank said while gently rubbing Derek's back.

"I lost him. Oh my god. I lost my best friend. Joey's gone."

Tank continued to hold Derek while he cried, closing his own eyes in the process. "Let it out. It's okay. Just let it out." While holding his friend and brother in arms, Tank lifted his lids to meet Kiro's gaze. Kiro's heartbroken eyes mirrored his own.

THERAPY 7
Break

Chief Travis caught up with Derek upon his return to the station. "Steve filled me in," he told Derek. "Go ahead and take the rest of the shift off, and if you want, you can stop by Doc Majors today rather than tomorrow. He'll be expecting you either way."

Derek shook his head. "Yeah. I'm sure he is."

"I'll get you home, Doc," Tank offered.

"No," Derek said. His voice was calm, almost indifferent.

"Doc?"

Derek raised his eyes, still bloodshot from his earlier breakdown. "Take me to Dad's?"

Tank smiled. "Yeah. Sure. Let's go." With a nod to the Chief, he led Derek to his car and dropped him off at Derek's childhood home.

Derek surprised his dad when he walked inside in civilian clothes on a day he was supposed to be on shift. His dad's welcoming smile disappeared the moment he saw Derek barely holding himself together.

He'd only seen that look on his son one time before: when Derek stepped off the plane the day he brought Joey's body home. Except, unlike that day, it seemed like today, Derek really would break.

"I lost it, Dad," Derek said as the tears fell.

Abe pulled his son into his arms. "Ah, son. What happened?"

Derek dropped his backpack on the floor and returned to his father's embrace. "I lost it."

"I've got you, son. I've got you."

A few hours after breaking down a second time at his father's house, Derek texted Doc Majors, who immediately welcomed him inside his office as soon as he arrived.

To anyone else, it was a beautiful day. The sun had risen in the sky and burned off the clouds that gave it a typical dreary, cold-weather-in-Ohio start. Sure, the day was still cold; it was December, after all, but the fresh air did Derek good on his walk over.

"I'm glad you made it," the doctor said as he closed the office door and grabbed his signature clipboard off his desk.

"Yeah."

Derek plopped down on his usual spot on the couch. After telling his father about Carl's accident and his subsequent breakdown on the way back to the hospital, his dad encouraged him to keep his appointment with Doc Majors.

Foregoing the usual start-of-session questions about sleep, food, and his shift, Doc dove right into the deep end. "I heard you had a rough start to your day. Want to tell me about it?"

Derek raised his bloodshot eyes and met the gaze of the doctor who probably knew more about his inner demons than anyone else Derek knew, save Tank. Ignoring the strong pull to keep it all inside, he opted not to hide what the doctor probably already knew; he recounted the day, adding in how he broke down a second time at his dad's.

"How did your father take it?"

"He's my dad." Derek swallowed down a nagging desire to break again. "He's always been there for me. I'm thirty-five years old, and I fucking cried in my dad's arms like a baby."

"You're allowed to show emotion, you know."

Resigned to the fact that today was going to suck no matter what, Derek agreed. "I guess."

"I'm glad you have someone who can support you like that. Someone you can go to."

"I normally can't."

A crease formed in Doc Majors' brow. "What do you mean you normally can't?"

"I mean, Dad is the one the Army notified when Joey died. He's been through enough."

Derek took almost as much time releasing his deep breath as he did drawing it in. "After Joey died, I found a letter that he'd written me. A death letter. In it, he said that," Derek swallowed. "That he understood if my dad's first thoughts were of me rather than him when the officer and chaplain arrived."

Doc Majors gave Derek the time he needed to continue.

"Joey wrote that it was okay because he was my dad first. Though I don't know why he said that. Joey was every bit a son to my father as I was." Derek sniffed and quickly wiped the moisture from his eyes. "I keep his letter in my locker at work." Derek wiped his hand down his face and blinked a few times. "God, I miss him."

"I know," the doctor agreed to the most obvious sentence of Derek's story. "We've all lost friends."

Derek's head jerked up. He'd never asked before, but he couldn't stop himself. "Where were you?"

"Iraq and Kuwait. Desert Storm."

Derek nodded. "Branch?"

"Air Force. PJs."

"Pararescue. Were you a medic, too?"

Doc Majors bobbed his head from side to side. "Yes, but it was more in line with rescue operations when it came to downed pilots and the like." He pulled his pant leg up to reveal a prosthetic leg. "Got two of these for my efforts on my last mission before I started teaching at Fort Bragg."

"Where I trained to be a medic."

"Yes. You were already serving in Afghanistan by the time I got there, but yeah. One and the same."

Not breaking his gaze, Derek took a few moments to take in what the doctor just said. "So you get it."

"Yeah. I get it."

Derek nodded slowly as the realization hit him. "Then you know I didn't kill Joey."

"I've known the whole time, Derek," he confirmed. "You just needed to figure it out for yourself."

Chapter 36

New Life

"IF YOU'D LIKE," ABE SUGGESTED WHILE FLIPPING THROUGH pages on his clipboard, "we can schedule the demo as early as February."

Callie's brow furrowed. "In the middle of winter?"

"Sure."

"Won't it be too cold? It's only December, and it's not so bad, but I imagine it'll be colder by then."

"Well, yes. It'll be cold, but we can at least clear the place out and take it down to the studs. After that, we can wrap it in an enclosure during the coldest months for the actual reno work."

Callie shivered at the thought when her phone rang. She only planned to be in Ohio for a couple of days before returning to D.C. for a week. Then, she would be off on another assignment. "Those will be the months your crew is working on it, right?" She asked as she pulled her phone out of her pocket and glanced down to see who was calling.

Abe chuckled. "Right."

"Whew." She held up her phone. "Excuse me a second. I need to take this." She walked toward the other end of the workshop.

"Hey, MAT," she answered her brother on the other end of the line. "What's up?"

"It's Grandpa, CAT."

Her stomach dropped upon hearing those few words.

"He's taken a turn for the worse. Uncle Graham had to call an ambulance this morning."

"How's he doing?"

"Not well, I'm afraid."

When her brother didn't continue, her thoughts veered toward the worst. "MAT? What aren't you telling me?"

He exhaled on the other end of the line before answering. "They're saying this may be his last time in the hospital."

"Well, that's good, right?" Then it hit her. "No. No. MAT, you don't mean ...t" Her eyes welled with tears.

"They say he'll probably have to be put on a ventilator before long. Once he's on it, though, they don't anticipate being able to take him off it."

She turned and met Abe's gaze on the other side of the room. His concerned expression told her he'd heard enough to know the news wasn't good.

"I'll change my flight and get back as fast as I can."

"I'm sorry you have to change your plans."

"I'll send you my new flight info."

"Love you, CAT."

"Love you, too."

She ended the call with silent tears while frantically opening up the travel app to change her flight. She clicked a few times to make the changes, but accidentally dropped the phone to the ground. "Shit." When she leaned down to pick it up, she jammed her finger on the floor. "Ouch!" She stuck her finger in her mouth, shook out her hand, and then tried to pick it up again. Tears in her eyes made it hard to see, and she dropped the phone again just as she thought she had it. "DAMMIT!"

Frustrated, she covered her face with her hands and tried to breathe.

"Callie? Are you okay?"

Callie's shoulders were shaking, but she stopped the moment Abe spoke. She sniffed and leaned down, more slowly this time. "Yeah. Fine." Her voice was much higher-pitched than she'd have liked, but, without turning around, she hit confirm to change her flight.

"Callie?" Abe's voice was gentler this time. Closer. "What's wrong, dear?"

Callie turned and couldn't keep the tears at bay. She may be in her early thirties, but she couldn't hide her emotions when it came to her closest family members, including the only grandfather she'd ever known. "My grandpa," was all she got out before Abe pulled her into a comforting hug.

"It'll be alright, dear."

Callie appreciated the hug for a few moments and then pulled herself together and wiped the tears from her cheeks. "I was planning to be here for a couple of days, but my brother called to say Grandpa had to be taken to the hospital in an ambulance. I just changed my flight and need to call a rideshare to the airport."

"Need me to take you?"

"You're sweet, and I appreciate the offer. I do. However, I don't want to impose, especially with no notice. I'll be fine." She wiped her eyes again and sniffed. She huffed out a humorless laugh. "At least I didn't unpack my bags." She rechecked her phone. "The driver will be here in a little while."

After returning from getting her bags, she apologized. "I'm sorry. I know we were going to set a date, but–"

"Don't worry about a thing. We'll get it all scheduled when you're ready."

The driver pulled into the driveway. Callie confirmed the driver and his car and loaded her luggage into the trunk. She turned to say her goodbyes to Abe and froze. "Oh shit!"

"What's wrong?"

"I was supposed to meet Derek for dinner tonight to catch up. Would you please let him know I can't make it? I'm sorry. I don't mean to–"

"Don't worry. Just get home to your family." He paused, then asked. "If you think of it, shoot me a text when you get to the airport and again when you get home so I know you made it safely."

"I will," she promised. "And Abe? I'm so sorry."

"It's okay, Callie. Don't worry. Just be safe."

With a final wave, she slid into the car and headed out to the airport.

Derek sat down at the bar and ordered a beer. "Thanks, Mike."

"You bet."

As Mike popped off the top for him, Derek shot off a text message to Callie.

> Derek: Dad told me about ur grandfather. How r u doing?

> Callie: Ok. He's not doing well.

> Derek: Sucks. I'm sorry.

> Callie: Yeah. No kidding. Everybody's here. Even my brother.

> Callie: Sorry I had to cancel on you.

> Derek: Family takes priority.

> Callie: Thanks. But friends do, too. You ok?

Derek took a sip of his beer, then typed out a text. He was pissed because of the week he had, and he just wanted to be with somebody that he didn't want to get rid of after a quick hookup. He actually wanted to spend time with her. And not that it was her fault that she canceled, but yeah. He was definitely pissed. He just couldn't take it out on her. He texted her back.

Derek: Yeah. I'm ok. Take care of yourself, k?

Callie: OK

He placed his phone, face down, on the bar. He probably smacked it against the bar a little harder than was necessary, but he didn't much care at the moment.

"You look like your date stood you up."

Derek closed his eyes and exhaled. He hadn't even noticed that Berneta Forsythe, one of the town's infamous Tres Widows, had sat down next to him. She and her two lifelong best friends were forever getting themselves into trouble. They'd all outlived their husbands and were practically as old as the town itself.

But when anyone in town needed moral support, help getting through a funeral with a hot meal or cleanup, or help watching the kids, the Tres Widows —Berneta, Abigail, and Lizzie —were the first ones to volunteer. They were there when his mom passed away, going on twenty years ago. They would come in and boss everyone around like drill sergeants to get others to pitch in, but their biggest skill, even at funerals, was ending up with a date along the way. No matter the occasion, they'd flirt their way to a dance at Jo's, lunch out, or drinks.

"Something like that." Derek took a sip from his bottle. "She had a good reason."

Were she forty years younger, he might have taken her home

with him, but he could at least offer a drink to one of his grandmother's friends.

Figuring he should cut his losses now, he turned to the tall African-American lady next to him. "Can I get you a drink, Miss Berneta?"

"Glad you asked," she said while reaching back to ensure her always-perfect and mostly gray chignon was in place.

Mike was across the bar when Derek flagged him down. "Add hers to my tab, Mike."

"Be a dear and get me an Old Fashioned, please. Ah!" Berneta held up her finger with a disapproving arched brow when Mike started to turn away. "With a twist, Michael."

"Yes, ma'am," Mike snickered while dutifully mixing her cocktail.

She turned her attention back to Derek. "Now tell me, young man. What's going on? It's not like you to drink alone."

If only she knew.

"At least not here. What's troubling you? Since I've been here, at least two women have come over to flirt with you, and each one has left disappointed."

"My plans were canceled."

"Mmhmm. So you said. And what reason did she give you?"

Derek breathed out an overly dramatic sigh just as Mike set Berneta's cocktail in front of her. She picked it up and took a sip. "Delicious, Michael. Thank you."

Mike chuckled. "You bet."

"You're welcome," Derek mumbled under his breath.

"Now, Derek. Don't give me any attitude. It's unbecoming."

When he turned, she met him with an expectant gaze.

Resigned to tell her, he gave her a quick summary. "She had to cut her trip short because her grandfather's been sick. Sounds like he's not doing well."

"And you believe her?"

This time, it was Derek's turn to convey his impatience with a stern look that nearly rivaled hers. "Yes. That's why she was here to begin with."

He probably didn't need to be so short with her.

When a crease formed between Berneta's perfectly shaped brows, Derek took a breath and explained. "Her grandfather wasn't well enough to travel, so she came out to oversee the renovation of the house. Of Brockmoor."

"Ahh." Her face lit up in a genuine smile. "Brockmoor was a beautiful home in its day."

Surprised, Derek set down his bottle. "You remember when it was nice? I've only ever seen it all run down and falling apart like it is now."

"Oh, yes," she assured him. "It was beautiful, with colorful flowers in the spring and the most festive decorations at Christmas. They threw some of the most lovely garden parties when I was a girl. And then, in the 1980s, it went through a series of many owners who either didn't want or weren't able to keep it up. As you well know, it's a large house. I can't imagine having all that upkeep."

She smiled and rested a hand on Derek's arm. "Darius and I never had a need for so much space, but I imagine it would be perfect for a larger family."

"Maybe." Derek smiled. "Though I can't imagine having a family at all now."

"Now, don't sell yourself too short, young man. You're a handsome thing and have a good job." She took in his wary expression, messy hair, and unshaven face and then smiled. "Obviously a bit rough around the edges, but the foundation is good. I'm sure you'll find the right person for you."

Her description made him laugh. "Thanks, Miss Berneta, but I can't picture that anymore. Maybe a long time ago, perhaps, but now?"

"But now, what?" she nearly snapped, causing Derek to lose all pretense of playing along.

"What do you mean, what? Since I've come back? I don't want to settle down–"

"Pfft." She waved him off before he had a chance to continue. "Enough of that. Darius said the same thing when he came back from Vietnam. He was a changed man, but still every bit the good man I married. A bit more hardened, yes. A bit more haunted, definitely, but a good man nonetheless. He often fretted about how coming back from war was a new life for him, but didn't think I should have to suffer through it with him."

"What happened?"

She took another sip of her drink. "I told him he was a fool for thinking I'd ever give up on him. And if he didn't like his new life, he should change it. End the new life that had been thrust upon him and start an even better one, making his own choices." She pointed with each syllable for emphasis. "So he did."

Her no-nonsense take on things was no surprise to Derek, but she did offer food for thought.

"Sometimes, Derek, it's deciding to make a change that is what's difficult, not the change itself. Now, pay for our drinks and walk your date to her car."

"My date?"

She grabbed her coat, then leaned in with a mischievous grin. "Me, Derek Mitchell. Me!"

Chapter 37

Go Home

Derek arrived at the station for his shift the next morning, sporting a pair of sunglasses to cover his bloodshot eyes.

"Fuck." Kiro jumped off the couch and ran to the locker room to intercept Derek. "What the hell are you doing here?"

"I'm working," Derek snapped as he shoved his pack inside his locker.

"You're getting worse."

"Fuck off, Kiro. I'm fine. I'll be in back, okay?"

"Probably not a good idea today."

Derek leaned his head back and squeezed some eye drops into each eye, blinking a few times before replacing the bottle on the locker shelf.

"Eye drops." Kiro shook his head. "You really think that's going to help?"

"Fine. I'll drive." Derek slammed his locker door shut and stepped back, nearly losing his footing when the back of his leg came into contact with the bench in the aisle way.

"What the hell, D? You can barely walk."

"What the fuck do you want, K? In the back or driving?"

"Neither. You can't even walk in a straight line. I don't want to die because–"

"I'm fine."

"You are NOT fucking fine," Kiro answered, perhaps a bit too loudly. He took a deep breath and lowered his voice. "If you were fine, you'd be able to stand up and walk in a straight line. If you were fine, your eyes wouldn't be so bloodshot. And if you were fine," Kiro now stood toe to toe with Derek. "your nose wouldn't be bleeding."

Derek's hand snapped up to his nose. "Shit."

Steve entered the locker room just as Derek pressed a folded washcloth to his nose. He leaned against the door frame while Derek and Kiro argued.

"When's the last time you actually drank something for the purpose of hydration?"

Derek glared at his friend because he couldn't answer.

"Go home, D."

"I'm not going home."

"Yes. You are. You shouldn't be here."

"No. I'm–"

Kiro turned to Steve as he walked in. "Steve, you're with me in the rig today."

"What the fuck, K?"

"Go home, Derek."

Derek snapped his head back in surprise at being addressed by his full name. It had been since Kiro was in middle school when he'd last called Derek anything other than his first initial, D. "What are you doing to me, K?"

"Not a damned thing ... except saving both of our lives - and the life of whatever patient we're picking up."

"Fuck you."

"Fuck me what? Wanna cuss me out? Do it." Kiro stepped back and spread his arms wide. "Have at it. But I am not letting you go out there. Not today and not with me. Now look, we can drop you back home. That'll get you inside before your dad arrives and starts working. He won't have to see you get home. He won't know."

"And you don't think Steve will ask why?"

"I'm sure he will, assuming he hasn't figured it out already," Kiro said, a bit more matter-of-factly than Derek would have liked.

Steve approached them. "I don't need to ask, Mitchell. You don't hide it as well as you think."

Derek exhaled, not yet resigned to take the loss.

Kiro sniffed. "Jesus D, I've seen you hungover a million times, but you smell like you're still drunk."

Derek stared his friend down. "I'm fine."

Kiro took a step back, heartbroken at how his friend was acting. "Don't lie to me, Derek. Jesus. Lie to anyone else, but do not lie to me. You've never lied to me."

Derek dropped his chin like Kiro had finally taken the wind out of his sails.

"You're going home," Kiro said. "We'll tell the chief you're not feeling well. It won't be a lie, but it won't share details either. Come on."

Tank stood at the door, having observed Derek and Kiro's exchange.

"D's not feeling well, Tank. Steve'll be with me today. We're taking him home."

Tank nodded.

In a last-ditch effort, Derek leaned closer to Kiro. "It's not your call, K."

"Yes. It is, Doc," Tank answered. "As senior medic, it is his call. I'll let the chief know of the change."

Derek's heart sank when Tank turned and walked away without another word. This was a new low in his new life's never-ending downward spiral.

Chapter 38

Collapse

THE BUZZ OF THE DOOR PULLED DEREK FROM HIS THOUGHTS. It was bad enough that Kiro and Steve dropped him off that morning, but he wasn't exactly up for company. Derek had made a beeline for the door, plugged in the correct code on the second attempt, and went straight upstairs to his apartment. He slept for a few hours before his buzz had faded. He'd drunk a few beers since then to get it back.

The door buzzed again. "Shit, you know the code," Derek said to no one, voicing his displeasure at what was probably Kiro checking up on him. He leaned back against the couch and closed his eyes.

A knock on the door startled him. He slowly turned to stare at the door, as if willing it to remain closed.

Another knock. He took a breath and called out, "Come in. It's open."

Derek closed his eyes again. The door opened.

"Leave me alone, K. I think you've done enough today."

"Uh, hi," a familiar voice spoke out. A familiar voice that didn't belong to Kiro.

Derek arched one brow, then opened an eye as he slowly directed his not-so-clear gaze toward the door.

"Doc Majors?"

"Yeah. Hi. Your dad? I think? Let me in."

"Making house calls now?"

"Sure."

"Seriously. What the hell are you doing here?"

"I was told you went home early today."

Derek took his time standing up, struggling to stay upright. "News travels fast." His words slurred, making it come across as *newsh travelsh fasht.*

Hanging back near the door, the doctor scanned the mostly tidy apartment and then took in Derek's appearance along with a couple of bottles on top of the small kitchen island. "Chief Travis called to let me know you might not make tomorrow's session."

"They said I was drunk before, but I wasn't. But now? Definitely." Derek waved him off with a laugh. "But, I'm fine."

"Is that what you think?"

"Yeah, Doc. I'm good." He took a drink out of his bottle. "So good."

"I see that." He reached into his bag and pulled out a folder containing some papers. He held it up. "Here's the info on applying for a service dog."

"Really. Why bother? I don't get one, do I? You said I don't qualify."

"You will. Eventually."

"*Evenshually?* Pfft."

Doc perused Derek's shelves with a carefully folded flag preserved in a triangular frame, surrounded by pictures. He picked up the picture of Derek, Tank, and Joey. "Is this Joey?

"Don't touch that," Derek snapped.

Doc Majors' brows dropped. "Are you okay, Derek? You look pale." The doctor turned around to look at the other pictures on the shelf.

Derek extended his hand in an attempt to point. "Put it ... back."

He took one step forward and froze. His bottle fell out of his hand onto the carpet, and his vision darkened. "Doc ..." Unable to complete his sentence, he collapsed into a heap like a tossed-out ragdoll.

Doc Majors snapped around to see Derek lying on the floor, unmoving. "Derek?" He dropped his bag and rushed over. "DEREK!"

When he didn't respond, the doc shook his shoulders. "Derek?" He leaned closer to listen for breathing, any sign that Derek had just passed out. "Shit. Come on, Derek. Talk to me." He felt for a pulse. "Fuck." He reached into his pocket for his phone and dialed 9-1-1. He hit the speaker button and immediately started chest compressions.

"9-1-1, what's the location of your emergency?"

"4-3-7 Adams Street. Carriage House apartment. I'm Doctor Zachary Majors. I have a thirty-five-year-old male in respiratory distress. Was drinking heavily and collapsed. No pulse. He's unconscious. I'm administering CPR. Possible alcohol poisoning."

"I'm dispatching an ambulance to your location now."

***

Kiro laughed and smacked his card on the table. "Four points, baby!" Grinning, he high-fived Tank, who sat across the table. "Yes!"

Tank tossed his cards into the center of the table. "Thank god you had that loner. I've never been so happy to not have to call suit. We'd have been screwed!"

Tim groaned but collected the cards and shuffled them for a minute or two.

Emerson sagged in his chair. "Deal me some good cards this time around, would you, Tim? We can't lose to these guys again."

Kiro rubbed his hands together in excitement. "I'll still have the lead, so here's hoping I can stop you right out of the gate."

The alarm sounded overhead, causing them all to pause and listen.

"GC Medic. 437 Adams Street. Thirty-five-year-old male, unconscious and in respiratory distress, possible alcohol poisoning."

Dispatch had barely finished relaying the information when Kiro and Tank's eyes met.

Tank shot up. "Shit!"

"4-3-7 Adams," Emerson said while standing up. "That's just down the street."

"That's Derek." Kiro smacked Steve on his way to the ambulance. "Come on."

"Everybody up," Chief Travis commanded. "Let's go."

***

"Steve, get the gurney." Kiro grabbed his kit and sprinted up the drive the second they parked the ambulance. It was barely two minutes after receiving the call at the station. He punched in the code he knew by heart and dashed up the stairs. "DEREK!"

Forcing the door open, Kiro ran into the apartment to find a man performing chest compressions on Derek. "You got here fast. Started chest compressions roughly three minutes ago. No change in the interim."

"What was he doing?" Kiro asked while checking Derek's eyes. "Pupils are non-reactive."

Steve entered the room and kneeled next to the doc. "Here. I've got this."

"Thanks," Doc Majors said as Steve took over compressions. The doctor shook out his arms and backed away to let the medics do their work.

Kiro opened Derek's mouth. "Throat looks clear." He felt Derek's neck. "No pulse."

"You." Kiro turned his attention to the doctor. "Did he get sick at all?" As he asked, he reached into his bag for an oxygen mask and started pumping air into Derek's lungs.

"No. Zach Majors. Doctor Zach .... No. He didn't aspirate."

"His body doesn't want to work. He's out cold. Dammit, D. Breathe."

"He's been like that since he collapsed."

"How are you even here?" Kiro asked while he worked.

"I was dropping off ... doesn't matter. He was clearly drunk, but he was standing. Kind of. He collapsed mid-sentence."

"Don't shut down on me, D."

"Derek!" Abe called out. He followed the firefighters into Derek's apartment and stopped, stunned at what was happening. "Kiro, what happened?"

"Not now, Abe." Kiro's calm voice belied his concern as he watched for Derek's chest to move. He pressed the bag a few more times, but there was no change. "He's not taking in oxygen." Kiro opened Derek's mouth again. "He's swallowing his tongue. I'm going to intubate." Kiro tore open a package from inside his kit. He raised Derek's chin and forced his mouth open to insert the device that would help get much-needed oxygen to his lungs.

"What are you doing to my son?"

"He's saving his life." Tank placed his hand on Abe's chest and gently backed him away. His low voice had an unusual edge to it, stemming from worry for his friend. "Let him work, Abe. Let him do his job."

"Jesus, he's not fighting this at all," Kiro whispered as he worked the laryngoscope and tube into Derek's throat.

"Shit," Steve muttered, not letting up on the chest compressions.

"He has no gag reflex. Not good. Not good." Kiro pulled out the stylet and attached the bag-valve mask. "Tank, help me."

Tank dropped to his knees and took over the oxygen while Kiro listened with a stethoscope to confirm oxygen was getting into Derek's lungs.

"Good. It's in." Kiro felt again for a pulse. "And he's got a pulse. It's weak and thready, but it's there."

Steve stopped compressions.

"Okay. Let's get him on the gurney." Kiro instructed. "He needs more help than we can give him here."

Tim set the Stokes basket with a backboard next to Derek. He then grabbed his shoulders to help put him in there so they could carry him downstairs. Tank maintained the oxygen mask.

"Make room."

Abe backed into the hallway but followed them down to where Emerson waited with the gurney.

Once downstairs, they rushed Derek to the ambulance. Kiro jumped in. "Emerson, get us to Grady."

"On it," Emerson called out on his way to the driver's seat.

Kiro jumped in and secured Derek. "Steve? Stay in the back with me in case he needs compressions again. I'll get the IV going."

"We'll take Abe and meet you there," was the last thing Kiro heard before Tank closed the door to the back of the ambulance and ran up front to get their friend to the hospital.

Chapter 39

At Grady

Kiro was grateful they made good time to Grady Hospital. He had already hooked Derek up to an IV and administered fluids by the time Emerson opened the ambulance door. Derek was still unconscious, but he hadn't coded along the way.

The doors to the Emergency Department swooshed as Kiro rattled off Derek's vitals.

"Just what we need," the doctor muttered with obvious annoyance as they pulled Derek into a trauma bay. "Another drunk."

"So what if he's another drunk?" Kiro spat out in anger. "He needs you to do your fucking job, Doctor. Preferably without the judgment."

"Yeah, yeah, yeah. I'm just sayin'–"

"NO," Kiro yelled. "You're not saying shit. You have no idea what he's been through."

The doctor acknowledged Kiro's outburst as he grabbed the sheets. "Move on one, two, three, move." They transferred him from the gurney to the hospital bed. "Why do people do this to themselves?" The doctor asked while he examined Derek and barked orders to the nursing staff. "I don't care if you broke up, lost your job, or even if your best friend died ..."

The firefighters stilled, filling the air with tension so thick they could have cut it with a knife.

"Hey, Brent," Doc Majors said, his calm voice cracking the tension in the room. "He's one of them." He motioned to all the firefighter-paramedics crowding around the trauma bay. "He's one of us. A medic."

"PJ?" The doctor's attitude changed in a heartbeat.

"Army Ranger in the 3/75."

"Apologies, gentlemen." The doctor's attitude immediately changed. "We'll take good care of him."

"You'd better," Doc Majors countered with a glare.

Fortunately, Abe missed the doctor's words when he followed Doctor Majors into the treatment bay.

Over the course of the early evening, they stabilized Derek, which required adding fluids after pumping his stomach.

Once Derek was stabilized in the ER, the doctors had to assess the extent of the damage his drinking had done. With nothing more they could do, Kiro, Steve, Tank, and the others returned to Grant's Crossing. They'd done their part. Now, all they could do was wait.

With privileges at Grady Hospital, Doc Majors stayed while Derek was being treated. He made sure a visibly worried Abe was taken care of when they moved Derek into the ICU. Once there, the attending doctor gave an update to Abe. Simply put, Derek wouldn't be going anywhere anytime soon.

Later that evening, Doc Majors entered the station, stopping all conversation. "Derek's dad, Abe, gave me permission to give you an update."

"How is he, Zach?" the chief asked.

"Not good." Zach wore a grim expression, but gave the men a moment to close around him so they could all hear. "You all saved his life today. His blood alcohol was at a near-fatal level when you took him in. They pumped his stomach and, in addition to giving him fluids, are keeping him in a medically-induced coma for a few days while his body detoxes."

Their heads dropped upon hearing of the severity of Derek's condition.

"Shit," Emerson said while Tank muttered the equivalent in Spanish. Kiro listened in with an unreadable expression as Steve dropped a comforting hand on his shoulder.

"He's got a rough road ahead of him," the doctor continued. "We won't know the full extent of the damage to his body for a few days at least. His ribs should fully heal after a while, too. Seems I might have cracked a few while performing CPR."

"Could have been either one of us," Steve said with a shrug.

Doc Majors nodded in response, appreciating Steve's words.

"Anyway, he won't be back for a while. Going through detox is no simple thing. He's not going to have an easy time of it." He turned to Chief Travis. "Chief. Got a minute?"

While they disappeared into the chief's office, the rest of the men returned to what they were doing prior to the doctor's arrival. Kiro didn't move at all, still staring into space with the same indifferent expression he wore as Doc Majors delivered the news.

Sensing someone was nearby, Kiro swore under his breath. "I should have reported him sooner. I should have forced him to go to rehab. Something. I should have done *something*."

Tank pulled him into his arms for a quick hug, then looked him in the eye. "You did everything right, Kiro. You did everything a good friend would do. Until something like this happened, or until he decided to take action himself, you couldn't force anything on him. All you could do was support him, and damn if we all couldn't use as good a friend as you."

Kiro met Tank's gaze, but didn't respond.

"Come on and sit down for a while. He's in good hands. He's getting the help he needs. All we can do is support him."

"Dad?" a groggy voice called out. "Dad. Help."

Abe lifted his head after hearing his son's voice for the first time since they reduced the sedatives that had kept him in a medically induced coma. Derek lay in a bed that raised his upper body. Abe reached for his son's hand. "I'm here, son."

"Dad. Dad." Derek's hand fumbled for purchase until Abe gripped it between his own two hands.

"I'm here. Derek? I'm here," Abe said. He brushed some hair off Derek's nearly unrecognizable face. His beard was growing in as thick as Abe's when he didn't keep it trimmed.

"Dad," Derek scanned the room, frantically looking from place to place, unable to make sense of where he was. "Where am I, Dad? Where? Help." He lurched forward and emptied whatever was in his stomach down his chin and all over his hospital gown. Having been on feeding tubes for the last few days, there was nothing but liquid.

"You're okay, son," Abe assured him as he coughed a few more times before he repeated the process. "NURSE?" Abe called out while steadying Derek. "Shit." Abe tore out of the room and called out to the first person he saw wearing scrubs. "Nurse? NURSE? My son needs help!" He motioned toward the inside of the room. "Something's wrong."

A middle-aged woman rushed into the room, took one look at Derek, and grabbed a small, plastic dish just in time to catch Derek's third round of being sick. She was followed by Derek's doctor, Dr. Landherr, who began examining him and rattling off instructions.

Derek was dry-heaving at this stage, but had already made a

mess of himself. Unfazed by the mess, the nurse followed the doctor's instructions, which included adding some medicine to Derek's IV. "This will help with the nausea," she explained more to Abe than to Derek, who had leaned back with his eyes closed.

The nurse raised the bed so Derek was sitting more upright than before. She left the room and returned with fresh sheets, a new hospital gown, and a warm smile. "I know it's not the most stylish, but it's clean."

While Abe waited outside the room, the nurse patiently cleaned Derek, still groggy from having just come out from under anesthesia. She made quick work of changing his hospital gown and sheets. Abe reentered the room as she spoke words of comfort to Derek. Abe couldn't hear what she said, but Derek didn't utter a single word in response and rarely made eye contact. Occasionally, a tear escaped down his face, which he slowly wiped with the back of his hand.

Once done, she gathered the soiled linens and welcomed Abe back inside the room. He thanked her and returned to his seat by Derek's bedside.

"Dad?"

Careful not to disturb the IV, Abe grabbed Derek's hand as another tear slipped down his son's cheek. "Ah, son. You'll get through this."

"What happened?" a groggy Derek asked.

Abe barely spoke a sentence before Derek slipped back to sleep. While sitting at his son's bedside, he resigned himself to wait out Derek's recovery. Since his son arrived, he'd pretty much been living in the hospital, often joined by a steady rotation of the other firefighters when they weren't on shift, and sometimes, even if they were.

"He'll be in and out like that for another day or two, depending on how much he was used to drinking and for how long."

Abe was startled from his thoughts upon hearing Dr. Landherr's voice behind him, but kept his eye on Derek. "I knew he drank a lot when he was out, but I had no idea how much he drank at home." He released a long exhale. "He lives alone. Our schedules don't always align. I should have–"

"You had no way of knowing. Alcoholics get quite good at hiding their addiction."

"Alcoholic," Abe whispered. "Addiction."

"Yes." The doctor's tone was sympathetic. "He'll want to go into rehab if he truly wants to get better."

Abe brushed some more hair off Derek's face.

"We'll get him through the detox, but it's only a short-term solution."

"A short-term solution that saved his life."

"Yes," the doctor agreed. "He was lucky."

"Lucky," Abe repeated.

"He's alive, Mr. Mitchell, which means he has a chance," the doctor explained. "In the meantime, it's going to be a rough road while his body gets over its addiction. Physically, he'll get through this. Psychologically, however, he's got a long road ahead of him."

Abe nodded.

"He's actually doing well, all things considered. We gave him something for the nausea. It will help for the next time he wakes up, but it'll be rough to get through and rough for you to see. If all goes well, we should be able to get him into a private room within the next day or two." The doctor patted Abe on the shoulder. "Hang in there. We'll be in and out to check on him, but find one of us if you have any questions."

THERAPY 8

A knock on the door drew Derek's attention. He set the half-eaten container of Jell-O back on the tray table and pushed it away as Doctor Majors walked in.

"Since you're not going to make it to my office for a while, I felt a visit was in order." He grabbed a chair and pulled it closer to the hospital bed where Derek lay.

"Yeah. I haven't exactly been around," Derek said, his voice far more subdued than usual. "I'm sitting in the hospital eating what they tell me is food."

Doc Majors smiled and sat down. "How are you feeling?"

Derek scoffed. "Really?"

The doctor held up a hand in surrender. "Have you been sleeping?"

"Yes, but maybe a little too well lately." Derek shrugged then attempted to sit up. Doc Majors leaned over to help raise the bed when Derek struggled to get it in the best position. He made a face and pulled his arm against his ribs.

"Still hurt?"

"Yeah. The doctor said I have three cracked ribs."

"Sorry about that. I might have been a bit heavy-handed with the chest compressions."

"It still hurts when I take a deep breath, but thanks for that." Derek lifted his gaze. "No. Seriously, thank you."

"You're welcome." Doc Majors smiled. "Want to talk about it?"

Derek drew in a long breath and exhaled. "Guess I need to, huh?"

"Wouldn't hurt. We're going to need to talk about where you plan to go when you get discharged, too."

"Not so honorable this time around, huh?"

Doc Majors smiled. "That's all a matter of perspective. You'll be getting help. There's honor in that."

"I'm alive because of you."

"You're alive because of a lot of people, Derek."

"Well, I'd offer to buy you a drink, but ... " he trailed off.

A mischievous grin formed on Doc Majors' face. "I wouldn't say no to some of that Cajun food you're always talking about making for the guys at the station."

Derek smiled for the first time in nearly a week since being admitted to the hospital. "I'll let you know the next time it's my night to cook."

"Fair enough. Now. Let's talk about what's in store for the next thirty days."

Derek closed his eyes nearly an hour later, his discussion with Doc Majors interrupted only by the occasional nurse who came in to check his IV and vitals.

After the doctor left, Derek's dad went home for a shower and a change of clothes. He'd barely left his bedside since Derek was admitted.

Derek's thoughts wandered to Kiro, Tank, and the other men at the fire station. His dad told him that they'd been in and out to check on him. Now that he was awake, Derek had no idea what he'd say to them the next time they saw each other. After all, they'd done more than their fair share in helping keep him alive the last two and a half years since he re-entered the civilian world.

Now it was his turn to make the effort.

Chapter 40

Old Friends

Two years and five months after Joey Parker died

DEREK PACKED THE REST OF HIS CLOTHES AND SHAVING KIT into his duffle bag. He'd been sober for nearly six weeks now, over a week in the hospital and thirty days in rehab. And while he still had nightmares, he also had a clear head for the first time since he could remember. He made a final check of the sparsely furnished bedroom to make sure he had everything and zipped up his bag.

"Ready to go home, Derek?" A cheerful nurse standing in the doorway asked him.

One last look at the place that had kept him safe during the nightmares, during the cravings, during the times his body was sick out of habit rather than necessity. One last look at the room that contained his screams when he couldn't have a drink. That first week had been the worst, but he'd gotten through it. Somehow.

He missed his friends and couldn't wait to see them. He hadn't been allowed visitors while in rehab because they couldn't risk an outside influence tempting him with the vice that sent him there in the first place. After two weeks, he was allowed to speak to his dad for a short while. Despite not seeing them, he knew he owed them all big time, especially Kiro, who never once gave up on him.

Too nervous about returning to his apartment, where he

would be alone, Derek planned to stay with his dad for the foreseeable future. Walking toward the lounge where his dad was waiting, Derek's thoughts wandered to Callie. He hadn't heard from her since before he was taken to the hospital, and wondered how her grandfather was doing. He worried about her as well. Was she working on a new story? Writing her book? All he knew from the last time he spoke to his dad was that she hadn't yet returned, which meant renovating her grandfather's house was on hold again. But that was a thought that could wait for another day.

Abe waited in the lounge area as Derek emerged wearing a timid smile on his face.

Derek approached his dad and set down his bag. "Hey, Dad."

"Hi, son." Abe pulled his son into his arms. "It's so good to see you."

"I feel good." Derek chuckled. "I think."

Abe pulled back and grasped Derek's shoulders with his hands. "That's a good start."

Derek had been home for two days when Tank and Kiro stood on the doorstep of his childhood home.

Kiro practically knocked him down with an overly enthusiastic hug. "So good to see you, D!"

Derek broke into a grin and returned the embrace, followed by the same with Tank.

"You're looking terrific, Doc."

"I've missed you." Derek pulled back and smiled. "How's your mom, K?"

"She's so happy you're home. Ready to stuff you full of food."

"I'll never say no to her cooking," Derek laughed. "And Celi?" he said to Tank. "The kids?"

He clapped Derek's shoulder. "They all miss their Tio Derek, and Celi wants to have you over soon for dinner."

"Sounds good." Derek laughed, hugging them both again. "Damn, it's good to see you both."

"Good," Kiro said as he stepped inside the house without closing the front door behind him. "Because we have a surprise for you today."

Derek's forehead creased. "A surprise?"

"Can we come in yet?" a voice called out from around the side of the wraparound porch. "It's colder than a well-digger's butt out here."

It had been nearly three years, but Derek would recognize that Texas drawl anywhere. He grinned at Tank, whose excited expression mirrored his own. "Rass?"

"It's not that cold," a second voice spoke up. "And while it's not as cold as Nebraska, I gave up a whole weekend with no kids for this! Let us in already."

Still stunned, Derek huffed out another laugh. "Jonesy?"

Tank nodded to Derek, but called out in response. "He's right," Tank leaned his head back and called out without looking away. "It's not that cold out."

"You corn-fed boys are too damned much!"

As if on cue, Tank and Kiro exchanged a conspiratorial glance.

"Okay, D," Kiro said while pushing Derek backward into the large living room where he'd been reading in front of the fireplace. "You have to wait right here."

"Huh?"

Kiro placed a hand on Derek's shoulder. "Alright, Tank. He's good to go."

"Okay, boys. You can come in now."

Two men, one still shivering, emerged from their hiding place outside and stepped inside.

"That ain't right," Rass said with no shortage of indignation, causing Tank to break out in laughter. "Keepin' us outside in the middle o' winter like that. It ain't right."

"Shut up and get inside." Tank urged him inside and closed the front door.

"DOC," Jonesy called out with a grin as he rushed Derek and wrapped his arms around him in a tight squeeze.

"Jonesy!"

Jonesy had messy brown hair and was sporting a full beard, which he stroked with his hand. His look wasn't quite hipster, yet not quite punk. It was most definitely a work in progress.

No sooner did Jonesy let go of Derek than Rass took his turn smothering Derek in a hug.

"Hey, Doc. Great to see you, man."

Rass was clean-shaven, but his straight black hair had grown out and was half in a ponytail and half hanging down his back. He held a black cowboy hat in his hands.

Derek's gaze bounced from Rass to Jonesy and back. "How are you here?"

"You can blame this boy right here," Rass explained while smacking Tank in the arm. "He called us up and said you could use some extra friends." Placing his hat back on his head, he moved closer to the fireplace and held out his hands to warm up.

"How long have you been here?" Derek asked.

"Long enough to have already settled into your apartment," Jonesy explained.

Confused, Derek stared at Tank and Kiro. "My apartment?"

"Yeah," Rass motioned to a grinning Kiro. "Your boy there let us in after we all had lunch today."

Jazz music played from someone's phone. "Oh, that's me." Kiro jogged over to where he'd hung his jacket to pull his phone out of the pocket. He answered the phone and stepped into another room while Tank explained.

"Your dad figured you wouldn't mind opening it up to a couple of old Army buddies."

Derek shook his head, gobsmacked at the unexpected reunion. "Not at all, but Tank here is the old one."

"Hey," Tank laughed. "Only by a couple of months."

"Yeah, but don't worry," Rass assured him while rubbing his hands together in front of the fire. "Jonesy and me, we've already gone through all your stuff. Disappointed you didn't have anything in the fridge. Might wanna work on that the next time we're here. I'm not yet impressed by your Midwestern hospitality."

The room filled up with friendly laughter.

Kiro returned a few minutes later. "Okay. That was Celeste, so I've gotta run. Great to meet you both."

"You, too," Jonesy said with a handshake.

"Tell your mom we'll be back again before we leave town," Rass promised.

"She'll love that. D? Glad you're home." He waved on his way out the door.

"Thanks, K."

"Good guy, that one," Rass said.

"The best," Derek agreed. He shook his head as if clearing out the cobwebs. "Tell me, how did you guys get here? I mean, I haven't seen either of you since ... "

Their faces dropped when they all realized they hadn't seen each other since the day Joey died, but they all nodded in agreement.

Jonesy spoke first. "Tank's been trying to get us to come out here for a while now, but with our families and adjusting to civilian life, it's been hard to find a time." He stared at the fire for a moment, then glanced at Rass, who shrugged. "We weren't sure you'd want to see us after, well, after we lost Lieutenant Stephens and Sergeant Parker."

Derek didn't know how to respond. They weren't wrong.

"Yeah," Rass sat next to Derek on the couch. "You patched us up so many times," he laughed. "Like that time that damned wall fell on me. Joey said I should always stay away from it, but I didn't listen."

Jonesy and Tank laughed. Derek didn't have enough energy to laugh, but smiled just the same.

Rass continued. "Or that time I tried to do a backflip off the barracks and broke my arm."

This time, a hearty laugh escaped Derek's mouth. "You were such an idiot."

"Well, sure, but you said it was a complication from an injury from our last mission the day before, so I wouldn't get in trouble from the CO."

"Yep. I did."

Tank shook his head. "Still can't believe you did that."

"You always had our backs, Doc," Jonesy said.

"Jonesy's right, Doc. There was no way we couldn't be here for you," Rass agreed. "You saved our lives. Tank thought we should help save yours."

"Damn. I appreciate you guys." Derek struggled to hold back tears, but blew out a long breath. "It's been rough. No, that's not right. It's fucking sucked."

"I bet," Jonesy agreed. "Shit. I jump anytime something falls on the floor."

"Or when a car backfires," Rass added.

"I change directions or at least look for alternate routes when I see someone standing in a doorway on the square," Tank admitted.

Derek met Tank's gaze. "I didn't know that."

Tank nodded. "It's true."

"Anybody watch fireworks?" Rass asked. "I've only been back since last summer, but hated when everyone set them off at New Year's."

They all agreed.

"Anyway," Jonesy hesitated a few seconds before continuing,

"Tank let us know you were having a tough go of it and asked us to come out."

Rass picked up where Jonesy left off. "Thought you could use some friends."

Derek looked up and blinked back the unexpected moisture welling in his eyes. A combination of hurt, anger, and resignation flashed across his face.

"Doc, I thought it would be good if–"

"No, Tank." Derek leaned forward enough to grasp Tank's forearm while Rass and Jonesy's faces were showered with concern. Derek nodded as if reassuring himself. "No need to explain. You were right. You were right. Thank you." He turned to his friends. "You, too. Thank you. I mean it. Thank you."

Derek lifted his gaze and froze while looking at a picture on the mantle of Tank, Joey, and himself. It was the same picture he had in his apartment. They were in full combat gear, having just returned from a mission on their second or third tour out of Bagram in Afghanistan.

A hand dropped onto Derek's shoulder.

"We miss him, too, Doc."

Derek turned toward Rass. "Me, too."

"Uh," Jonesy said slowly. "We were thinking, Rass and me, of paying our respects to Joey. If that's alright."

Rass held up his hands. "You don't have to go if you don't want to."

"No," Derek smiled. "I want to go. It's been since before ... " He glanced over at Tank, as if seeking assurance. "Well, it's been a while."

"Want to go now?" Tank asked. "I have plenty of loose change in my car."

"Yeah," they all agreed.

Tank drove them to the cemetery and pulled up by the large oak tree that Derek had hit with his truck all those months ago, on the day he passed out drunk on top of Joey's grave. He put his large SUV into Park and cut the engine. They all stepped out, but Tank stopped long enough to grab the cup into which he always tossed his loose change. He grabbed a handful of coins and started handing them out to everyone. When he grabbed his own, he set the cup back on the console and shut the door.

"It's right over here," Derek said, leading his friends to Joey's grave. Someone had recently put fresh flowers on his and his mother's gravestones. A small flag stuck in the ground occasionally flapped from a periodic breeze.

Tank didn't speak. He stepped up and placed a penny, a nickel, and a dime atop Joey's gravestone to show he visited, and also that he went through Basic training and served with Joey.

Visiting was a mostly silent affair, but Derek's breath hitched when Rass and Jonesy spoke.

"Hey, Parker," Jonesy started. "I'm sorry I haven't been here before now. Rass and me, we're here checking up on Doc. Seems he needs us to take care of him for a change." He chuckled. "We'll never do as good a job as he did. But we'll try to care as much as you always did." Jonesy set a penny, a dime, and a quarter on top of the gravestone. He visited. He served with Joey. And he was with Joey when he died.

Jonesy turned to step away, exchanging a nod with Derek before he joined Tank about ten feet away from them.

Rass stepped up next, removing his cowboy hat and holding it against his chest.

"Parker," Rass spoke to Joey, his voice suddenly gruff. "I'll forever be grateful to you for pushing me out of the way that day, but damn, I wish you were still here with us."

Derek dropped his head, remembering when he first learned

Joey had pushed Rass out of the way just before the RPG hit them that day in Afghanistan.

"I told my wife about you. My kids, too. I don't ever want them to forget the man who made sure their daddy made it back home to them." Rass went silent for a minute or so before he continued. "I may be down in Amarillo working my daddy's ranch, but even from Texas, I'll do better about checking in on Derek for ya. Clearly, he needs someone to look after him." Rass turned and faced Derek with a smirk before saying one last thing. "We'll take care of him, okay?"

Like Jonesy, Rass placed his penny, dime, and quarter next to the others. He touched his gravestone. "Rest easy, Sergeant."

With a friendly bump to Derek's shoulder, he stepped away and joined Tank and Jonesy.

"Hi, Joey," Derek said, stepping up to Joey's gravestone. "So, uh, I'm sorry I haven't been here in a good long while. I just haven't been doing too well lately. I drank too much and landed my ass in the hospital. I haven't had a drop of the stuff for about five or six weeks now." He breathed out a humorless laugh. "I think that's a new record for me. I'm gonna try to stick it out, though, because I need to believe I should stick around to make sure people remember how amazing a friend you were. God, you should be here. But for your sake, I'm going to try to be more like you. We should all try for that." Derek turned his head slightly and spoke louder. "Even Rass over there. Rass, who's shivering like a Michigan fan who can't even wear a T-shirt out in January."

"What?" Rass called out, sticking his hands deep in his pockets. "Come on, man, it's colder than a witch's tit out here!"

Derek laughed this time. "I'll do better, Joey. I promise. And this is a promise I really hope I can keep." Derek placed his four coins next to the others, noting that together, their coins totaled one dollar and twenty-nine cents.

"I love you, brother." Derek placed his hand on Joey's grave. "I'm so sorry I couldn't keep you with us."

Chapter 41

First Meetings

Two years and seven months since Joey Parker died

Derek sat in his chair in the center of the room as part of a circle with fellow veterans working through their issues. "I'm not sure what to say. Um, I'm Derek, and I've been drinking since before my enlistment ended. I never drank a lot until," He held his breath for a few moments and then swallowed hard. "Until my best friend died on our final mission in Afghanistan."

He took a few seconds to hold himself together. "That's been since August 17, 2014, so I guess that makes me an alcoholic." He laughed nervously. "Anyway, I was the combat medic on that mission, and I couldn't save him. We were ambushed. My head knows he wouldn't have made it, but damn if I didn't do everything in my power to keep him alive. For the longest time, I convinced myself I didn't do everything I could, and that it was my fault he died. I just ... I still can't believe he's gone, but I'm starting to believe that maybe it wasn't because of me. That maybe it really was because of the RPG that hit."

He unscrewed the cap of his water bottle and took a few sips. Replacing the cap, he continued. "I, uh, work as a paramedic now. And a few months ago, I broke down after a call. We saved the patient, but it all came flooding back. The severity of the injuries, I don't know. I went home, got drunk, but didn't stop drinking. Apparently, I collapsed and stopped breathing. Someone happened to stop by my place for the first time that day. If he hadn't, I wouldn't be here now."

Derek wiped his eyes with the palms of his hands and sniffed. "Maybe that was Joey watching over me or something. I don't know. I don't remember much from that day. I woke up in the hospital a few days later. I spent about a week there detoxing and then a month in rehab. I just started back to work a month and a half ago, which means I've been sober for about three months now. I always drank to forget. It never helped, but I thought it let me escape. I mean, it did, just not for long. Not long enough.

"I think in some way, I'll always blame myself for not saving Joey, but I'm getting better at accepting the fact that he's gone. Or at least living with the fact that he's gone. He was always there for me, you know? He was my best friend and ... " Derek choked back a sob and barely got the words out. "I really miss him."

Derek wiped the tears off his face, acknowledging the man next to him who squeezed his shoulder in support.

"The night before I almost died, a lady in town was telling me about her husband, who served in Vietnam. She said he spoke of how his post-war life was his new life. When he tried to push her away, she refused, telling him she was with him no matter what." Derek cleared his throat. "She said he decided to end that new life and create another one. I guess that's what I'm doing now that I'm sober. My new life after the Army consisted of drinking myself into oblivion while mourning my best friend. Going through rehab ended that new life, so now I get to create a different one."

"Thanks for sharing your story, Derek," Troy, the leader of the group, said. "And welcome." He looked at each of the veterans sitting around the circle. "We've all lost friends here. We've all lost some part of our lives that we can't get back and have to learn to live without. By sharing our stories, we can help keep ourselves on track. I hope to see you come back. I hope to see all of you come back. Ups and downs are a part of dealing with our addictions, but sharing our days and our stories, well, it helps keep us all accountable to ourselves."

Chapter 42

Briggsy

Three years and six months after Joey Parker died

"Sergeant First Class Mitchell? This is your service dog, Briggsy."

Derek reached down and held out his hand for an adorable chocolate lab to sniff. The lab licked his hand a time or two until Derek scratched him behind the ears. "Hi, Briggsy." He was one of three service dogs in the room, each one meeting their new veteran they'd be caring for.

"Briggsy," the trainer explained, "is eighteen months old and full-grown. You'll spend the next three weeks together learning how to guide him and learning what he's trained to do."

Derek sat on the floor, and Briggsy immediately crawled into his lap and nudged his chin with his nose. Derek laughed. "Your nose is cold." Briggsy reached up and licked Derek's face.

"He can tell you're nervous," the trainer said. "He can tell your heart rate is higher than usual. Just pet him and take deep breaths."

"He can sense that?"

"Yes."

Derek scratched Briggsy behind the ears again. After a few

minutes, his new service dog turned on his side and made himself comfortable between Derek's legs.

The trainer started explaining the signs the dog would make and what he would do when he sensed Derek was having a rougher-than-usual time with his PTSD.

"And will I have to crate him when I fly back home?"

"Not at all. As a service dog, he's legally entitled to go wherever you go. He's a trained service animal. When he's working, he won't react to any other animals or people. That's a big part of what differentiates a fully-trained service animal from an emotional support animal. Service animals are trained to support their humans. That includes inside the cabin on an airplane. While on the plane, he'll sit on the floor between your legs."

"Between my legs?" Derek's gaze switched between his new service dog and the trainer. "He's got to be what? Fifty or sixty pounds at least?"

"He's just under seventy pounds," the trainer confirmed. "He'll sit on the floor facing you and will rest his head in your lap. The same applies to restaurants, especially if the space is tight. If not, he'll lie down on the floor at your feet. It might be a bit tighter of a fit at a sporting event, but most places have ADA seats that offer you a bit more space."

"Wow. That's good to know since we're all going to a hockey game right after I get back home," Derek admitted.

"He'll automatically stay close to you, but when there are lots of people around, you'll want to work to keep him especially close. He's a dog. And he's cute." She smiled. "Everybody will want to pet him. And though most people are getting better about not bothering service animals, there are many who will still try to approach him. As his handler, you'll have to get good at saying no.

"Now, working as a paramedic may be tricky. You'll have to figure out what works best for you on the job. In an ambulance, other paramedics keep their service animals up front as opposed to with their patients. They definitely shouldn't go into fires. But at the station, they do a great job of keeping their humans calm."

"What about public places like restaurants? What if they don't let me in?"

"Legally, they're required to let you in. The ADA requires it."

"Okay."

"They're also allowed to ask only two questions."

"Only two? What are they?"

"The first is whether or not this is a service animal, to which you would answer yes. He's a service animal."

"And second?"

"They're allowed to ask for what task he's trained. To that question, you're allowed to just say PTSD. You're not required to provide any more detail than that."

"Will he help with ... " Derek swallowed. "With nightmares?"

"Absolutely. He'll sleep near you or at your feet, but when he senses you're having a nightmare, he can do a few different things to help you through it."

"What kind of things?"

"He'll nudge your hand or face. He might lick your face, too, if you don't wake up right away."

Derek nodded as she explained what Briggsy could do, already impressed with his abilities. He laughed at the next thing Briggsy was trained to do.

"He's also trained to flip a light switch and wake you up with light."

"That'll go over well at the station."

"Yeah," she joined his laughter. "I've heard some fun stories about those kinds of situations. On top of that, Briggsy here is trained for deep pressure therapy, or DPT."

Derek's brow furrowed. "What's that?"

"It's a form of therapy that applies pressure to the whole body.

In a way, it simulates being held, being cocooned. Are you familiar with weighted blankets?"

Derek nodded in the affirmative.

"Same concept, but on an as-needed basis. When Briggsy senses your heart rate climbing or senses that you're tossing and turning, he'll climb on top of you and lie down on your chest." The trainer smiled. "Trust me. You'll notice when you have an extra seventy pounds on your torso."

Derek laughed. "I don't doubt it."

The trainer spoke more about his particular breed of dog. "Labrador retrievers are bred, as the name implies, to retrieve, so you'll want to give him plenty of exercise, including throwing a ball or a stick for him to bring back. As I understand it, you like to run?"

"Yes. A few times a week."

"Good. That'll be good for him. You should also know that Labs are eager to please, but they're also a very intelligent breed, which is why they're so good at being service dogs."

Derek petted Briggsy's head and back for a while, letting the rest of the world around him fade away.

"Your heart rate must be dropping."

"What? How can you tell?"

"Briggsy isn't licking your face as much. He's relaxing because you're relaxing. See? He's already doing his job."

Derek smiled. "Good boy."

Epilogue

Nationwide Arena, Columbus, Ohio - First Responder Night

Columbus, Ohio - *Winter 2018*

"Tarasenko, Steve? Really?" Derek shook his head at Steve's St. Louis Blues hockey sweater. "We're at a Blue Jackets game and you're wearing Vladimir Tarasenko's number?"

"Doc's right," Tank added. "You should at least be like us, with Jenner and Werenski on our hometown sweaters."

"This is *my* hometown sweater," Steve countered, wearing a proud smile.

Derek and Tank shook their heads as they stepped out onto a floor mat covering a small portion of the ice rink on First Responder Night at Nationwide Arena in downtown Columbus. They were accompanied by the Columbus Blue Jackets' national anthem singer, Leo Welsh.

When the spotlights focused on them, the rink announcer's voice sounded overhead. "We'd like to welcome three firefighter-paramedics and military veterans from Grant's Crossing Fire Department in Grant's Crossing, Ohio. Corporal Steven Cook with the U.S. Marines, and U.S. Army veterans Sergeant Juan "Tank" Palacios and Sergeant First Class Derek Mitchell, here with his service dog, Briggsy." The announcer continued. "We'd now like to ask you to please remove your hats and, if able, to stand for our national anthem."

Exchanging amused smirks at being the center of attention for a brief moment, Derek, Steve, and Tank all removed their hats. Briggsy sat still next to Derek's leg, tail swishing back and forth.

"Ladies and gentlemen, please welcome Mr. Leo Welsh."

As is tradition at Nationwide Arena, the sell-out crowd immediately responded by yelling, "LEO!"

Despite not being in uniform, Derek, Tank, and Steve each saluted the flag hanging over the shoot-twice side at the opposite end of the hockey rink while the deep, rich tones of Leo's voice filled the arena.

They dropped their salutes as Leo pumped his fist with an enthusiastic 'woot' to the applause of all the fans in attendance. Leo then shook their hands, and they all retreated into the tunnel to find their seats.

Late in the first period, when the Blue Jackets held a 2-0 lead over the Blues, a waving flag appeared on the Jumbotron above the ice to the organist's accompaniment. Within a few seconds, it showed a live picture of Steve, Tank, and Derek in their respective team sweaters, standing in a suite reserved for tonight's game, especially for first responders.

All three men watched the Jumbotron as they were introduced to the crowd, which started its non-stop applause.

The PA announcer began speaking over the loudspeaker as the crowd stood and showed their appreciation with continued applause. "Originally from St. Louis, Missouri, Corporal Steven Cook served in the U.S. Marines from 2007 to 2012 in Operation Iraqi Freedom in Iraq, Operation Enduring Freedom in Afghanistan, and Operation Unified Response in Haiti. During his service, he received a Silver Star for gallantry in action. He now serves as a firefighter-paramedic with the Grant's Crossing Fire Department."

The pictures on the Jumbotron quickly transitioned to show Steve during his active-duty service in the Marines, including one with his best friend, Mace, who traveled down to see the game with him. They even flashed a picture of him in his utility uniform standing next to Nicky at their family's farm in Illinois, as well as one in his Dress Blues on his and Tara's wedding day, before transitioning over to a picture of him in his full turnout gear while cleaning up after a fire a few months earlier.

The pictures transitioned to a shot of Tank, Derek, and Joey inside an airplane during their airborne training just prior to their first jump. The announcer continued, "Sergeant Juan 'Tank' Palacios & Sergeant First Class Derek Mitchell enlisted after 9/11 and served together in the U.S. Army with the 75th Ranger Regiment, 3rd Battalion."

More active duty pictures followed. Derek leaned closer to Tank. "You know nobody here's gonna believe that your nickname, Tank, comes from a high school football game."

Tank chuckled in response.

"Sergeant Palacios served in Operation Iraqi Freedom in Iraq and Operation Enduring Freedom in Afghanistan. While serving in Afghanistan, Sergeant Palacios was wounded and spent six months at Walter Reed Army Medical Center, where he was awarded a Purple Heart before being honorably discharged in 2010. He now serves as the captain of the Grant's Crossing Fire Department."

The applause of the crowd continued throughout the presentation.

After another picture or two, including one while he was at Walter Reed going through physical therapy, and a family picture with Araceli and all their kids flashed by before switching to pictures of Derek providing medical care to his fellow Rangers.

"Sergeant First Class Derek Mitchell served as a U.S. Army Ranger Combat Medic with the 3/75 in Operation Enduring Freedom in Afghanistan from 2001 to 2014, where he was awarded a Purple Heart and two Bronze Stars. He now serves as a firefighter-paramedic."

The Jumbotron showed a recent picture of all three men in their turnout gear, including a smiling Derek, kneeling next to an adorable chocolate Lab who'd since become his trusty sidekick.

He gave Briggsy a scratch behind his ears just as the picture changed to show Joey Parker smiling with the years 1981-2014 directly below.

Tank clasped Derek's shoulder as the announcer spoke.

"Sergeant Palacios and Sergeant First Class Mitchell would like to honor their good friend and fellow U.S. Army Ranger, Sergeant First Class Joseph Miles Parker, who enlisted with them after 9/11 and served honorably in the 3/75 until he was killed in action on August 17, 2014. Sergeant First Class Parker was posthumously awarded the Purple Heart and Silver Star for gallantry in action."

As the announcer spoke, Derek swallowed hard while directing his attention to the pictures they'd provided the Columbus Blue Jackets PR team, including a picture of Derek, Tank, and Joey from the summer before fifth grade, when Joey had just moved to Grant's Crossing. They shared a picture from their first camping trip together when they were barely teenagers, their high school graduation, basic training, and a picture while serving at Bagram in Afghanistan. The final image was of Joey and his boyfriend, Logan, together, smiling.

The crowd's applause showed no sign of slowing down, and even the players on the ice, who were gearing up for their next face-off, tapped their sticks out of respect.

"At this time, we'd like to present each of you with a special Columbus Blue Jackets sweater in appreciation of your service to our nation. We thank these four men, and all veterans, active-duty military, and first responders, for their service to our communities and nation."

The camera returned to Derek, Tank, and Steve in the stands.

The general manager himself appeared in the spotlight next to their seats and handed them each a military-colored sweater with the Blue Jackets logo on the front and the word "HONOREE" on the back. He shook all their hands until the applause finally dwindled and play resumed.

"I'm happy they now get to know Joey a little bit, too," Tank said in Derek's ear.

With four minutes and 30 seconds remaining in the first period, they took their seats after the next face-off. Briggsy returned to her spot, sitting between Derek's legs with her head on his lap, nudging his hand with his cold nose after the cannon fired after the Jackets' next goal.

Tank leaned closer to Derek as play on the ice resumed. "How are you feeling?"

Derek took a moment to inhale and consider his answer. He smiled at Callie, who was seated on his left, and squeezed her hand. "I'm good." He exhaled slowly, scanned the crowd around the arena, then faced Tank again. He scratched Briggsy behind his ears and smiled before answering. "For the first time in a long while, I can honestly say I'm good."

Bonus Epilogue - 6 months earlier

Three years after Joey Parker died

GRANT'S CROSSING, OHIO - LATE SUMMER 2017

Callie opened the door to Jo's just as Bryan Reynolds was exiting with his dad, who now walked with a cane. She held the door open, receiving a thank you from Bryan in return. She waited until they'd rounded the corner before walking inside.

"Hi, Jo." Callie set her bag on a chair and leaned up against the bar.

"Hey, Callie." Jo set a coaster down in front of Callie. "I heard you were back. Good to see you. What can I get you tonight?"

Callie placed an order for a grilled turkey and Swiss with seasoned fries.

"Sure! Get that right up for you."

"Thanks!"

Jo set a Diet Coke in front of Callie, then went back to the register to place her order. Taking a sip, Callie noticed Kiro and Celeste sitting in a booth on the side with the pool tables and walked over.

"Hi! Mind if I join you for a few minutes?"

"CALLIE," Celeste squealed as she jumped up and greeted Callie with a hug. "You're back!"

Kiro hugged her as well, though without the squealing.

Callie laughed. "Great to see you both."

"Have a seat." Celeste scooted over to make room for her. "Are you back for good?"

"I don't know about for good, but I'll definitely be here for a while since we'll be demoing the house soon."

"I'm so sorry about your grandfather."

"Thanks, Celeste. I appreciate that. I didn't mean to be away for so long. After he passed away, there was so much to take care of. Then I was sent away on assignment, and so much has happened since. It would take too long to tell you everything."

Callie glanced over at the bar to see a woman with her arms wrapped around Derek's neck, laughing at something he'd just said. Her good mood drained as the woman reached over to take a sip of the drink the ponytailed bartender set down in front of her, just as Derek paid the tab.

Was that disappointment on Derek's face? The bartender added a second drink. Rum and Coke, maybe?

Kiro's eyes followed Callie's in time to see the woman follow Derek to a table where he was sitting with two other friends. He was probably waiting for the right time to take her home for the night. She assumed that was still his usual M.O.

Celeste tried to distract Callie while she waited for her food. "So, what do you have left to take care of in your apartment?"

"What?"

"Your apartment. What's left to do?"

"Nothing, really. Most everything was set up before I had to head back home." Callie took a drink of her Diet Coke, shooting a quick glance over toward the dance floor.

"Oh, good."

"I should have you over sometime." Callie laughed. "I can't cook, so maybe we can order pizza or something."

"Sounds fun," Celeste said. "Do you play euchre by chance?"

"Euchre? What's that?"

"It's a Midwest thing. A card game. It's played with partners, but it's a little confusing with the jacks, so you may want to learn in a group where everybody else already knows how to play."

"Confusing, huh?" Callie laughed. "I suppose I can give it a try, and I'd love to have the girls over." Her gaze returned to Derek.

"He's missed you, you know."

"What?" Callie turned to Kiro, speaking half to herself. She forced a laugh. "No. No. No. I don't think so."

"He does."

"Kiro." She exhaled. "We've actually kept in touch, kind of." She tilted her head back in Derek's direction. "He seems to be doing pretty well these days."

Jo waved at Callie, who scooted out of the booth. "Looks like my food's ready. Have a good night, you two."

Celeste turned a stern look toward Kiro when Callie returned to the counter. "What was that?"

He shrugged. "What do you mean? She'd be good for him."

"Yes, but he needs to figure that out on his own, baby."

Kiro's shoulders sagged as he watched his best friend do nothing but work on his latest one-night stand. Derek had stayed sober, but his need for one-night stands persisted. "Yeah. You're probably right."

"I am right," she confirmed with a proud smirk. "And, she needs to want that, too."

Kiro caught Derek watching Callie as she waved goodbye and slipped out the door. When his eyes met Derek's, Kiro nodded toward the window and mouthed, "She's here. Go!"

Derek walked his date back to his apartment. As soon as they turned down the drive, his eyes were fixed on Callie's silhouette through the curtains in her apartment. His date was talking, but he wasn't listening.

"Derek?"

His eyes didn't move from Callie's window as they walked.

"Derek?"

"What?" He stopped to look at her.

"You didn't hear a word I just said, did you?" Her voice lacked accusation; she was simply stating a fact.

He didn't. His heart just wasn't in it. With an exhale, he looked at the ground for a moment before returning his eyes to her. "I'm sorry, Mandy. I just can't tonight."

She smiled and looked up at Callie's window for a moment before returning her gaze to him. "Thanks for the drinks, Derek. I had fun tonight." Pointing toward the window, "You should go talk to her. Let her know how you feel."

"Mandy, I'm sorr—"

"It's okay." Her lips curled up in mischief. "I wasn't looking for anything beyond tonight, anyway."

"I'm ... "

"It's okay." She tilted her head toward his truck. "Mind giving me a ride home at least?"

He looked at her for a moment, all while feeling guilty at being distracted by another woman. He smiled. "Sure."

Callie looked out the window just as Derek climbed into the driver's seat and backed out of the driveway. Not ten minutes later, the headlights on his truck pulling back in drew her gaze through the window. She paused the movie long enough to watch him step out of his truck and walk toward the door alone.

At least his date didn't have to walk home.

She hit play on her movie again, reaching her hand down for another seasoned fry as Mary Astor entered the scene with Humphrey Bogart, and said, *"I wish I knew how to handle him."*

THE END

Watch for Don't Call Me Ma'am, a Grant's Crossing Romance Book 2, coming Spring 2026.

Official Website: www.hmsbrown.com

Find all my Grant's Crossing Novels and stories at https://linktr.ee/grantscrossing

Heroes of Grant's Crossing novels are available wherever books are sold online.

They are also available via Hoopla, Libby, and in paperback.

Ask for them at your local library!

Bibliography

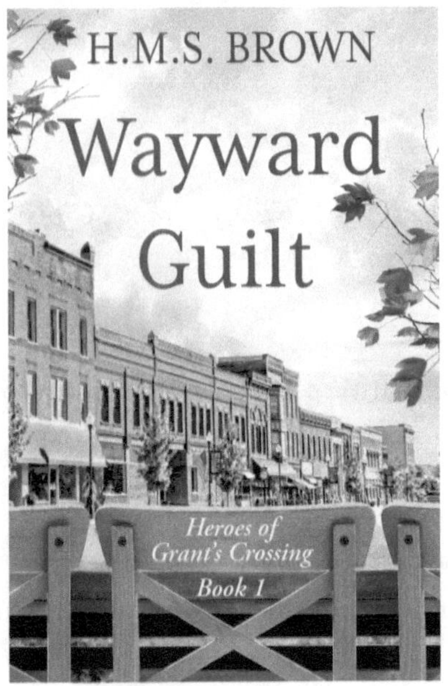

Wayward Guilt
Heroes of Grant's Crossing Book 1
Available now in ebook and paperback: https://books2read.com/u/38WRM7

Three friends leave home to serve their country. Only two make it back.

After the Twin Towers fall, Derek Mitchell enlists in the U.S. Army with two of his best friends. He dreams of helping people, whether in the field of combat or back home in Grant's Crossing, Ohio.

Juan dreams of marrying his high school sweetheart and starting a family.

Joey dreams of being happy and living his own truth.

Together, they serve in multiple deployments until Juan and Joey are each grievously injured in separate combat missions. Thirteen years after initially enlisting, one doesn't make it back.

Four months after the funeral, friends and family gather to celebrate Derek's return to civilian life. With each story shared, he relives their final missions together, carrying the guilt of having saved one friend but not the other.

What do you do when the one friend you've always turned to is no longer there?

Safe Now
Heroes of Grant's Crossing Book 2
Available Now in ebook and paperback: https://books2read.com/u/3Jn15P

Some secrets can't be kept.

Some people can't be protected.

Some brothers can't be stopped.

Bibliography

Growing up in a small town outside St. Louis, Missouri, Steve and Nick Cook struggle to balance their own aspirations with their strict parents' desire to mold their sons into a picture-perfect and obedient family.

But when Nick is outed, their parents make life worse for both. Steve promises to get his little brother somewhere he can live without fear, even if that means delaying his own dream of becoming a Marine.

When fate intervenes, Steve takes Nick far from their childhood home to live with extended family. Believing he is safe, Steve finally enlists and serves multiple deployments in the Middle East.

With Steve fighting for his country, Nick risks the only safety he's ever known to set out on his own. When Nick disappears, Steve vows to do what the local authorities can't—setting on a new mission that takes him across the Midwest, from Chicago to the seediest neighborhoods in Detroit and Columbus, to find him.

Now, living in a community of friends who don't hesitate to share his burdens and with a family willing to share his pain, can Steve complete one more mission and save his brother?

Don't Call me Sugar
A Grant's Crossing Heroes Romance
Pre-order: https://books2read.com/DCMS

 Tara

After her father is injured in a serious accident, Tara Bailey puts her big-city life on hold to help her parents' flailing business in her beloved hometown of Grant's Crossing.

While there, Tara meets a motorcycle-riding first responder who sparks a fire within her she once thought lost.

Will this newfound passion be enough for her to stay and give love another shot?

 Steve

Marine Corps veteran Steve Cook is starting a new chapter in his life. With his brother in rehab nearby, Steve finds himself drawn to the slower pace of life in this central Ohio town.

Shortly after starting a new job at the local fire department, Steve falls for a strong-willed shopkeeper who puts up walls as quickly as he breaks them down.

Will his perseverance pay off before she moves back to Chicago?

Don't Call Me Sugar is a slow-burn Grant's Crossing Romance - where family and friends mean everything, and happily-ever-afters are guaranteed.

Acknowledgments

Authors can't write books without a solid support network. Sure, we're alone most of the time, writing, but the love and support I receive from my family and friends is absolutely invaluable.

Dan and Kalie - your feedback makes my stories make sense - especially when I don't. THANK YOU!

Liberty - I'm so glad I was able to get more of your favorite character in here. And yes - you'll see more of Kiro, I promise!

Kristy, Deb, Rachel - Thanks for your support, and Kristy - my book release twin! I'm so excited that we're releasing our books on the same day! YAY!

Amy at Sagewood Publishing - There are no words to express how much I appreciate all you do to make my book better. Even 72,000+ words in here are insufficient to say how much you help bring my characters to life.

Kylie at Cover Culture - your covers are so gorgeous! Thank you!

Mom and Dad - my own personal PR departments. I love you! THANK YOU!

To all my friends and family who have shown amazing support by reading and reviewing my books, sharing posts, talking me up to anyone you meet, encouraging me to keep writing, and - finally - not bringing up the fact that the CBJ First Responder night was actually in December against Toronto, rather than in January 2018 against St. Louis as I wrote in my epilogue: THANK YOU!

Thank you all! - Heather

About the Author

H.M.S. Brown stumbled into writing during lockdown in 2020 after complaining to her mom about a book she didn't like. When her mom challenged her to write her own, the town of Grant's Crossing was born.

When not cheering for her Columbus Blue Jackets, H.M.S. Brown can be found at a neighborhood cafe working on her next story or at her day job so she can maintain a roof over her library and yarn stash.

End of a New Life is H.M.S. Brown's third and final installment of her Heroes of Grant's Crossing series, which tells stories of veterans navigating their way through civilian life in the Midwest. Like Wayward Guilt and Safe Now, it can be read as a standalone book.

In the meantime, check out all of H.M.S. Brown's novels, found at your local library and wherever books are sold online.

goodreads.com/hmsbrown

bookbub.com/authors/h-m-s-brown

amazon.com/author/hmsbrown

threads.com/@grantscrossing

instagram.com/grantscrossing

x.com/GrantsCrossing

bsky.app/profile/grantscrossing.bsky.social

youtube.com/@GrantsCrossing